WORTH
fighting
FOR

AMANDA KELLEY

1

If I could describe bliss, this would be it. There's nothing. No worries. No pressure. No stress. Only total weightlessness. It's like I'm floating through a dense black fog and nothing can touch me here. It's the most peace I've gotten in ages.

But...that's not true.

This isn't right.

There's something I need to do. Something I should know. I can sense it, drifting just beyond the edges of the fog.

I try to grasp it but that weightlessness I felt becomes heavier, almost suffocating, holding me back from where I need to be. The more I fight it, the heavier it becomes until my body feels like it's made of stone.

I can't move.

I try to sit up—or at least, I think I do—but nothing happens.

I was wrong. This isn't bliss. This is much worse.

Something is seriously wrong with me, but I can't think here.

I know I need to leave, that I don't want to be here anymore.

I try moving my legs, but nothing happens.

I'm pinned down.

There's something on top of me, and it's crushing me. If I don't budge it soon, I won't be able to breathe.

Immediately, panic overrides everything.

I can feel my heart slamming against my ribs as my pulse begins to race.

My fight-or-flight switch has been flipped, but I can't do either if my muscles refuse to respond.

I put all of my concentration into moving.

Beads of sweat begin to form on my brow from the effort.

Finally, my arm wiggles free, and I blindly reach out, grabbing something soft.

Wait.

How can something soft be so heavy?

Nothing makes any sense.

Frustrated and panicking, I swing out with a closed fist definitely connecting with something solid.

Again and again, I beat at it, but it's no use.

No matter how hard I try, I move in slow motion, only to connect with the force of a butterfly.

The panic grows until it's a living thing coiling inside my chest.

I can't fight, and I can't run.

A frantic scream claws its way up my throat, burning and violent. But nothing comes out.

I'm pretty sure I'm going to die here.

Ali jerked to a sitting position in her full-sized bed, her poofy red comforter falling to her waist.

It took her a full minute to pull in a solid breath and another minute after that to stop the trembling in her hands. Her small bedroom was still dark, but her eyes could make out the outline of her tall dresser and the pile of unfolded laundry contorting the wide chair in the corner. Without looking, she reached for her phone sitting on her nightstand and illuminated the screen. The sudden brightness all but blinded her as she checked the time—*5:27.*

Never had three extra minutes of sleep seemed so precious. Annoyed, she threw her phone at the end of her bed just a smidgen more violently than she'd meant to, causing it to bounce onto the floor.

Blowing out a long breath, she dragged her palms down her cheeks.

This is getting ridiculous.

What happened to the dream where Charlie Hunnam was waiting with open arms on a beach, but when she tried to run across the sand, she never got anywhere, no matter how hard she tried? Or how about the one where her teeth started falling out one by one throughout the day until she was a poster child for a hillbilly meth addict? She'd take either of those over this bullshit any day.

It'd been the same damn dream for over a year now. At first, it had come maybe once a month, but recently, it'd been more persistent than ever. Always the same. From the crushing weight to the blind panic, but underneath all of that, the thing that bothered her the most was the spaghetti arms. The absolute inability to help herself.

Before Ali could dwell on it any longer, her bedroom door flew open, and her light flicked on.

"Rise and shine, my valentine!" Her roommate bounced into the room with far more enthusiasm than any one person should have before the sun came up.

Shelby was maybe five-three and cute as a button with the personality to match. She easily made friends wherever she went and never met a stranger she couldn't win over. Basically, she was Ali's opposite in every way. It didn't surprise Ali at all that Shelby was already fully dressed, and her chin-length, curly blonde hair looked like she'd just walked out of a salon.

"It's March," Ali grumbled as she shielded her eyes.

"Fine. Stretch and yawn, my leprechaun." In response to Ali's raised eyebrow, Shelby simply rolled her eyes. "What? I'd like to see you rhyme with leprechaun at five a.m."

Yeah, right.

Ali was the furthest thing from a morning person as anyone could get. But, alas, adulthood had reared its ugly head and demanded she earn a living.

"Coffee?" she grumbled hopefully.

"Do you really think I'd come in here, unarmed?"

Only then did she notice the giant pink coffee mug that her roommate held out toward her. Her brother Jase had given her the mug on her last birthday. It was princess pink, which she loathed, but that could be forgiven because the elegant black script read, ~~Fuck off~~. *I mean, good morning.*

She took the offering and cradled it close, breathing in the rich aroma like a fat kid entering a doughnut shop.

"Thanks."

"Rough night?" Shelby squatted down to pick Ali's phone up off the floor before sitting on the end of the bed, handing it to her. "Is the dream back?" When Ali nodded, her friend's eyebrows pinched together. "That's the second time this week, isn't it?"

"And the fourth this month."

Not like I'm counting or anything.

"Were you paralyzed again?"

"Yeah."

"You know," Shelby started gently, "you should really listen to what your dreams are telling you. Especially since it's getting worse. Paralysis indicates you feel a lack of control or even helpless—"

"I know what it means," she abruptly cut Shelby off with a snap. Immediately regretting it, Ali closed her eyes and took a deep breath. "Sorry. Just don't shrink me today. Please. Save your mumbo jumbo for your patients."

"You mean, my customers?" Shelby snorted and then continued with a wistful sigh, "What I wouldn't give for actual patients."

Ali bumped her foot into her friend's knee. "One of these days, you'll be able to put that psychology degree to use on someone more appreciative than me."

"Ah, but for now, I will settle for solving the problems of every caffeine-addicted patron at the Rise and Grind. Speaking of"—Shelby checked her slim rose-gold watch—"I've gotta go. Fresh pot in the kitchen, and I folded your laundry and left it on the table. Now, go wash your ass. The young minds of the world are depending on you. And you might want to consider some mouthwash because…damn."

Before Ali could kick her, Shelby bounced off the bed and out the door with a tinkling laugh that hung in the air.

How the gods had seen fit to curse her with such a roommate she'd never know, but she was forever grateful for it. Everyone needed a Shelby even if, like her, they didn't deserve one.

When Ali whipped into a parking space behind West Grove Elementary, she was pleased to notice her white car was one of only three in the lot. Early in the year, she'd made it a habit to get here early despite her aversion to mornings. She'd learned that, if she got here after everyone started to arrive, she was bombarded with work gossip and nosy coworkers. That alone was enough to fry her brain. But, mostly, she needed the quiet, so she could finish waking up before the tiny humans descended upon the school.

Sliding out of her sporty little Mustang, she folded the seat forward and snagged the bulging tote bag out of the back while simultaneously juggling her purse, coffee, and keys in her other hand. With her hands full, she shut the door with a bump of her hip before making her way to the front of the building.

Last fall, shortly after Ali had moved back home, she'd landed a job as one of three kindergarten teachers. Two weeks into the school year, the previous teacher had quit abruptly when her husband was transferred out of state for work. Ali had spent the better part of the first quarter playing catch-up, but now that they were in the home stretch for the year, she felt like a veteran. An exhausted, jaded veteran. She'd seen some shit. Literally. Kindergarteners could be seriously gross.

Just inside the set of double doors, she spotted Daryl, her favorite janitor, washing the office windows, and she gave him a quick salute with her monogrammed tumbler. Reaching out, he picked up his own mug from the ledge next to him and raised it to her in return with a wry twist of his lips as she made her way past the office and down the hall to the left. She and the old man had become fast friends over the last six months. They didn't need fancy words. He understood her need for some downtime in the mornings, and she understood his need for fancy-ass coffee and artery-clogging pastries, which she supplied him with regularly.

The two of them had an ongoing game they played where she would try to guess his age, and he would tell her she was wrong. He had one of those faces that was weathered from years spent working outdoors for the oil field and a close-cropped head of white hair, but paired with the twinkle in his eyes and his bright smile, he could be anywhere between fifty and eighty years old. It had become a mystery she was bound to solve for no other reason than the fact that he refused to tell her. One day, he would mention 8-track tapes like he knew how to use one, and then the next, he'd whip out his smartphone and text faster than a teenager with good gossip. Someday, he was going to slip up, and she'd be waiting with a jaunty hat and a wooden pipe. Of course, she could always bribe the secretary to tell her, but that would be cheating.

Opening her door, she flipped on the row of light switches with her free pinkie, illuminating her room with a harsh fluorescent glow. To anyone else's eyes, her room would look cluttered with not a spot of counter or wall space available. But she saw perfectly organized chaos.

In one corner, she had a cozy reading area full of pillows and beanbags, bracketed by two stunted bookshelves that were overflowing with used children's books she'd picked up at garage sales. Between the smart board and the five hexagon-shaped tables lay the kids' favorite multicolored rug. Alphabet cards wrapped around the top of the walls, complete with their corresponding pictures, while the old white dry-erase board contained their daily schedule and class rules. There were also last week's monster projects the kids had made out of square tissue boxes lined up under the cabinets on the counter. Those would go home today, only to be replaced with this week's creations. Things were always moving, always changing, and she wouldn't have it any other way.

Her desk sat in the far corner of the room and was just as chaotic as everything else. After unloading her things onto her chair, she walked around and unstacked the pint-sized chairs. Then, she changed the sight words for the week before adding a few drops of eucalyptus and tea oil to her warmer. Breathing in the calming aroma, she sat down to answer her emails and print off today's math sheet before making her way to the front office to make her copies.

By now, the building was buzzing with teachers and office staff, but she was still the first one in line at the copier. That didn't happen. As in *never*. That was like being the first one to Starbucks when they released their pumpkin spice latte in September or the tenth caller to the radio station to win Thomas Rhett tickets. Basically, it was the holy grail for elementary teachers. Giddy as could be, Ali did a little happy dance as she punched in her code.

"Well, aren't we in a good mood this morning?"

Ali fought to keep her smile in place as she turned around to address the woman who was about to rain on her parade. To the kinder, more tenderhearted people of the world, they were nice words, but she'd heard them for what they were. She herself was well versed in the art of bitchcraft.

"Morning, Sarah."

The raven-haired woman waited behind Ali with her arms crossed over her ample chest, which threatened to topple her tiny frame over, with a single sheet of paper dangling from one manicured hand. She was wearing a summer dress that hit way too many inches above her knees and more makeup than Ali owned layering her face. Sarah was better dressed for a date than she was for teaching third graders.

Maybe today will be the day she busts her ass in her three-inch, knee-high boots.

One could only hope.

"Oh, dear." Sarah winced, examining Ali's face with mock sympathy. "You look like you had a rough night. But kudos to you for finding the silver lining to things this morning."

And there it was.

Too bad for Sarah, when it came to a battle of wits, Ali could play all day.

"Well, we can't all be photo-shoot ready every day, but of course, *you* can understand that." She'd tried not to put too much emphasis on the *you* and failed.

Okay, so maybe she hadn't tried that hard.

Turning back around, Ali gathered her copies and left Sarah with a tight smile. She wasn't exactly proud of the way she'd handled that.

Sarah was that one.

No, not *the one*. But *that one*.

That one person who was bound to hate you no matter where you worked or where you went to school. There was always at least one, and she was it.

In her younger years, she would have been drawn into Sarah's petty little agenda, but these days, Ali was attempting to turn over a new leaf and build a life for herself.

Obviously, some days were harder than others.

On the harder days, she tried to remember that she was a, more or less, mature adult with responsibilities and a level head on her shoulders.

The harder days made her want to punch a wall.

Jab. Cross. Hook. Jab. Cross. Hook.

Ali expelled a quick breath with each extension as she alternated arms. The satisfying sound of her padded fists connecting with the leather went a long way to reducing her stress levels. The muscles in her arms and shoulders had reached the numb stage while the strands of long brown hair that had escaped her elastic tie stuck to her sweaty face and neck as she pounded out her frustrations on the heavy bag.

Maybe, if she wore herself out enough, she'd skip the dreaming part of her night and slip right into an eight-hour coma.

Boy, had she lowered her expectations these days.

Hank's Gym was in an old, run-down building, bracketed by a tattoo parlor and a pawnshop. The once-white walls had long since faded, sporting random patches of exposed red brick that she knew weren't an interior designer's nod toward authenticity. Neither was the duct tape that held together more than a few of the bags, and nor were the worn gray mats that covered the cracked concrete floor. It might not be much to look at, but it gave her something that she couldn't get at the gym back in West Grove.

Anonymity.

There was something to be said about being able to walk into a place where no one knew her last name, let alone about that time when she was fifteen and had gotten caught making out with Matt Baker behind the concession stand after the homecoming game. Small towns were a pain in the ass most of the time, as their memories were long and well informed. So, whenever she had the time or just the inclination to hit something, she'd drive thirty minutes outside of West Grove to come here.

Luckily for her, people didn't come to Hank's to socialize. The Sarahs of the world wouldn't set foot in a place like this in their brand-new tennis shoes and designer leggings to stand around, taking selfies in the mirror with their pristine makeup still in place. Hank's was rough with an even rougher-looking clientele. And it might smell like the inside of her brother's old gym bag, but in here, she wasn't Ms. Crawford, Lee and Maggie's little girl, or even Mase and Jase's little sister. She was simply Ali.

"So, who is it today?" Max's voice growled behind her as she continued through her sequence.

Ali smiled to herself.

It had taken a long time for her to realize that Max wasn't actually mad at her. That the growly tone to his voice was involuntary from too many smokes a day for too many years. He'd taken over this place when his dad, Hank, died more than twenty years ago. He was a fit old man with a trimmed gray beard that contrasted drastically with his midnight skin.

"What do you mean?" Ali panted out between reps, never losing focus.

"Don't play dumb with me, girl. It's unbecoming. Whose face is on that bag you're trying to maim?"

"If I said he broke my heart, would you offer to maim him for me?"

"We both know you don't need me to fight your battles for you. What you do need me to do is tell you when that bag's had enough for one night. Now, go cool down before I have to get out the duct tape."

Ali reached out to steady the swaying bag and looked over her shoulder at the grump. "Careful, Max. People might start to think you care." She wiped at the sweat running down her forehead with her arm, pushing her hair out of her eyes.

With an annoyed huff and a few muttered words, Max turned and walked away.

Okay, so maybe they won't.

But Ali smirked at his back. He could walk around, growling and grumbling all he wanted. At least she saw him for the big ole, squishy marshmallow he was. Either way, she knew he was right. It was time for her to go home.

Walking over to her bag along the wall, she gingerly pulled the fingerless gloves from her hands, wincing when she freed her knuckles. They were swollen, sore, and more than a little red, but at least she hadn't ripped any skin off this time.

As she tossed her gloves in her bag, the front door banged shut behind her. Ali looked at the group of women who'd entered before glancing at the large industrial clock on the wall, realizing how late it had actually gotten. Monday nights at seven, Max taught a women's self-defense class with the help of volunteers from some of the surrounding areas.

Ali had taken a self-defense course in college and loved it. Her teacher had been a tiny Asian man who could make the likes of Chuck Norris flinch. Looking at the women who were trickling into the gym to warm up on the mats at the back, she categorized the wide range of personalities.

There were the few who stood in a group, giggling with one another. They were no doubt here more to ogle the instructors than learn, but in the end, they might just walk away with a few helpful tips.

Then, there were the two who stood, stretching on the mat, laser-focused and ready to kick some male ass.

But it was the two girls in the corner that tightened Ali's stomach with sympathy. They looked terrified. They weren't here out of curiosity or willingness. They were here out of necessity. They were the few who would benefit from what they learned here more than any of the other women. But her twisting gut told her that help might be coming too late for one, if not both of them.

Swallowing hard, Ali looked away as she shrugged on her hoodie and hoisted her bag onto her shoulder. When she turned to leave, her eyes swung past the weights area in the back where she stopped short, locking eyes with a man who was leaning his forearms across the bar of the bench press.

He was dressed in loose blue track pants and had on a black T-shirt that hugged his thick biceps. But it was his pale eyes that held her attention as he studied her without apology. He wasn't leering or ogling; it was more like he was working through a difficult math problem. When he didn't look away, she raised her eyebrows in a *can I help you* gesture. But the man simply dipped his head as his full lips pulled into the faintest of smirks before he pushed off the bar and walked away.

"Oh-kay," she muttered, turning toward the front.

Kellen watched as the little firecracker pushed open the front door with more than a little attitude before strutting her firm ass right through it.

He'd seen her here a few times. She was a hard one to miss. Built like a wet dream, and she knew how to work the bag. She might have caught him staring tonight, but if she just took a look around once in a while, she'd realize that, at one point or another, she drew the eyes of every guy with a working dick and a beating heart. Even some of the chicks gave her a good once-over, either wishing she batted both ways or contemplating switching teams themselves. And, as far as he could tell, she never noticed any of them. She was too busy working her shit out on that sack of sand. Some people smoked; others drank. Some ran or went to yoga. Some used their fists. Some handled it better than others, but everyone worked their shit out one way or another, or it destroyed them.

Max fell into step beside him as they made their way over to the mats to get class started.

"Little tip?" the old man asked, giving him the side-eye.

"Doesn't matter if I say no. You're still gonna tell me."

"Keep your eyes to yourself 'cause that filly will eat you alive, boy."

"Noted," Kellen replied with a deep chuckle.

"It's your funeral." Max gave a shrug.

"But what a way to go."

Addison came to stand with them just then, so Max simply gave him a look that said he agreed before he stuck his thumb and finger in his mouth, letting out a sharp whistle, gathering the women around.

"Evening, ladies! I'm glad to see everyone back tonight. Last week, we talked about awareness and all the ways we can reduce the risks we take by being smart and vigilant. But, no matter how careful you are, sometimes, shit happens, and you need to be ready for anything. Tonight, Kellen and Addison here"—Max jerked his thumb out to indicate them standing at his side—"are going to show you how to defend yourself in close quarters."

"That's right," Addison began, stepping forward. "Kellen here might be built like a mountain, but that can be used against him. Let's face it; in most cases, men are bigger. Men are stronger. This isn't an opinion. This is a fact. They are simply built different than us. But this doesn't mean they get to win. Ever. You don't need to be bigger or stronger. You just need to know how to use what the good Lord gave you."

Kellen gave the women standing around them an encouraging smile. "Self-defense is about survival. It's as simple as that. There are no rules. There are no limitations. You do what you have to do in order to survive, and we are going to give you the tools to do that."

Addison wasn't wrong. He was a big guy—six-two and topping two hundred–plus. That being said, he was resigned to the fact that he was going to be sore tomorrow. It was literally his job to get his ass kicked tonight. And Addison wouldn't go easy on him. Hell, she was going to enjoy it. These women needed to see the five-foot-nothing Army Ranger take him down. Then, they needed to do it, too.

They went slow, and the women gained more and more confidence as the night wore on. By the end of their class, he'd been flat on his back a total of twenty-seven times. Every woman there had taken him down at least twice.

Everyone, except Mia.

But she'd practiced with her sister, Hayley, and Addison. She had the moves down, but she wasn't ready to take him on. The girl shook like a leaf if he got within five feet of her, so he kept his distance, confident that she'd get there in her own time. Hell, at least she could look him in the eye now. It might not seem like much, but for Mia, it was a huge hurdle that she couldn't manage last month.

Kellen sat on the bench, stretching out his stiff back, as the women gathered their things and mingled around. When Addison finished talking with a group of the girls, she plopped down next to him.

"Wanna go grab a drink? I'm buyin'. It's the least I can do after knocking you on your ass half a dozen times."

"You're right. It is the least you can do, but I have to take a rain check. My shift starts at nine."

"Oh, that's right. You'd rather slink around in the shadows, fighting evil, than face it in the light of day like the rest of us." Suddenly, she slapped him on the thigh. "Holy shit! You're Batman!"

"Fuck off, Corporal Daley."

He battled down his grin, causing Addison to throw her head back with glee as she happily clapped her hands.

"It's okay. Your secret is safe with me."

"Joy."

He got up and shouldered his bag. Addison followed suit as she waved good-bye to Max.

"You know you love me. Speaking of, Adam wanted me to remind you about poker night next Saturday and to, I quote, 'make sure the fucker doesn't pick up an extra shift.'" Adam was Addison's husband and his closest friend.

"I'll be there." He held the door open for her and followed her out to the street.

"With beer."

"With beer," he agreed.

"And pizza." When Kellen just looked at her, Addison continued, "What? You should know by now that I'm not going to cook."

"Fine, beer and pizza. But get your mom to make that spinach dip I like."

"Deal." She beeped the locks on her black 4Runner and paused with the door open. "Be careful out there tonight."

Even though she could never pass up an opportunity to give him a hard time, he knew she worried about him. She was like the little sister he never had.

"Yes, ma'am."

With one last nod, she got in her car and started it up.

Kellen waited until she pulled out into the street before he headed for his Dodge Ram parked down across the lot and back to West Grove to start his shift.

2

"The ricotta pancakes look delicious. Oh! They have s'more waffles!" Callie browsed the breakfast menu a little manically before slapping it down on the table. "Ugh, why does everything sound so good? This kid is determined to make me break the world record for growing out of fat jeans."

Damn, Callie was right. The ricotta pancakes were the bomb, but so were the biscuits and gravy.

"Who cares?" Ali shrugged her shoulders as she contemplated getting an extra order of bacon. "Get both, and then we can go maternity clothes shopping when we're done."

"You're an enabler."

"You're not wrong," Ali agreed without looking up from her own menu. "I'm going to spoil that kid to within an inch of its life, so you'd better just get used to it now."

"Have I ever told you how awesome you are?"

Ali laid down her menu and leaned into the table, staring into Callie's gleeful eyes. "Possibly but tell me more. Better than Jase, right?"

Her sister-in-law's face broke into a smile as she giggled.

Callie was one of those people who lit up a room. Even on her tough days—and she'd had her fair share—she could still manage a smile for a complete stranger. When Mason had brought her home for Thanksgiving the year before last, Ali had instantly loved her. She had known that growing up with two annoying, overprotective, gross, amazing brothers was going to pay off one day. Gaining a sister like Callie was worth every wet willy and rubber snake.

"Fine." Callie ignored her with a grin, never willing to pick favorites. "But, when I'm the size of a barn, it's going to be your job to tell me I'm pretty at least twice a day."

"Oh, please! If my brother doesn't have that job covered, it will be *my job* to kick his ass."

"What's this I hear about my ass?"

Mason appeared and planted two hands on their table. With a smile, he leaned over his wife, who beamed up at him and greeted her with a quick, albeit thorough, kiss.

"Excuse me." Ali patted the Formica tabletop to get their attention. "You're crashing girl time. Go away."

"See how she treats me?" Mason asked Callie, completely ignoring her. "How are you feeling?"

"Honey, I'm fine. I'll be better once I feed your offspring. Seriously, if these last few weeks are any indication of how much this kid is going to eat after he pops out, we're in trouble."

"Any nausea today?"

"Yep. Right over here." Ali swallowed hard, fingers to her throat, earning a glare from her brother.

Callie simply gave her a cheeky grin as she gripped Mason's hand, pulling his attention back to her. "Eight days and counting. I think it's safe to say, we're past that stage. You need to stop worrying so much."

"Babe." Mason raised his brow, saying everything with that one gentle word, and his wife got the message loud and clear.

"I love you, too."

Honestly, if two people were ever meant for each other, they were it. Ali didn't even have it in herself to poke fun anymore. These two had something the rest of them could only hope for. So, in a rare show of restraint, she kept her mouth shut and let them have their moment.

"Did you seriously come all the way down here just to check on me?"

"Of course not. I'm grabbing Kade and me some breakfast to go. I had no idea this was where chick time was happening."

"Mmhmm."

There wasn't a person at this table who believed that.

"Speaking of…" Ali prompted.

"All right, I'm leaving." With another kiss for his wife, Mason turned to Ali. "Take care of her for me."

"I've got her, Mase."

"Hello? I'm right here! I'm carrying a baby, not missing my legs."

Ali crossed her eyes at Mason as he grinned before walking to the counter to collect his order. Callie could complain all she wanted, but it wasn't going to change a thing. She should know that by now.

Callie was watching her husband walk out the door, carrying the white sack, when he turned and smirked at her with a wink, like he knew she was ogling. And she totally was. Unrepentant, Callie blew him an air kiss in return. Ali would be completely grossed out if she wasn't so damn happy for them. But a person could only take so much cuteness.

"So, where were we?"

Without missing a beat, Callie's mind switched right back to the dilemma at hand. "Ricotta heaven or sugar coma?"

"Right."

"Ooh, and French fries."

Ali laughed at her sister-in-law's exuberance. "Whatever floats your boat, preggers."

After their waitress brought their order, Ali watched in awe as her pixie-sized sister-in-law demolished her Frankensteined order of pancakes, waffles, fruit, and, yes, French fries.

"Okay, I give." Callie pushed her plate away and slouched back into the booth in defeat. "Let's go buy me something with an elastic waistband."

Ali felt Callie's pain as she finished off her last strip of bacon.

Placing some bills on the table, Ali stood up from the bench seat. Grinning down at Callie, she asked, "Am I going to have to roll you out of here?"

Callie slowly joined her. "That is so close to true; it's not even funny."

Ali was still smiling as Callie pushed her way out of the diner doors. They headed toward her car that was parked at an angle just up the street. Before Callie rounded the front of Ali's Mustang, she turned back and started to say something, but instead, she looked down the sidewalk beyond Ali and waved.

"Hey, stranger!" She beamed at whomever she'd spotted.

"Callie," the deepest, rumbliest, *sexiest* voice Ali had ever heard replied a few feet behind her left shoulder. "I hear congratulations are in order."

Ali casually glanced over her shoulder to sneak a peek at the owner of that voice and immediately jerked her head back around.

No fucking way.

Her astonishment must have shown on her face because Callie gave her a strange look before addressing her friend.

"Thank you! I'm halfway through my fourth month already. It's going by so fast. Have you met my sister-in-law yet?" She gestured to Ali, ignoring her subtle head shake. Callie's smile was somehow smug and giddy at the same time. "Ali, this is Officer O'Connell. Kellen, meet Ali Crawford."

Now, she had no choice but to turn around and did so with a strained smile on her face. She would not, under any circumstances, insult Callie's friend.

"Hello. It's nice to meet you."

The infuriatingly handsome man from Hank's Gym merely looked at her when she faced him, but slowly, his lips pulled into a sexier-than-sin grin that made her heart speed up.

She'd be lying if she said he wasn't attractive.

Hell, attractive is an understatement. Eatable? Nope. Fuckable? Definitely.

She wasn't sure if she'd ever been face-to-face with anyone she'd describe as fuckable before.

Soft lips were surrounded by dark stubble that was at least a week past needing shaved. And all six-foot-plus of him was solid, tight muscles and slim hips. He wore that dark blue uniform like some men wore a tailored three-piece suit. And, even though his mirrored aviators hid his eyes from view, she could still feel their intensity burning holes through her composure. That did nothing but fan her irritation even more until she wanted to smack that ridiculously wicked grin off his face.

But, instead of acknowledging what he made her feel, she let her bitchiness surround her like a warm blanket.

Finally, he spoke—in reality, only a few seconds had passed since she turned around—"Ms. Crawford, I believe the pleasure is all mine."

"Oh, I know it is," she replied with a sugary smile before she turned back to her car.

Yanking the door open, Ali slid inside and shut the door more gently than she'd thought possible, letting the quietness of the interior surround her. With the push of a button, she started the car before studiously fiddling with the air settings to keep from looking out her windshield, allowing her irritation to bubble.

He has some nerve!

First, he'd crept on her at Hank's, and now, he had the audacity to stroll down the street of her hometown, in front of her diner, like he owned the place.

Where does he get off? Is no place sacred anymore?

Ali was well and truly peeved by the time Callie daintily slid into the passenger seat, quietly shutting the door.

"Not to complain, but you're kinda stealing my thunder." Callie stared her down as she crossed her arms on top of her tiny baby bump.

"Say what now?"

"My thunder, Ali. You're stealing it. Me, the woman who is carrying around your niece or nephew, is the only one here who gets to throw a bitch fit and get away with it. And I get to blame it on my hormones. What's your excuse?"

Under the scrutiny of the unbelievably patient pixie next to her, Ali's irritation faded away as fast as it had come on.

What's wrong with me lately?

"I'm sorry." She sighed long and thorough. "You're right. I have no excuse. From here on out, I will leave the bitch fits strictly up to you. Deal?"

"Thank you. I'd appreciate that."

Ali put the car in reverse and looked out at the sidewalk in front of the diner with a pang of guilt. Kellen was nowhere to be seen as Ali backed out of the space and headed toward the only maternity store within a hundred-mile radius.

It only took a few minutes for Callie to lay a cleverly placed jab, which caused the tiny flicker of guilt Ali felt to spread like a cancer. Apparently, Callie wasn't going to let her off as easily as she'd hoped.

"Did you know the first time I met Kellen was the night my garage burned down?"

"No, I didn't know that."

The year before last, some psycho had gone off the deep end, and in the process, decided to set Callie's garage on fire. It'd happened right after Mason and she got together. To say the two of them had had a rough beginning was a colossal understatement.

"Yep, he showed up in the middle of all our crazy and was never anything other than solid." Callie waited a beat as she looked out the window at the passing trees. "He's one of the good ones, Ali."

The soft way she'd said it only served to make Ali feel worse.

"Next time I see him, I'll apologize." Ali gripped the steering wheel. She didn't break promises, so she didn't make them lightly. Even if it killed her, she'd make good with Officer McPain In Her Ass.

"You'll probably sleep better if you do."

Ha! If that was all it took to get some sleep, she'd grovel at his feet.

Kellen pulled the old file out of his desk and flipped through it until he found what he was looking for.

Alyssa June Crawford, 22. Senior at Montana State University.

"Fuck me." He lounged back in his chair.

There wasn't a picture attached because he'd never had to dig that far. After the fire, he'd looked into everyone, including each of Callie's and Mason's families and friends. Alyssa—excuse him, *Ali* had never even been considered because she lived out of town at the university at the time of the incident.

Of all the people he'd thought the girl from the gym could be, he never thought she was Mason Crawford's little sister. According to her DOB, that would put her at twenty-four now. It fit.

Kellen picked up a pen and absently spun it around his fingers.

Now, he had questions.

Basic questions, like: *Is she just visiting, or did she move back?* He'd only seen her at Hank's a few random times. Maybe she just worked out there while she was in town. *But, if she did move back, where is she living? Where does she work?*

Then, there were the more complicated questions, like: *If she lives back in West Grove, why would she drive to a different town just to go to the gym? And what exactly did I do to piss her off so fast?*

He also wanted to know why there were shadows under her eyes.

But, most importantly, and regardless if he should want to or not: *When can I see her again?*

Fortunately, he had no qualms about running her name as he opened the search engine on his computer. Seconds later, he had the answers to his more basic questions.

Good news? Chances of running into her again just went up tenfold. Bad news? Now, he needed the answers to his other questions.

"O'Connell!"

Kellen looked up to see Travis Brooks striding toward his desk.

Sighing to himself, Kellen closed out the window on his computer.

"What do you want?"

He didn't have the patience to deal with this prick most days, and today was not an exception.

"Heard you helped Beatrice Watkins with her groceries this morning." The officer—and he used that term loosely—propped his ass on the edge of his desk. "You didn't happen to save Whiskers from a tree while you were at it, did ya?"

"Well, not everyone can sit around with their dick in their hands all day, now can they?"

Brooks's eyes hardened as he tried again. "What exactly were you protecting the old lady from? Killer carrots? Or maybe she was in danger of breaking a hip?"

"I know you're slow, Brooks, but you do realize it's 'To Protect and *to Serve*,' right? Or did you miss the day at the academy when they covered that last part?"

Having run out of anything else clever to say, Brooks mumbled a, "Whatever," before walking away to annoy someone else.

Kellen hadn't had to deal with the asshole for over a week while he was out of town on vacation, and if he was lucky, Brooks would decide to transfer to wherever the hell he'd been and make all of their lives better. Hell, Kellen would settle for not being called in to work to deal with his shit for the next two days, so he could enjoy his days off.

As he placed Callie's file back in his desk and locked the drawer, his phone vibrated in his pocket.

Sarge: See me before you leave.

With a few clicks of his mouse, he shut down his computer before dropping his paperwork off at the front desk on his way to the back office.

The door was open, and his boss sat behind his cluttered desk, squinting down his nose through his glasses, cussing at his computer screen.

Schooling the grin on his face, Kellen rapped a knuckle on the doorjamb, causing the older man to look up.

"You wanted to see me, Sarge?"

"Yeah, get your ass in here."

Kellen stepped into the office but stayed standing as Sergeant Hoffman spun around and grabbed a sheet of paper that was sitting on the printer.

"You like kids?"

"I guess you could say that," he answered cautiously.

"Perfect." Sarge jutted out the paper he held. "Take Reedman with you."

Quickly skimming the email, Kellen huffed out a laugh.

"Problem, son?"

"No, sir."

He'd just been handed a request to come in and speak to the kindergarten classes at West Grove Elementary where, twenty minutes ago, he'd learned a certain brunette worked as—wouldn't you know it?—a kindergarten teacher. Kellen didn't know what kind of Karma he'd racked up to earn this, but he wasn't going to complain.

Grinning at his boss, he suggested, "How 'bout we take Rogue, too?"

Sarge pointed a finger at him. "I knew you were the right choice. I'll have Reedman call and clear it with the school."

3

Shit. Shit. Shitty shit.

Two more hours. She could make it two more hours.

In the corner of her room by the door, Ali leaned heavily on the counter in front of the sink with her eyes closed, fighting off the dizziness.

She'd woken up this morning with a pounding headache and a foggy brain after another restless night. With her eyes full of sympathy, Shelby had tossed her a bottle of pain relievers from across the room, holding the sleeve of her sweater over her mouth and nose. They'd been down this road a few times already since she started her new job.

When she'd thought of becoming a teacher, she'd dreamed of shaping the minds of the next generation and that amazing feeling she'd have when the light bulb went on for a struggling kid who finally got it. What she hadn't thought about were the germs. About the classroom full of germ-infested, booger-picking, snotty, sneezing, hacking, projectile-vomiting five-year-olds. Her room was a revolving door of infections and viruses. Hand sanitizer was her best friend at this point.

After too short a time, the recess whistle sounded with a too-loud screech outside the window across the room.

Her reprieve was over.

Turning on the tap, Ali splashed some cold water on her face and popped two more pills before she went to collect her kids.

At least the rest of the day was going to be a breeze. Their regular schedule was being substituted for a few guest speakers from both the local fire department and police station as well as a couple of paramedics. They'd been learning about the importance of community and how it played a role in their everyday lives. And, since they weren't able to get permission from the school board to take all of the children on a field trip, they'd decided to bring the field trip to them.

Joyce Galloway had been teaching here since before Ali attended elementary school in West Grove, and she'd made it her personal mission to get all of the first responders here today. The woman was a force to be reckoned with. She'd made phone calls, written emails, and personally visited each and every station until she made it happen.

As Ali pushed out the double doors, she squinted against the spring sunshine and found her class lined up, ready to go.

"Yo, class," Ali barely croaked out above the excited chatter.

But the familiar line got the kids' attention as they straightened out and turned toward her with a strong, "Yo, Teach!" in response.

"Remember, today is a bit different than normal, so we are going to walk quietly to our room, hang up our coats, and line back up as quickly as we can, okay?" Her voice cracked again on the last few words, but they got the message.

As calmly as a group of excited five-year-olds could be, they made their way back to the room and followed directions. Then, Ali led them down a different hallway and into the small gym.

The gym looked like what Ali suspected every elementary gym in the country looked like. The floor was gleaming light-colored wood, just big enough for a basketball court, complete with hoops on the walls at each end and a few extras placed around the perimeter of the room. The back wall held a six-foot-high climbing wall with blue mats on the floor beneath it. The opposite wall faced a set of wide stairs that led to the retractable separator, which opened into the cafeteria where they held their school programs. This was where she walked her students now and had them sit in the row behind Mrs. Anderson's class facing the stairs. After Mrs. Galloway's class took the row behind them, the three teachers made their way to the front of the room where their guest speakers were gathered.

There were three volunteers from the fire department, all of whom were wearing blue T-shirts with the department logo on the chest and matching blue cargos. As well as two paramedics wearing similar blue uniforms, including her uncle Ben. Uncle Ben was shaved bald, having lost most of his hair decades ago, with a thick gray mustache that he refused to shave, no matter how much crap she'd given him for it. He was adamant that he looked like a young Sam Elliot. He winked at her as she walked by, and she smiled in return. But, as her eyes drifted over the two uniformed police officers next to them, she faltered in her steps.

Next to the woman she recognized as Officer Reedman, known from an unfortunate incident involving a regrettable night at sixteen, stood Kellen in all his glory. If her head hadn't been so cloudy, she might have had the capacity to wonder if he'd be one of the volunteers today, but it honestly hadn't crossed her mind. On her way past, she gave him what she hoped was a polite smile before standing to the side as Mrs. Galloway stood front and center to get things started.

"All right, I need everyone to settle down and look up here." The kids quickly began to focus and quiet down as she held her fingers up and softly counted, "Three…two…good. As you know, these last few weeks, we've been learning about our community and how all the different parts work together to make our town the wonderful place that it is. Today, we have some special people who have taken time out of their busy schedules to come and share with you. So, I need all of you to do your best to be quiet and be respectful to our guests. I know you will have a lot of questions, but let's leave them until each department is finished, and then you can raise your hand and wait to be called on. We'll try to get through as many of your questions as we have time for."

Mrs. Galloway turned and smiled at the man behind her before she stepped aside to come and stand with the rest of the volunteers, Mrs. Anderson, and Ali. The three firemen stayed where they were and stepped forward, promptly earning the kids' rapt attention.

Ali knew her kids had been looking forward to this all week. It had been all they could talk about. Eighty percent of the time, if you asked a five-year-old, especially the boys, what they wanted to be when they grew up, they'd say a fireman, a cop, or a soldier. These were their heroes, and they watched in awe as the men spoke.

While the kids were held captive by one of the men donning a heavy tan fire suit, Ali felt someone come stand beside her. She glanced to her right and found Kellen. He seemed much bigger, standing shoulder-to-shoulder with her, than he had the other day. Ali wouldn't consider herself short, and he still had at least six inches on her.

"You doin' okay?" he whispered, keeping his eyes trained forward.

"Aces. Why do you ask?"

"Oh, I don't know. Could have something to do with the pale skin and choppy breathing. Or maybe it's the way you're swaying on your feet."

Crap.

She hadn't thought it was so noticeable.

She caught the eye of one of her students who'd turned to talk to the boy next to him and motioned for him to be quiet and pay attention before she whispered back, barely moving her lips, "Occupational hazard. I'm fine."

"Of course you are, but why don't you have a seat before you fall over?"

Ali gritted her teeth. More than a little annoyed that he'd noticed. Annoyed that she felt like crap. Annoyed that he'd ordered her around. And annoyed that the pills were barely keeping her on her feet. "I said, I'm fine."

"Whatever you say, Ali Cat."

"Excuse me? Did you just call me an alley cat?"

When he didn't respond, she glanced up at him and found him completely relaxed, calmly watching the firemen, who began taking questions from the kids.

That only annoyed her further.

"You know, in polite society, people don't go around, pointing out how crappy someone else looks."

"And, if you'd retract your claws a little, you'd realize I never said you looked crappy. I was simply asking if you were feeling okay."

Double crap.

Ali closed her eyes.

He was right, and she was being a bitch again.

She had ninety more minutes before she could head home and quarantine herself—and her bitchiness—in a hot bath where she couldn't infect anyone else.

But there was something she needed to do first.

"I'm sorry."

"Accepted," Kellen easily returned.

"No, not just for today," she continued. "For last week in front of the diner. I was snippy that day, too, and you didn't deserve it then any more than you deserve it now."

"Has everyone been graced with your sunny demeanor lately, or am I just that lucky?"

She huffed out a surprised laugh. "You've been luckier than most."

"Any particular reason?"

None that she was going to share. "Luck of the draw, I guess."

"Fair enough."

"And I appreciate your concern. Thank you for checking on me."

See, I can be nice.

"Anytime."

A few moments passed in silence as they listened to the firefighters wrap up the kids' never-ending questions. One of her kids started getting a bit restless, so she knelt down next to her row to discreetly remind them to be respectful, but when she stood back up, the room went a little topsy-turvy as black spots danced in front of her eyes. Before she could right herself, Kellen's warm hand gripped her elbow to steady her.

"You're not okay."

"I'm fine," she replied automatically, still feeling the head rush.

"*No, you're not.*"

It was the first time she'd heard a bit of steel enter his voice, and it surprised her enough that she turned her head to really look at him for the first time today.

She'd only ever seen his eyes from across the room or covered with sunglasses, but up close, they were incredible. The light cornflower blue was surrounded by a dark ring that blended toward the pupil. The effect made it look like the plasma ball she'd had when she was younger. Although, if the muscle flexing at his jaw was any indication, they could just look that way because he was seriously miffed.

"Why didn't you call in sick?" he demanded quietly, still gripping her elbow.

"Are you kidding? It's easier to just pop some cold meds and suffer through the day than to get a lesson plan drawn up in time for a substitute. And that's assuming there is even one available. Chances are, the other teachers would have had to split my kids up into their classrooms, and that would have just made their days harder. It was easier this way."

She gently tugged her arm back, and he let her go.

Ali was tired to her very core. She didn't have the energy to spar with him right now. Making a small compromise, she walked to the wall and leaned against it for support. She didn't have it in herself anymore to pretend she was even the slightest bit functional. The meds she'd taken obviously never kicked in. What she needed was a hot bath and about twelve hours of sleep.

She must have zoned out because, the next thing she knew, Kellen's deep timbre sounded from the front of the room where he stood with Officer Reedman. She'd completely missed her uncle Ben and the other paramedic.

Sixty more minutes.

Kellen stood in front of the school with Rogue sitting by his side. She was a beautiful three-year-old German shepherd, but unlike the traditionally colored breed, she was mostly black with only a few tan highlights on her chest and belly. Rogue was one of their drug dogs. Kellen had known she'd be a hit with the kids.

They'd moved the herd of kids outside, so they could check out Officer Reedman's squad car along with the fire truck and ambulance. While they waited their turns, he allowed the kids to come over and pet Rogue a few at a time. The K-9 was lapping up the attention. It wasn't often they were allowed to spoil the dogs like this.

While Rogue rolled over, so the kids could have a clear shot at some belly rubs, Kellen looked across the yard and found Ali. She was sitting on a short retaining wall, leaning forward with her weight on her hands, next to the ambulance, watching the kids explore. Even from this far away, he could see how pale she was.

What the hell was she thinking?

Anyone with two working eyes and a brain in their head could see she was sick. She tried to hide it, but she wasn't doing a very good job. Those shadows he had seen under her eyes last week looked even more pronounced next to the color of her skin. She needed to be in bed.

Before long, one of the other teachers blew a whistle, and the kids quickly stopped what they were doing to form three separate lines in front of their teachers.

Jesus, they're better trained than Rogue.

The dog, having abruptly lost all of her tiny hand massagers, accusingly looked up at him.

"Don't look at me like that. It's not my fault you're an attention whore."

Rogue apparently took offense and turned her back to him. Kellen smirked at the dog and then looked up to see Officer Reedman walking over to the grassy area he was standing in. When she rested a hand on Rogue's head, the dog's tongue lolled out, happy to have someone touching her again.

See? Attention whore.

"I think that went well." Tina smiled up at him.

She had been on the job for twenty years and was tough as anyone he knew, but she had a soft spot for stuff like this. It was why Sarge had sent her.

"Yeah, the kids seemed to have fun."

"It's okay to admit you had fun, too, ya know." She eyed him for a few seconds, seeming to mull something over. "You were a good fit today. They responded to you, and you handled every question thrown at you without scaring them. It was almost like you knew what you were doin'. You got a bunch of kids somewhere you forgot to mention?"

Kellen huffed out a laugh. "Not unless there's someone out there with a big-ass secret I don't know about."

"Well, you're a natural. You'll make a good dad someday."

Kellen was saved from responding when Mrs. Galloway walked over to them. The tall, fifty-something brunette was the absolute definition of what he'd call a kooky kindergarten teacher. She was wearing a knee-length dress that had birds all over it. The fact that she had on yellow tights and about five too many necklaces only made it worse. That being said, it was obvious the kids loved her. She seemed like a truly kind person who loved her job.

"Thank you, thank you, thank you!" She stopped in front of them, clasping her hands over her chest. "The kids were in heaven! They'll be talking about this the rest of the year!"

"We were happy to do it," Tina said while Kellen simply dipped his chin in acknowledgment.

"I can't thank you enough for taking the time to do this." Mrs. Galloway looked behind her and noticed Ali and Mrs. Anderson leading the kids inside as they waved good-bye to the guys from the fire department and ambulance. "I've got to get the kids in and ready to head home, but I hope to have you guys back again someday!"

"You can count on it." Tina smiled at her, genuinely meaning it.

With one last grin in their direction, Mrs. Galloway caught up with her class just as they walked through the front doors.

"I'm going to take Rogue back to the station. You headed out, too?" Tina took the leash he handed her.

"Not yet. I've got something I've got to do."

"Whatever you do, make sure to get gone before school lets out. Nothing like an armed policeman at the school to freak the parents. Rose will have your ass if she gets bombarded with calls from worried parents."

Rose was a little terror of a woman who ran the front desk down at the station.

"I think Rose is going to have a busy afternoon regardless." Kellen scanned the parking lot and the street beyond to see it was already filling up with parents waiting to get their kids.

Three buses were just now pulling in behind their three vehicles, seeing as they were all parked at the curb in front of the school, which was obviously the bus lane. If an armed policeman was enough to freak them out, then two armed policemen, a K-9 unit, a cruiser, three firemen, a fire truck, two paramedics, and an ambulance were going to cause an absolute panic.

"Well, shit." Tina looked around and came to the same conclusion. They could already see some of the parents talking on their phones and taking pictures. "Nothing to do about it now." She shrugged her shoulders and then headed for her car with Rogue.

Kellen acknowledged the paramedics pulling out right after her with another dip of his chin. The firemen were almost done packing up the equipment they'd had out for the kids when he walked over.

"Hey, man. What a day, huh?" Wade greeted him as he gripped Kellen's hand, slapping his back with the other.

"Can't say I've ever had one like it."

Wade was a solid guy. Kellen had met him when he joined Adam's poker games a few years ago. The man gossiped like a sixteen-year-old girl and cussed like a sailor, causing people to forget that he was as smart as they came. He could be living large, making millions if he wanted to, but for whatever reason, Wade lived here in town in a little two-bedroom house close to the station, making pennies.

"Saw you talking to Ali in the gym." Wade raised his brow, fishing for information.

"Yeah." Didn't mean Kellen had to give him anything. Especially since there wasn't anything to share.

Wade tried a different angle. "Heard she's seeing somebody out in Wellington."

"I wouldn't know." Kellen shrugged. Although Hank's was in Wellington. Could explain why he saw her at the gym.

"Whoever he is, he's one lucky son of a bitch. She might have looked like death warmed over today, but I gotta say, I still wouldn't kick her out of my bed the next morning."

"Now, you're just bein' a dick."

"What? That was a fuckin' compliment!"

"Only you would think that."

Wade simply grinned, not caring.

Knowing he was opening himself up to Wade's speculation, Kellen risked asking, "How well do you know her?"

Wade eyed him seriously for a second, his mind working overtime behind his stare, before a slow smile worked its way across his face. "Only by reputation. I went to school with her brother Jase. She was hard to miss. Even back then. I haven't seen her in some years, but those years have definitely been kind to her."

Kellen couldn't argue there.

Just then, the bell rang, signaling the end of the school day and cutting off any further comment from Wade. It took only seconds for the side door that led into the fenced-off playground to burst open. Kids poured out like wasps from a nest that had just been kicked.

"All right, man, you guys had better get out of here." Kellen slapped Wade on the shoulder. "I'll see you at Adam's tomorrow."

"Later." Wade stepped up into the passenger seat, giving Kellen a two-finger salute before the truck pulled out and drove off.

Turning away from the madness, Kellen headed for the front doors of the school.

Ali stood on the playground, waving off the last of her students with a smile that probably looked as tired as she felt.

I did it.

She'd made it through the day.

Breathing out a weighted sigh, she walked back to the building and swiped her badge that was hanging off of the lanyard around her neck. The panel by the door turned green as the locks clicked open, allowing her to open the door. On the other side, there was a student rummaging through the Lost and Found.

"Hey, Ms. C," the third grader looked up, greeting her.

"Hey, Camilla. What did you lose today?"

It seemed the girl was always searching for something. A few days ago, it had been her coat, and last week, she'd somehow misplaced her socks. How she'd managed that while she still had her shoes on was one of the many mysteries Ali would never solve.

"My lunchbox. There was still half a tuna sandwich in there. If I leave it here all weekend, my mom's gonna kill me." She'd already made it to the bottom of the bin, but she was still searching like it was Mary Poppins's magic bag, and her lunchbox would show up if she just kept digging.

"Did you check the bin inside the lunchroom yet?" Ali suggested.

Camilla's little blonde head popped up so fast that her hair went flying. The quick movement made Ali dizzy. "The lunchroom!" Camilla spun and took off running down the hall. "Thanks, Ms. C.!"

Ali didn't have it in her to remind Camilla not to run. Besides, the girl was already rounding the corner at the end of the hall. So, instead, Ali headed for her room. The sooner she got out of here, the sooner she could curl up in her bed.

By now, the rest of the school was fairly quiet with only a few students lagging behind in the halls. Most of the teachers' rooms were dark and empty as well. On Fridays, the building cleared out fairly quickly. Both the students and the staff were ready to be anywhere but here.

Once she reached her room, she started stacking chairs and picking up the tables. With the excitement at the end of the day, they'd cut their time incredibly short, so none of their normal end-of-the-day routines had been kept. They hadn't meant for the first responders to stay as long as they had, letting the kids explore every inch of their vehicles. Ali didn't mind picking up the room though. The experience the kids had had was more than worth a few extra minutes spent gathering a few pieces of paper and a pencil—or twelve.

She was just straightening the beanbags in the reading corner when she heard the soft knock on the door. Glancing back, she saw Kellen standing in the threshold, looking as broody as ever.

"Hey," her voice barely squeaked out the word. She swallowed before trying again. "I figured you'd be gone by now." Ali picked up a few discarded books, putting them back on the shelves.

"Thought I'd check on you. See if you were able to get home okay."

Taken aback, Ali stopped picking up and turned to look at him. He was leaning a shoulder against the frame of the open door with his arms crossed over his chest.

"Why wouldn't I be able to get myself home?" For once, with Kellen, it hadn't come out bitchy. She was genuinely curious.

Uncrossing his arms, he walked into the room, stopping a few feet from her. "Considering you were having trouble staying vertical twenty minutes ago, I thought I'd see if you'd accept a ride home."

"Oh." Ali paused, blinking a few times. "Well, that was nice of you."

His eyes went soft at her tone, as did his voice. "Just tryin' to help."

Before she could figure out what to do with the cop in front of her, Callie rounded the doorframe, already talking, "Finish up, sister mine! I'm declaring tonight girls' night at your house." Callie stopped short when she saw Kellen, worry clouding her eyes. "Is everything okay?"

"All good," Kellen assured her. "I was just here to talk to the kids."

The worry vanished as she beamed up at him. "I bet they loved that." Callie turned to look at Ali, and her smile disappeared, sympathy taking its place. "Aw, honey. You look like crap."

Ali glared at her sister-in-law, but when she saw Kellen was fighting a grin, she turned her glare on him. He held his palms out to her in an *I didn't say it* gesture.

"Oh, you know I love you." Callie flicked her wrist, brushing off Ali's glare. "But I'm going to nix the idea of girls' night. You need sleep and meds—and possibly quarantined."

"I'm way ahead of you." Her plans were to do just that.

"Do you need a ride home? I'll have Mason get your car for you later."

Ali gave in, thinking that sounded like the better option, considering those black spots were starting to make a reappearance the longer she stood here.

"Sure," she said at the same time Kellen said, "I've got her."

"Wait, what?" Ali looked back at him.

"I said, I've got you." Kellen tipped his head in the direction of her desk. "Grab your stuff."

"No."

Just NO. I didn't agree to that.

"Really, Kellen, it's no trouble," Callie assured him. "I can take her."

"See." Ali gestured toward her sister-in-law, but she might as well have been talking to herself, for all the attention they paid her.

"No offense, Callie, but you should steer clear." Kellen looked pointedly at her baby bump.

Callie placed a protective hand over her little belly, apologetically looking back at Ali. "You do kinda look contagious."

This is ridiculous.

"I got myself here. I can drive myself home."

"No, you won't," both Callie and Kellen said at the same time.

"I'm not getting in the back of your cop car." So far, in her life, Ali had avoided that scenario. She'd like very much to keep her streak going.

"I've got my truck."

"You drove your truck to work?" Now, Ali was confused.

"I'm not working."

"But you're here." Ali pointed to him, indicating his uniform and all his cop-y glory.

"It's my day off." Kellen's jaw hardened, the only sign that he was losing patience with this whole conversation.

"You gave up your day off to come talk to the kids?" Callie gushed. "That was so sweet of you!"

"It's no big deal."

"Yes, it is. Okay." Callie clapped her hands together, having made up her mind. "Kellen's going to take you home. I'm going to go and grab Mason, and we'll get your car home.

I'll pick up some chicken soup on the way, and I'll leave it at your front door. You are to do nothing but sleep and rest this weekend. I'll call tomorrow to check on you, but just holler if you need anything before then, okay?"

Ali stared in disbelief.

I've just been railroaded by Tinker Bell.

But Ali didn't have it in her to fight anymore. She just wanted to get home. "Fine."

"Keys." Callie held out her hand.

Without protest, Ali walked over to her desk and scooped up her keys. Taking the key fob off of her key ring, she tossed it to Callie.

"I hope you feel better." Callie gave her a small smile.

"Thanks, Cal."

Callie blew her a kiss before turning to walk out the door, leaving her alone with Kellen.

How in the hell did this happen?

"Ali," Kellen called.

It took her a second, but eventually, she managed to look at him.

He tried not to laugh at the expression on her face. It was part-shock, part-resignation, part–pissed off, but tired definitely won out. It was that last part that made him lose his humor. "Grab your stuff."

"Right." She turned and walked back to her desk.

As she powered down her computer, she pulled on her coat and packed up a purse the size of a small suitcase.

Oh, nope. Not her purse.

That, she grabbed out of her bottom drawer.

How much shit can she possibly have?

Next, she grabbed her thermos and turned off the misty thing sitting next to her monitor.

Pausing, she looked around her room. "I think that's everything."

"You sure? I got a truck. We can fill it up."

The small smile she gave him was the first genuine one he'd seen from her, and he tried to ignore the way it made his stomach tighten.

"I'm sure."

As she passed him walking to the door, he snaked his fingers under the strap of the mini suitcase, transferring it to his shoulder.

Her big brown eyes shot to his, startled when the weight lifted, but she only paused a moment before muttering a quiet, "Thanks."

Kellen looked down at her, transfixed by the soft look in her eyes.

There's the sweet.

"After you." With a smile pulling at his lips, he shut the lights off and followed her through the doorway.

Just outside her room, coming down the hall toward them, was an older man rolling a large trash can behind him. The cluster of keys attached to his belt loop jingled as he walked.

He smiled easily when he got closer to them, his leathery skin crinkling at his cheeks. "'Bout time you headed home." He gave Kellen a curious glance but didn't comment on his presence.

"Don't you start in on me, too," chastised Ali.

"Won't say another word about it." The man zipped his lips and held his hands up before continuing, "But I did get a brand-new bottle of disinfectant just for your room."

Ali grinned a tired grin at the man. "You're a gem, Daryl. There's a Java Chip Frappuccino in it for you."

"Now, you're speaking my language." Daryl's face sobered, and his eyes softened. "Rest up, kid." Turning his stare to Kellen, the shorter man ordered, "Take care of my girl."

"Yes, sir." Kellen dipped his chin in a brief nod.

The older man nodded in return before heading around them.

They were all going their separate ways when Ali suddenly stopped and turned around to call out to the man's retreating form, "Fifty-nine!"

With a hearty chuckle, Daryl replied without a backward glance, "Better luck next time, girlie!"

"Damn it," Ali huffed.

Perplexed, Kellen asked, "What was that about?"

"Nothing. Just my sanity slowly chipping away," she muttered before walking away.

Whatever the hell that had been, he was glad she had people looking out for her. Kellen had a feeling she wasn't as tough as she liked people to believe. He couldn't help but grin at her back as he followed her down the hall and out the front doors where the wind immediately slapped them in the face.

Rolling in overhead were dark storm clouds that had obliterated the sunny spring day from earlier.

"That's me." Kellen pointed to his truck standing alone in the middle of the guest parking lot at the front of the building.

Silently, the pair made their way across the asphalt as the wind whipped Ali's long hair back and forth, tangling it around her face. She did her best to capture the unruly tendrils with her free hand, holding the bundle close to the side of her neck.

Hurrying ahead of her, Kellen opened the passenger door. "Up ya go."

She didn't waste any time, grabbing hold of the inside handle and stepping onto the footboard, hoisting herself in. Once Ali was seated, he shut the door before making his way around the front of the truck. Hopping in, he tossed Ali's bag in the backseat and started the engine. The diesel came to life with a rumble, and he reached over to turn up the heat.

"Where to?" he asked even though he'd seen her address when he ran her name through his computer.

"Head to Main Street." Ali ran a hand over her hair, smoothing it down.

Neither of them said another word as he pulled out of the lot. Ali looked spent as she settled into the seat, staring blankly out of the window. He knew that kind of tired, so he kept the radio at a low murmur and let her relax. But, as tired as she was, she didn't let the silence linger for long.

"So…a cop, huh?" she asked as he made the left onto Main Street.

"Yep."

"Was it the uniform?"

He cracked a grin and looked over at her. "Just the handcuffs."

She snickered out a laugh that ended on a weak cough. "And here I thought, you were in it for the doughnuts."

"You're not wrong." He stopped at the four-way, turning on his left blinker.

"Turn right here." She pointed in the opposite direction he was planning on taking, but he flipped his blinker over, following her lead. "Okay, now the real answer," she pushed.

His little Ali Cat had unknowingly stumbled on to a much deeper conversation than either one of them was ready for, so he kept it vague. "I imagine it's the same reason you had for becoming a teacher."

"The money." She nodded in understanding before propping her elbow on the armrest on the door, lowering her cheek to her fist.

Good to see her smart mouth wasn't inhibited by her cold.

"Definitely. I'll be buying that vacation house any day now."

She smiled but closed her eyes, not quite able to keep up the banter.

Kellen thought about giving her another smart-ass answer but settled on the least complicated version. "Truth is, I was young and needed a steady job."

And isn't that the tip of the fucking iceberg?

The rain started slow just then, a few drops smattering his windshield as he paused for a woman crossing the street with her two little dogs in tow. They hurried across with a wave of thanks, beelining it for the cover over the gas station seconds before the sky opened up.

His wipers were working double time now.

She mumbled something that sounded like, "And so the plot thickens," but it was hard to hear her as the rain pounded down around them. Raising her voice, she said, "Go straight and then take the second left."

Kellen continued to follow her directions even though they were nowhere close to where he thought she lived. In fact, they'd just passed his own apartment building when she had him take another left at the corner.

"That's me." Ali pointed up ahead to an older house on the right. One that sure as shit was not the address he'd looked up.

Kellen pulled to a stop along the curb and put the truck in park. This wasn't an apartment building like his own but rather a large two-story house that had been converted into what looked like four apartments. Two on the upper level with stairs off to either side and two on the ground level with their entrances facing each other in a large alcove.

"How long have you lived here?"

"Six months or so," she said tiredly as she unbuckled her seat belt.

Kellen watched her shaky movements and knew she was done. He wished he could ask more, but for right now, he'd let it go, as she was struggling to keep her eyes open.

"Let's get you in." He made a move to open his door when he felt a cold hand on his arm.

"What are you doing?"

"What does it look like I'm doing?"

"You're not walking me in."

He locked eyes with her as he clenched his jaw. She looked more awake than she had the last ten minutes. That fight was back. The same one she'd shown when he offered to take her home. He'd be damned if he was going to drive her all the way home and leave her and that damn suitcase to walk on her own to her door in the rain.

Fuck it.

Without another word, he opened his door, grabbed her big-ass bag out of the back along with his coat, and stepped out of the truck as she looked on with her mouth gaping like a fish.

His hair was quickly soaked though as he rounded the hood. The rain was ice-cold, dripping down his face, so he wasn't surprised to see it was starting to turn to slush as it gathered at the bottom of his windshield. When he reached her door, he jerked it open and stood back.

"Let's go." When she didn't budge, he held back his smirk but just barely. "You walk, or I carry you." He figured her preference differed greatly from his own.

Her chocolate eyes narrowed. "You wouldn't."

"Just give me a reason, sweetheart."

She moved then, grabbing her belongings. When she stepped out of the truck, he lifted his coat over both their heads. It wasn't perfect, but it kept most of her dry. The last thing she needed was to be out in this.

"Which one?"

"Bottom left."

They hurried until they were between the doors to the two bottom apartments. Under the cover of the overhang, Kellen lowered his coat as Ali flipped through her keys. Her hands were shaking enough to fumble the keys, but Kellen fought the urge to take them from her and unlock the door himself. He had a feeling she'd have more to say about that, and he just wanted to get her in where it was warm as fast as they could. Eventually, she got the door unlocked and turned to him with a sigh as she squared her shoulders.

"Thank you for the ride."

Kellen didn't bother to hide his smirk this time. "Did that hurt? It looked like it hurt."

"Bite me." But a smile pulled at her lips before she turned around and opened the door. Just inside, she set her keys on a small table and flipped on a light switch, illuminating the hallway beyond. "You were an unexpected surprise today, Kellen O'Connell."

"I'll take that." He could think of worse things he'd been called over the years. Handing over her bag, he continued, "Get some rest."

"That's the plan."

"Lock up."

"You're bossy. You know that?"

"You can call me whatever you want as long as you lock the damn door. I'll see you soon."

He didn't wait for her to reply as he turned and headed for his truck.

They'd definitely be running into each other again soon. He'd make sure of it.

4

Ali woke slowly. Keeping her eyes closed, she burrowed further under her covers. The sheets were soft and warm and far too cozy to abandon. There wasn't a sound to be heard besides the heat quietly blowing through the vent under her window.

Lying there, she took stock. Her head didn't feel like it was going to explode, her limbs were heavy with sleep but not aching, and her throat no longer felt like she'd swallowed a cactus. Overall, it was an improvement. She still didn't feel up to running a marathon, but she didn't feel like she was dying anymore either, so she'd take it.

Lifting the corner of her comforter, she peeked out. Her room was dark, and there wasn't any light coming in from around her curtains.

Stumbling out of her room, she made a much-needed stop in the bathroom before making her way down the hall and into the living room. That was where she found Shelby curled up in the corner of their deep-set, baby-blue couch with a bowl of popcorn, watching Netflix.

Surprised, Shelby looked up when Ali walked in the room. "Hey, sleepyhead! How are you feeling?" Setting her popcorn on the end table, she patted the spot next to her.

Ali happily lay down, resting her head on her friend's legs. "I think I'm gonna live."

"Glad to hear it. You want something to eat? Callie dropped off some soup if you're feeling up to it."

Ali's stomach growled at the mention of food. "That sounds great. I'm starving."

She moved to stand up, but Shelby held her down.

"I got it. You just take it easy."

"You're awesome." Ali snuggled back into the couch, snagging the blanket off the back, wrapping up in it. "What are you doing up so late?"

"I might not be a night owl like you, but I am capable of staying up past seven o'clock." Shelby laughed as she walked to the kitchen.

"It's only seven?" *Wait a minute…* "It's Saturday?"

"Yep."

"I've been asleep all day?"

"Yep."

"No wonder I'm starving." The last thing she'd eaten was a banana Friday afternoon at school.

"A mini coma can do that. You *did* surface for a few minutes this afternoon but just long enough to use the bathroom and take some more medicine."

Ali vaguely remembered that. She'd never looked at the clock though. Hell, she'd barely opened her eyes.

Shelby came back into the living room, carrying a tray, bending down to place it on Ali's lap. It had a bowl of steaming soup, some crackers, a glass of orange juice, a spoon neatly placed on a napkin, and some more cold medicine. "Eat up, buttercup."

"You're going to make someone the best wife someday."

Shelby grinned at her as she sat back down on the other end of the sofa. "Well, it's not going to be Eric."

"Date number three didn't go as planned, I take it?"

Last night had been she and Eric's third official date, and as far as Ali knew, they'd done no more than kiss good night.

"To say the least," Shelby agreed with a sigh. "Let's just say, the sparks were markedly absent."

"I'm sorry, hon."

"It's okay. Now, I can move on to better things," her friend said with a resolve that Ali envied.

"Still, I know how much you wanted it to work."

"I know. But you can't force what's not there, right? We both deserve better than that."

Ali knew she was right, but it still made her sad for her friend. She had the softest heart of anyone Ali knew, and she wore it on her sleeve. Shelby wasn't the kind of girl to leave anyone, guy or girl, wondering where they stood with her. If she liked you, you knew it. If she cared about you, you knew it. And, if she was pissed at you, you really knew it.

"To better things." Ali raised her glass toward her friend.

"Amen, sister." Shelby clinked an imaginary glass to hers. "Speaking of, who's Kellen?"

Ali choked on her orange juice, sucking it down the wrong tube. The acidy liquid burned like the fires of hell, scorching her lungs. She felt Shelby slapping her back as she tried to cough it all back up.

When she could breathe again, Ali looked at her friend with watery eyes. "What?"

"I think you heard me just fine." Shelby's eyes were full of glee as she tried not to laugh.

"Oh, I heard you. I just don't know how you knew to ask about him."

Shelby simply got up and walked back into the kitchen. Returning a few seconds later, she dropped Ali's phone into her lap and sat back down. "That's how."

Ali picked her phone up and looked at the locked screen. She had a missed call and voice mail from Callie. Another missed call from her mom along with a text asking her how she was feeling. And there, at the bottom of the list, was a text from a number she didn't have saved in her Contacts.

Unknown: It's Kellen. Just checking up on you. Hope you got some sleep.

How in the world did he get my number?

49

But the answer came to her before she even had to think about it.

Callie.

"So, I ask again, who's Kellen?" Shelby repeated.

"He's one of the police officers who spoke with the kids yesterday. He gave me a ride home."

"Oh." Shelby deflated a little. "That's not nearly as exciting of a story as I was hoping for."

"Sorry to disappoint."

It truly wasn't an exciting story. But it wasn't as boring of a story as Ali was making it out to be either. She told herself that, when she felt better, she would tell Shelby everything.

"You're forgiven. Now, eat your soup before it gets cold."

"Yes, ma'am."

Together, they settled back into the couch, and Shelby resumed her movie.

"I see your fifty, and I'll raise you another twenty-five." Adam dropped his chips into the growing pile in the middle of his kitchen table.

The beer had been steadily flowing for the last hour, and the pizza was long gone. Now, the guys munched on the chips and dip Addison had set out before she left to see a movie with her sister, leaving the six men sitting around the oval table, nestled in the bay window of her kitchen.

Adam and Addison lived in a four-bedroom house in a little cookie-cutter subdivision two blocks from the best elementary school in Wellington. All of their neighbors waved when you drove down the street, and they always stopped to say hello if they saw you outside when they walked by. Eighty percent of the houses on the block had bikes on their neatly trimmed lawns and basketball hoops in their driveways. His friends didn't have any kids yet, but he knew they'd been trying for the last few months. Kellen had no doubt that they'd make great parents.

The Daleys were so domesticated that it should be funny, but Kellen was envious. They even had the requisite golden retriever, named Sam, who was currently lying under Kellen's chair.

Give it a few more months, and Addison will have Adam driving a minivan before he knows what hit him.

Smirking at his own thought, Kellen matched Adam's bet. "Call." His chips rattled when they hit the others.

At this point, they were the only two left playing the hand.

"Burn and turn, baby." Wade sat to Kellen's right, flipping the fourth card down onto the table.

It was the two of hearts. Not a great card, but Kellen already had a pair of twos in his hand. This was made even better by the pair of red fives and queen of spades already on the table. Without a hint of emotion, Kellen rapped his knuckles on the wood.

"Oh, ho-ho, big man havin' second thoughts already? Gettin' a little gun shy on me?" Adam was a talker.

Most people would think it was a tell, but it didn't matter if he had a shit hand or a royal flush; Adam ran his mouth regardless.

"All right, let's make this interesting." His friend rubbed his hands together before he picked a black chip off his pile and flipped it toward the middle. "That's one hundred to you. If you think you can hack it."

Kellen mulled this over as he took a swig from his beer bottle, staring at his friend across from him. "All right." He set his drink down and plucked a few chips from his own pile, tossing them in. "I call."

"Get ready, boys." Adam looked around the table at the other men there. "I'm about to whoop his ass harder than Addy did a few days ago."

Jax, Wade, Thomas, and Stephan all laughed from their seats.

"The way I hear it, you spend the better part of Monday nights flat on your back," Jax said with a hoot, sitting to Kellen's left. Jax was Addison's little brother, home fresh from a four-year stint in the military. He was good people.

"You heard right," Kellen said with a grin of his own, giving in to the amusement.

The kid spoke the truth. Hell, he had the bruises to prove it.

Stephan, Adam's neighbor, got up to grab another beer out of the fridge. "Addy is one tiny powerhouse. You've got balls, O'Connell." He popped off the top of his beer on the way back to the table and flicked it into the trash before sitting down between Wade and Adam.

"I just don't get it," Thomas piped up from the other side of Jax. "Why would you sign up for that shit, man?"

Thomas was one of Wade's guys from the station. Kellen didn't know him all that well, and the parts he did know, he didn't like, so he chose not to comment. He didn't need to explain himself.

But Thomas wasn't looking for an explanation, as he continued, "All I know is, if I'm going to spend the night flat on my back, I'm damn sure gonna be enjoyin' myself."

Instead, Kellen asked Wade, who'd been silently watching the exchange, "Are we going to play or what?"

Wade grinned good-naturedly. "Burnin' and turnin', boss." He proceeded to discard the top card before picking up the final card, flipping it over next to the others. "Ten of clubs, gentlemen."

Again, Kellen chose to check.

"What'd I tell ya? Runnin' scared, boy, ain't gonna get ya nowhere." Adam picked up two chips and tossed them in. "That's two hundred to you."

"I call." Kellen added two hundred dollars' worth of chips. "And I raise you another two." Casting in the others, he sat back.

Adam narrowed his eyes at him from across the table. "Oh, it's like that?"

"It's like that," Kellen confirmed with a smile.

"Okay, okay. Officer O'Connell wants to play now." Adam picked through his remaining chips. "I'll see your two and raise you another two." The chips joined the others with a clatter.

Kellen finished off his beer before placing it behind him on the counter. Turning back around, he picked up his own chips, flinging them in with a flick of his wrist, matching Adam's bet. "Call. It's showtime."

"Read 'em and weep, baby!" Adam slapped his cards down, faceup. "Two pair, bitch!" He'd flipped over the three of hearts and the queen of diamonds to go with the two fives and the queen of spades already on the table.

"That's a good hand," Kellen admitted, causing Adam to start to do a weak-ass victory dance in his chair. "It's *almost* as good as a full house."

Kellen turned over his pair of twos one at a time and watched Adam's face fall.

"Motherfucker!"

Kellen's chuckle was lost in the hoot of laughter coming from the others as he scooped the pile of chips closer with a sweep of his arm.

"All right, let's go again." Adam slapped the table, rattling the beer bottles. "I've gotta win my money back."

Just then, Kellen's phone buzzed next to his beer. He paused stacking his chips to flip it over, and a smile spread across his face at what he saw.

> *Ali Cat: Sleep did wonders. I might actually live.*
> *Thanks for checking on me. Again.*

Callie had texted him last night with Ali's number. *Just in case you want to check on her*, she'd said with a winking emoji.

Callie had many strengths. Subtlety was not one of them. And, since she'd gone to the trouble of giving him Ali's number, he'd figured it'd be rude not to put it to use.

"Hey!" Wade snapped, not missing his grin. "You know the rules. This is a guys' night! No chicks allowed, and that includes text messages."

"Fuck off," Kellen ribbed without any heat, but he still wiped the grin off his face and dropped his phone in the pocket of his flannel shirt.

But it was too late. He'd already caught the attention of the others.

"What are you hiding over there?" Jax asked as he made a reaching grab for Kellen's phone.

"None of your damn business." Kellen easily slapped his hand out of the way as the younger boy laughed.

"You got a girl we don't know about, O'Connell? Who is she?" This came from Stephan.

Goddamn it, this is exactly what I wanted to avoid.

"Bet I could guess." Wade cocked a knowing eyebrow, and Kellen thought real hard about knocking that smug look off of his face.

"Wait a minute! What don't I know?" Adam demanded, looking between the two of them. "Do you have a woman?"

"He wishes," Wade supplied before Kellen could say anything.

"When the fuck did this happen? I talked to you three days ago, and you didn't say anything."

"When did this turn into a slumber party?" Thomas complained, and for once, Kellen could agree with the man. "Are we going to braid each other's hair now? I thought we were here to play poker!"

"Screw that." Adam dismissed him. Pissed to be out of the loop, he pushed, "Who is she?"

Kellen clenched his teeth as Wade answered, "Have you ever met Mason and Jase Crawford?"

"Yeah, once or twice."

"Ever met their younger sister?" Wade waggled his eyebrows.

"How the fuck do you know this, and I don't?"

Wade looked back at Kellen. "Go ahead. Tell him I'm wrong," he challenged.

Kellen glared at the self-satisfied son of a bitch. "You're worse than a sixteen-year-old girl. You know that, right?"

"So I've been told." Wade shrugged, unaffected. "And I'd like to point out, that wasn't a denial."

"That's because there's nothing to tell. She was sick, and I gave her a ride home. I checked up on her. That was her saying she's feeling better. End of story. Can someone hand me the cards, please?"

A round of "Aw!" went around the table, causing Kellen to grit his teeth.

I never should have opened my mouth.

Thomas was the only exception. He just rolled his eyes as he downed the rest of his beer.

"When was this?" Adam asked as he shuffled the cards, ignoring Kellen's outstretched hand.

Again, Wade answered him before Kellen could, "Yesterday, when we were at the school, talking with the kids."

"Seems like you went a little above and beyond your job description there, man." Jax popped a few peanut M&M's in his mouth, smirking at him.

This conversation needed to switch gears. Kellen didn't like sharing his personal business, especially in mixed company. Adam was good, and so was Jax. Even though Wade liked to run his mouth, Kellen still considered him a friend. Stephan was cool, too, but they were strictly just poker buddies. By mixed company, Kellen specifically meant Thomas. The guy was an ass. He ranked right up there with Brooks on his douche-bag list. How he'd managed to wrangle an invite from Wade was a mystery but one Kellen planned on rectifying post-fucking-haste.

Solidifying his opinion, Thomas piped up, understanding dawning on his face, "Wait, wait, wait." Thomas held out his hands, getting their attention. "Are we talking about that sweet little number from yesterday? The one with the long brown hair and the tight ass?"

Kellen breathed deep, his nostrils flaring. This was the exact reason Kellen hadn't wanted to say anything. Thomas had been one of the other firefighters at the school yesterday. Kellen had managed to avoid him beyond a nod of acknowledgment in his direction, but that didn't mean he hadn't seen him leering at Ali from across the gym either. If Thomas kept running his mouth, he was going to piss him off.

He kept running his mouth.

Thomas locked eyes with Kellen. "I'll tell you what. I bet she's got the sweetest—"

"All right!" Wade clapped his hands together, wisely interrupting whatever it was that Thomas had been about to say. "Whose deal?"

Still, no one made a move to deal the cards.

Kellen leaned onto his elbows, staring Thomas down. The other man merely sat back in his chair with a grin. The word *grin* wasn't right though because his had a mean edge to it that didn't set right with Kellen. He'd seen sneers like that before.

Thomas was the first to look away when he got up to get another beer.

Sitting back in his chair, Kellen looked over at Wade. "It's my deal." He held his hand out to Adam, who finally handed him the deck.

An hour or two later, things were beginning to wind down. Jax and Stephan were down to their last few chips. Kellen was still hanging on, but Adam and Wade were both kicking his ass. Thomas, however, was done for.

Kellen watched the cocky grin spread across Wade's face as he flipped his cards faceup on the middle of the table and knew it was over.

Wade had masterfully conned Thomas into going all in with just a pair of aces and easily beat him with a straight, queen high. Kellen chuckled under his breath when Thomas's jaw hardened at the sight of Wade's cards.

"How does your ass feel now, fucker?" Wade taunted while the other guys laughed.

"That's bullshit." Thomas glared across the table.

"Now, now," Wade said evenly. "You got fucked right and proper. Don't be a bitch about it." Not sparing the other man another glance, he stacked his chips in symmetrical piles.

"Whatever, man. I'm out." Thomas pushed his chair back and stood up. "I'll win my money back next time. You can count on it."

Kellen scoffed at that. There wasn't going to be a next time. Not if he could help it. The man was only out twenty bucks. He'd survive.

Thomas gave them all the one-finger salute and turned to walk out the door.

The five of them sat silently until they heard the front door slam shut.

Adam was the first one to speak up when he propped his elbow on the table and leveled a finger at Wade, "Never again."

Wade held his hands up in front of him. "Lesson learned."

Remarkably, they'd managed to keep it civil the last few hours, but Kellen wasn't sure if that was due to better judgment on Thomas's part or Wade's superior mediator skills. The man had an uncanny ability to defuse a situation before it had a chance to light.

With a flick of his wrist, Kellen folded his next hand and got up from the table.

Taking a break, he made his way outside and sat on the front step, looking out to the quiet street. It was just after eleven on a Saturday night. Only three houses still had their porch lights on, and the steady chirp of a cricket came from somewhere in the bushes.

His own apartment was located close to the station. It was never this quiet. If it wasn't the noise of cars passing by, it was his batty old neighbor's TV that she constantly left on or the dogs in the apartment below his, yipping at their shadows.

One day, he'd have this. The quiet neighborhood with the bikes on the lawns where he could sit on his front step and listen to the crickets.

After a while, muffled hoots and hollers sounded from inside.

Kellen smiled into the night.

That was probably either Jax or Stephan being knocked out of the game. He needed to head back in for the next hand, but first, he pulled his phone out of his shirt pocket and opened Ali's text from earlier.

The fact that she'd texted him back with more purr than hiss boded well. His little Ali Cat had shown him her claws, but he had a feeling there was a whole lot more to her than that.

The sound of the door opening behind him made him turn around just as Adam leaned through the jamb.

"Get your ass back in here, so we can finish you off. Jax is out."

"Comin'." Kellen typed out a quick text before he pocketed his phone and pushed up from the stairs.

Time to win his money back.

Ali thought that, after losing an entire day, she'd have trouble sleeping, but she was having trouble keeping her eyes open. It wasn't like Shelby's movie was dull. It was loud and full of explosions, but Ali wasn't even sure what it was about at this point. *Something about spaceships maybe?* She blinked her eyes wide and tried to focus.

Yep, they're definitely in space.

She was resting at one end of the couch with her head propped up on a couple of pillows while her feet were tucked up against Shelby's legs. The soft quilt was gathered around her like a warm little cocoon, but her eyes kept drifting to the phone that was resting on the couch by her face. She couldn't keep from looking at it every few seconds, no matter how heavy her eyelids became. Ever since she'd sent that text to Kellen, she'd been antsy, waiting to see if he'd text back.

It was truly pathetic.

She didn't even like him.

So what if he was beyond sexy? Looks didn't make the man after all.

There was also that whole Good Samaritan thing he had going on that some women might find attractive, but he had an intense broodiness about him that was definitely *not* attractive.

Nope.

Not at all.

Ali didn't have to check to see if her pants were on fire because she could feel the heat all the way in her cheeks. But the point was, would it kill the man to lighten up a little?

And what? You've got rainbows coming out your ass?

Bitchy Ali had a good argument, but the fact remained that she was not hung up on Kellen O'Connell.

Definitely not.

The short vibration jolted her eyes open. Sleepily, she lifted her head and looked around. The TV was off, the living room was dark, and she was alone on the couch. Shelby must have gone to bed.

Ali rubbed at her eyes with her knuckles. She didn't remember falling back asleep. With a groan, she stretched her arms out in front of her and pointed her toes, feeling her stiff muscles protesting. This couch was better than most, but it was still a couch. She was regretting not going back to her room earlier instead of trying to stay awake.

Flipping the blanket back, she started to push up from the couch when, suddenly, she remembered what it was that had woken her up.

With a quick check of the couch and the floor, she finally located her phone folded up in the covers. There, on the front of her screen, was exactly what she didn't want to admit she'd been waiting for.

> *Kellen: Glad you're feeling better. We'll talk soon.*
> *Get some more sleep.*

Ali dropped her head back onto her pillow, covering her face with her hand.

Okay, he might not be so bad.

5

The country music was low and quiet in the confines of Kellen's patrol vehicle as he drove through the deserted streets around the park. It was just after two a.m. on Tuesday night—or technically, it was Wednesday now.

It'd been a slow night in West Grove. Just the usual shit. An anonymous call complaining about a barking dog that had no longer been barking by the time he reached the neighborhood. Another about loitering teenagers at the local gas station who'd turned out to be harmless. Just a couple of kids from the high school, but the owner called on every kid if they didn't get in and get out after one of them had gotten busted dealing pot out of his trunk in the parking lot a few months ago.

His cell vibrated in his breast pocket, and he pulled it out, not surprised that it was the station.

"O'Connell."

"Hey, Kellen. It's Amelia. I just got a noise complaint from over on Ashland. Your GPS says you're the closest. Would you mind driving by?"

"I'm on my way." Kellen flipped a U-turn in the intersection. "And, Amelia?"

"Yeah?"

"Next time, use the radio."

"Okay."

She sounded like he'd just kicked her puppy, but he forged on.

"Remember, you're not asking us for favors. It's our job. Get on and tell us where we need to be."

"I know. I'm just afraid I'll screw it up again."

Amelia had just finished training, and this was her first night going solo. At the beginning of her shift, she'd gotten on and royally fucked up the call signs. Brooks, the prick, had been giving her shit all night for it. She was only nineteen and a single mom at that. She needed this job. She also needed to toughen up, or she wasn't going to make it.

"You will, but you've got to get over it. It's part of learning the ropes. Just don't get me killed. Deal?"

"No pressure." She gave a strangled laugh on the other end of the line.

"I'm pulling onto Ashland now. You're doin' fine, kid."

"Thanks, Kellen."

Without saying good-bye, he hung up the phone and turned off his music before he rolled down his window.

Off the bat, he didn't hear anything besides the sound of his tires creeping down the street. There weren't any parties going on, and all of the houses appeared quiet. Nothing seemed out of place. He was just about to call it a wash when he heard it. The *click, click, click* on the pavement. He rounded the corner and saw a moose and her two calves strolling down the empty road. Slowing to a stop, he kept his distance. The young ones were brand-new and all legs. The calves were the first he'd seen this season. It wasn't rare for them to wander into town, and the majority of the people were smart enough to leave them alone, knowing better than to get between a moose and her calves. But that didn't mean they couldn't cause a racket when you were trying to sleep.

Kellen picked up his radio. "This is O'Connell. The cause of the noise over on Ashland was just a mama moose taking her kids for a walk. The family looks like they're headed back to the woods. I'll tail them for a bit to make sure. Might want to put out a reminder for everyone to steer clear though. They're out early this year."

"Copy that, O'Connell," Amelia called out, sounding like a veteran already.

For the next twenty minutes, he kept his distance, creeping along behind the trio. The cow didn't like it one bit, keeping a close eye on his cruiser.

This time of night, the whole town was quiet as the group moseyed their way down Main Street, passing the blinking stoplights and the dark storefronts. It'd be hours still before the town woke up and started their day. Even the night owls were sound asleep by now.

When they reached the edge of town, the cow looked back with one last indignant huff that sent a cloud of warm air into the cold night before the family disappeared into the tree line.

Smiling to himself, Kellen thought, *Yeah, same to you, mama.*

Flipping another U-turn, he headed back toward the center of town. Without thinking of where he was headed, he found himself driving down Hickory Street. He knew exactly what had brought him this way, and she had a smart mouth and eyes the color of expensive brown leather. He made this same lap once or twice a night. It'd unintentionally become part of his regular patrol route, and he was okay with that. They all tended to patrol their own neighborhoods along with the areas that needed it the most. This hadn't been a street he took too often, but since it was just a block away from his place, he'd changed his route a little.

The whole block was dark, except for a few streetlights lining the walk, and everything seemed quiet. But, as he came up on Ali's building, he slowed when he saw a figure sitting on the front step, wrapped up in a heavy quilt. Their head was covered and bent low, preventing him from seeing anything else. Curious, he pulled the cruiser over to the curb and got out. Keeping his eye on the bundle of fabric, he made his way up the walk. The figure stayed huddled in the quilt, but fuzzy owl slippers peeked out from the front.

Clicking on his flashlight, he shone it on the lump of bedding and asked, "Everything okay here?"

An annoyed Ali looked up and shielded her eyes. "*Jesus,* turn that off. Everything's fine."

Kellen clicked the light off but not before he saw her red-rimmed eyes and blotchy face.

He'd seen her sweaty. He'd seen her sick. And he'd even seen her bitchy. He liked all those looks on her, but this one had his gut clenching.

"What's wrong?"

Just freaking perfect.

Why was it that this man seemed to always see her at her worst?

Tonight's dream had been beyond vivid, hitting her harder than normal. Ali didn't know what had made this one different, but she'd burst into tears as soon as she woke up and found herself in her own bed. She shared a wall with Shelby and didn't want to wake her, so she wrapped up in her quilt before sliding on her slippers and coming out front. She'd been losing it for a good ten minutes when she glanced up and watched the patrol car pull to a stop. She knew it was him before he even said anything. She'd made a vain attempt to wipe her face before she looked up, but she had known it wouldn't matter. She wasn't a pretty crier by anyone's standards. There was no hiding her complete meltdown.

So, she did what she always did. She lied.

"It's nothing."

Those wolfy eyes of his all but glowed in the night as they saw right through her. "That's bullshit, and we both know it."

Ali tried a little harder but couldn't quite force herself to look him in the eye this time. "It's those damn *Grey's Anatomy* reruns. They get me every time."

Kellen furrowed his brow but didn't comment again. Instead, he clipped his flashlight to his belt before sitting down next to her on the step. He didn't ask her any more questions. He just sat there, shoulder-to-shoulder with her, as another tear trailed down her cheek.

When he spoke again, his voice was low and rumbly as he all but whispered, "You're lying to me." She started to deny it again, but he continued, "And I'm going to let you because you don't know me. Not yet anyway. But I *am* going to sit here until you're ready to go back inside."

Ali sucked in an unsteady breath as another wave of tears filled her eyes again. He'd caught her raw, and she hadn't had any defenses ready for him tonight. If he had tried to push her or fix her, she would have been ready for that. But not for his quiet support. Everyone always tried to fix everything. Shelby, her brothers. Even Callie. And she loved them all dearly for it, but that wasn't what she needed.

Together, they sat quietly as the night carried on around them. Her tears eventually dried themselves up, and still, they sat.

"You probably need to go back to work, huh?" Ali asked, silently hoping he'd stay just another minute or two.

"No one's missing me. They'll radio if they need somethin'."

"Do you always work graveyards?"

"Most of the time."

"How'd you get stuck doing that?"

"I'm not stuck. I requested it."

"Why? Doesn't that screw with your sleep?"

"I'm used to it. As for the why, that's a longer story for another night."

She didn't push. She knew all about long stories.

"I should probably try to get a few more hours of sleep. Those kids will walk all over me if I don't."

"You going to be okay?"

She thought about lying again but instead said, "Thank you for sitting with me."

Avoidance was another one of her specialties. And he didn't miss her nonanswer.

"Answer me one thing."

She gave him a cautious nod.

"This happen a lot?"

She shrugged. "Sometimes."

Too often.

"Then, do me a favor. Next time you can't sleep, text me. I'm up anyway."

Ali wasn't sure she'd take him up on the offer even though she desperately wanted to, but she still found herself agreeing, "Okay."

"Okay." Kellen stood up then and reached a hand down to her.

Ali stared at his offered hand with its wide palm and strong fingers. It seemed so simple. She could easily stand up on her own and walk back inside, or she could accept a little help.

It might seem simple...but it wasn't.

Kellen stood patiently while she bit down on the inside of her cheek to keep the fresh tears she could feel burning behind her eyes at bay.

Slowly, she unfolded the blanket enough to release one of her arms, still keeping it wrapped around her shoulders, and placed her palm in his. With a firm grip and a gentle tug, he pulled her to her feet but didn't let go of her hand. Still feeling a little raw, she stared straight ahead at his throat instead of looking up to meet his eyes. His neck was strong and corded, and she watched, mesmerized as his Adam's apple bobbed with a swallow. While standing this close, Ali could feel the heat radiating off of him. She'd been freezing when she woke up in a cold sweat, and the quilt was never enough to fight away the chill. But his thumb blazed a streak across her knuckles where he rubbed, warming her hand.

"Whatever this is, don't let it eat at you."

She opened her mouth, but she stopped the automatic lie that had been about to fall out. Now that the tears had stopped, she was too tired to keep up the facade.

"I'm handling it." Although she didn't know if that was true anymore either.

"Well, if there ever comes a time when you're not, you've got my number. Yeah?"

Ali looked up at him then. His whole face had gone soft, losing some of his natural sternness. They were close enough now that she could see the thin scar below his right eyebrow and another hidden below the stubble on his jaw. She wanted to ask him about them. Anything to prolong his stay.

But she merely said, "Yeah."

This man, this once-unbearably cocksure man, had marched into her life like a battering ram. It seemed like, no matter how high she'd built her defenses, he found a way around them.

Kellen gave her a small nod before he ran his fingers into her hair and pulled her head into his shoulder. His breath caressed her ear as he whispered, "Get some sleep, Ali Cat."

Closing her eyes, she turned her head and rested her forehead against his jaw, her nose touching his neck. The deep breath she took was filled with the scent of his skin. Warm. Warm and comforting was the only way she could describe it.

Neither one of them moved.

His hand gently cradled her head, and his other held her hand. They were barely touching, but to Ali, it felt more intimate than anything she'd had in a long time.

It was amazing what the human body could live without. People got so caught up in the fact that they needed vital things like food and water that they forgot about the smaller things that, in the end, were everything. Things like this. The connection to another human. The feeling that we didn't have to go through things alone. Sure, we could survive without it, but we didn't realize how much our souls *needed* it until we felt it again. That was when we realized how much we'd missed it.

In that moment, Ali craved the feel of Kellen's rough hand cupping her slender fingers and the scratchy feel of his stubble against her forehead. She craved it more than anything, and that was why she pulled away.

Taking a step back, Ali let her hand slide from his.

She took a moment to readjust her quilt, covering her arm again and clutching it close before she met his eyes. "Good night, Kellen."

He had that look again. A look of pure, uninterrupted concentration. Like she was a calculus problem on an addition quiz. Kellen gave a single dip of his chin and rubbed the edge of his thumb on his bottom lip. Those intense eyes of his never leaving hers.

Unable to withstand his intensity, she turned and went back inside, softly closing the door before she latched the dead bolt.

As she passed the front window, she paused.

Kellen still stood where she'd left him. His head hanging down, one hand rubbing at the back of his neck. After a moment, he looked at her door one last time before turning back to his patrol car.

He'd surprised her again tonight. In fact, that was starting to become a habit of his. One she didn't mind at all.

Ali didn't know what tomorrow would bring, but for once, that didn't seem so daunting.

6

The brown grass that Ali was kneeling on sent a chill through her black slacks as she finished tying her student's shoe. Only a few green sprouts had started to make their way through the matted tangle of last year's grass. It was the first sign that spring might actually be on its way, no matter what that damn groundhog had had to say.

"All set." She patted Morgan's knee and stood back up.

"Thanks! Joey! Wait for me!" The raven-haired little pip-squeak took off at a dead run, chasing his friend across the playground, nearly knocking Joey over when he couldn't stop in time.

"Oh, to have that much energy," Joyce Galloway said on a wistful sigh as she came to stand beside her.

"Right?" Ali glanced over at her in agreement. Sometimes, these kids made her feel old.

As they watched the kids climb and run and scream, Ali's phone chirped from inside her coat pocket. Even without looking, she knew it was him.

In the harsh light of day, which had come far too early the morning after her meltdown, she'd felt like a total basket case. She was determined to forget the night before had ever happened and avoid any and all eye contact if she ran into a certain police officer anytime soon. But then she showered and dressed and was walking out the door when her phone went off in her hand.

Kellen: Good morning. I hope you got some sleep.

That was it.
Unassuming.
Nonjudgmental.
Sweet.
And, in true Kellen fashion, with a few easy words, he busted through the defenses she'd worked on putting up just an hour before.

Pausing in the threshold, she answered him back.

Ali: Enough. Thank you for staying.

Determined not to make a big deal out of it, Ali went about her day and chalked it up to a sweet gesture and nothing more. But then he sent another text and then another.

Over the last few days, he began to share little parts of his world with her. One night, it was a picture of a giant barn owl sitting on top of a fence. Accompanied by, *I thought you'd like this.* She was confused at first and then remembered the slippers she'd been wearing that night on her porch. She swore, the man missed nothing.

They'd gone back and forth a handful of times the past week. Always either before his shift or hers. Though she'd yet to take him up on his offer to call when she couldn't sleep.

"What is that?" Joyce asked her with a smile.

"What's what?" Ali looked around at the kids, wondering what she'd missed.

"That smile of yours." The older woman pointed at Ali's mouth. "I haven't seen you smile like that before."

Ali hadn't been aware that she was smiling. "I have no idea what you're talking about."

"Mmhmm. Your phone went off, and you got this smile. Who was it?"

"A friend."

"Honey, if he makes you smile like that, he's not just a friend."

"Who said it was a he?" Ali countered.

"Is it?"

"Maybe," she teased, amazed at Joyce's astuteness. "But he's just a friend. And a new friend at that." She paused, and then, not knowing why, she said, "He can be infuriating."

Joyce just gave her a knowing smile. "Well, I'll give you some advice you didn't ask for. I've known you since you were in school. I've seen you smitten. But I've never seen you smile like that. Especially as a grown woman. Maybe infuriating is just what you need."

Ali thought about the way Kellen pushed her buttons and saw right through her bullshit. She didn't like it...but that didn't mean it was a bad thing. Truthfully, these last few days, she'd found herself looking for him every time she saw a police car.

"Yeah, maybe."

"All I know is, we women need men who challenge us. Having a yes-man is boring. The day my Howard called me on my crap was the day I fell in love with him. Of course, I didn't know it *then.*" Joyce laughed at the memory. "*Then*, I wanted to snap his neck. But, looking back, that was the exact moment."

Ali had met the man a few times over the years, and he always had a smile on his face and a kiss for his wife of twenty years. "Howard seems like a good guy."

"One of the best," she agreed. Leaning in, Joyce whispered under the noise of the kids around them, "Do yourself a favor; the next time he's being infuriating, ask yourself whether you'd rather smack him and walk away or rip his clothes off. And be honest about it. Then, you'll have your answer."

Ali snorted out a surprised laugh. If anyone had told her ten years ago that she'd be having a conversation with her fifty-year-old elementary school teacher about ripping a guy's clothes off, she'd wouldn't have believed them. In fact, she probably would have thrown up in her mouth a little bit. This was another one of those moments when she realized grown-ups were regular people, too. Her first epiphany of that nature had happened when she was seventeen, watching her mother break down in tears because her brother Mason was going to miss his first Christmas. His flight had finally gotten canceled after twenty-four hours of delays due to a snowstorm that seemed to last for a week.

Since that day, she'd come to the conclusion that being a grown-up was relative. Everyone walking this earth, whether they were fifteen or eighty, had the same feelings. Lust, anger, love, or loneliness. They might mean different things at different ages, but in the end, we were all the same.

"You laugh, but you'll see." Joyce smiled and patted her on the shoulder before walking away.

Now that she was alone, Ali pulled her phone out and opened Kellen's text.

Kellen: Working a double shift through tomorrow.

The sudden disappointment Ali felt was unwarranted but unavoidable. She'd yet to bother him while he was working, and she wasn't about to start now. So, she replied with the only thing that mattered.

Ali: Stay safe.

Kellen: Always.

Putting her phone back in her coat, Ali walked around the playground until it was time to go in.

The rest of the day went by quickly even if the hours until tomorrow night seemed endless.

Kellen slid his glass forward and signaled the bartender for another whiskey.

Karen acknowledged him with a head jerk in his direction as she pulled a couple of pints for her waitress, who was waiting with a tray already lined with shots.

Perched on a stool near the end of the bar, Kellen surveyed the crowd with disinterest. It wasn't as packed as it'd be for a weekend, but Larry's was drawing a decent crowd for a Tuesday. Apparently, tonight was karaoke night.

God have mercy on his ears.

This was a bad idea.

Kellen propped his elbows on the bar, running his hands through his hair.

"What? You don't like this version?"

Kellen looked up and pinned Karen with a stare as she tipped the bottle to refill his glass.

Karen was a boisterous, full-blooded Russian woman with an accent that decades in this country had yet to dull, and she took shit from absolutely no one. She and her husband, Larry, had opened the bar more than forty years ago, and they ran a tight ship. The station rarely got calls concerning the bar. He'd known them since the first week he moved to town. They were good people.

Now, Karen's brown eyes twinkled with mirth as she smirked at him from across the mahogany bar, bracing her hands wide. The woman onstage was confidently screeching out what Kellen was sixty percent sure was supposed to be an Aerosmith song.

"I've heard better. Although you've got to admire her dedication to the high notes."

Karen barked out a laugh, turning heads their way. "You want to get up there and show us what you've got?"

"Not gonna happen."

"It's all in good fun, eh?"

"I'd rather empty a meth house, carrying a lit flare."

"Oh, so dramatic. What's it take to loosen you up? More whiskey?"

"I loosen up just fine."

"If you say so, *moy mal'chik*." *My boy*. She patted his hand with an affectionate smile before she walked to the other end of the bar where her waitress stood, signaling to her.

He'd just gotten off from his double shift, but his apartment was the last place he wanted to be tonight. Today had been one of the days that wore on his soul. Most of the time, he loved being a cop. Helping people. Making a difference. But the days when he could help no one, no matter how much he wanted to, tested his composure.

He went home, showered the mud from his body, and grabbed a slice of leftover pizza out of his fridge when it hit him. Throwing the pizza in the trash, he sat down heavily on his couch with his head in his hands.

The old man had never stood a chance.

Kellen was the first officer on the scene of a 911 call. The older couple lived in a cabin up the mountain about a mile from town. Everything was starting to thaw, making the ground slick with mud. The old man had tracked it up the steps as he brought wood in from outside. On his second trip up the steps with an armload, he slipped, falling in a heap at the bottom. His wife called it in, but he'd broken his neck when he hit the muddy ground. There was nothing anyone could do.

Days like today made it hard to go home to an empty apartment. Sitting on his couch with a beer in his hand, he listened to the noise around him. The sound of his neighbor's TV came through the wall, muffled explosions and gunfire rattling the Sheetrock. Car doors slammed out on the street, friends calling to one another. And the yip yaps from the apartment below him were barking at their shadows again. Getting up, he'd grabbed his keys and headed for the door before he lost his fucking mind.

Eventually, another song started, and a couple got onstage to serenade each other in a semi in-tune version of "Islands in the Stream." Kellen sipped his drink, thinking there was no way this was the better option, but it seemed healthier than drinking at home, alone.

If he was being honest with himself, he wasn't sure which bothered him more. The quiet house or the noises the quiet seemed to amplify. The noise never used to bother him—or at least, he hadn't noticed how loud the cars on the street sounded from his bedroom or how deafening his neighbor kept the volume on his TV. But it'd been a long time since his house was this quiet, too.

Finn had been gone almost nine months now, and Kellen still looked for his shoes by the door or his backpack hooked on the back of the kitchen chair when he got home. He hadn't gotten used to this new normal of theirs yet. He wasn't sure he ever would.

His brother was down in Bozeman, finishing up his first year at Montana State University. Kellen didn't see him all that much anymore, which would be standard for most siblings, but their life wasn't exactly the pinnacle of family goals.

For the first time in almost ten years, he didn't have anyone to look after.

He couldn't help it; he missed the little shit.

Karen only joked about him loosening up, but she'd known him long enough now for there to be more than a little truth to her teasing.

Some days, he felt like he'd lived two lifetimes already. Both of them on fast-forward.

His childhood sure as shit hadn't been what was considered normal. He hadn't gotten to play little league or go to the zoo. He had been forced to grow up too damn quick. Quicker than any kid should. And here he sat, at nearly thirty, having already raised a kid who was off to college.

That shit definitely wasn't normal.

Now that he was on his own, sometimes, he didn't know what to do with himself.

The newest torturer was announced, and Kellen threw back what was left of his whiskey.

Fuck this.

He stood up and pulled his wallet from his back pocket, tossing a few bills on the bar. Catching Karen's eye, he nodded his good-bye to her and turned to leave just as a new song began. But he paused at the commotion coming from down front.

"Get 'em, girl!"

"OW!"

"Yeah, baby!"

The catcalls and whistles all came from a table of women he could barely see in front of the corner stage as one of them walked up and took the mic off the stand.

The little blonde's face was beet red as she flipped off her friends and raised the mic. "I hate you. I hate you all."

Her words held as much venom as a baby seal, and it made his lips twitch into a faint smile.

Then, she opened her mouth to sing.

Kellen was expecting another ear-screeching performance, but what came out of that girl's mouth was anything but. Kellen folded his arms as he leaned back on the bar and listened to her belt out a version of "Church Bells" that would make Carrie Underwood proud.

The whole bar turned to take notice. She was a breath of fresh air after the last few performances.

When the last note trailed off, the crowd erupted.

But none were louder than the three women left at the table, who all stood and enfolded their friend as she hurried off the stage.

Well, I'll be damned.

Callie stood with her friend Brooke, whom he had met the night her garage was set on fire.

But it was the third girl who got his attention.

Dressed in tight black jeans and a low-cut red top, Ali was grinning so big that his breath caught.

Shelby tried to glare up at Ali, but the smile on her face kinda ruined the effect. "I should kill you for that."

"Oh, please." Ali threw her arms around her friend. "You totally rocked it, and you know it."

Ali was over the moon. Shelby would never admit it, but she'd had fun up there. The girl was a born singer.

Unable to deny it, Shelby pulled back with a smirk tipping up the corners of her mouth.

"Holy shit, girl! Who knew you had it in you?" Brooke hugged her as well.

"Seriously!" Callie added. "That was awesome!"

Shelby brushed off the praise with a giggle, but her smile was going to split her face in two if it got any bigger.

Shelby was strictly a shower singer, but when she committed, she *committed*. That was why, about twenty minutes ago, Ali had slipped their waitress a note, adding Shelby to the lineup, knowing she'd never get up there on her own.

"Next round's on me." Ali looked around but didn't see their waitress nearby, so she took everyone's requests and headed for the bar.

Larry's seemed more crowded tonight than usual. Weaving her way through the crowd, she smiled politely at an older gentleman who scooted in his chair, so she could get by.

Callie had introduced her to karaoke night about a year ago when she came home from school for a few days. Apparently, it was Brooke and Callie's tradition, and they'd eagerly pulled Ali into their night of *debauchery*. That was Callie's word for it. It sounded seedier than it was. So, ever since Ali had been back, the three of them met once a month for girls' night out for a few off-key performances and far too many drinks.

Eventually, she made her way through the tables and leaned her forearms onto the bar as she propped the toe of her boot against the gold foot rail, looking for the bartender. Spotting Karen at the other end of the counter, Ali held up her hand and smiled as the woman made her way down to her.

"What can I get you, my dear?"

"Could I get two Coronas, a strawberry daiquiri, and one Sprite, please?"

"Coming right up." Years of running the bar made her movements second nature as she expertly added the ingredients to the blender against the back wall. Less than a minute later, Karen set the daiquiri on the bar before pulling a couple of bottles from some unseen place under the counter, prying the tops off. "Your girl, she's got a set of pipes on her." She wedged a lime slice to the rim of each. "You should trick her into singing more often." Karen winked at her before she filled the glass full of ice for Callie's soda.

Ali grinned at the older woman. Nothing got past her in here.

"I will do my best. But that trick might only work the once."

"I'm sure you have your ways." Her thick Russian accent fascinated Ali to no end. "All us women do. We must use it for good where we can, yeah?"

Once the last glass hit the bar, Ali started to hand over the bills when a large tan hand covered her own before handing over the money.

"I got this."

Oh, Lord, help me.

That voice did dangerous things to her insides.

It was one thing when she was completely sober, but she was far from that at the moment.

Looking over to her right, Ali pursed her lips and eyed Kellen. He was angled into her with his chest nearly brushing her arm as he regarded her. A small smile gracing his tempting mouth.

Has he always been this big?

Maybe she'd just forgotten how much space he occupied.

Schooling her features, she met his eyes. "You know, if I didn't know better, I'd say you were following me." Cocking her head to the side, she batted her lashes. "Now, correct me if I'm wrong, Officer, but aren't there laws against that?"

She was trying hard to ignore that he was wearing another one of those made-for-him T-shirts that showed off his chest and arms. This one was white, and Ali really wanted to see if those muscles were as hard as they looked.

On their own, her eyes drifted down to linger on his thickly muscled forearm that he had leaning on the bar next to her. The sound of a stool scraping across the floor caused her to jerk her eyes back up to meet his.

Damn it! Eyes up, Ali!

His stare was intense, but his lip twitched upward at the corner, making her think she wasn't as subtle as she'd hoped.

"You can think whatever you want, Ali Cat."

That was the third time she'd heard him call her that, and the new nickname had her eyes narrowing. "Why do you keep calling me that?"

Instead of answering her, he slowly leaned down until his mouth was next to her ear. "I need you to stand up."

She was so focused on the feel of his breath tickling her ear that it took a moment for his words to sink in. "Huh?" She pulled her head back, furrowing her brow. "Why?"

With his face only mere inches away from hers, she could smell the rich aroma of whiskey on his breath. She'd never been a whiskey girl herself, but at the moment, she was willing to reconsider.

"Two reasons. For one, that ass, in those jeans, should come with some kind of a warning label."

Ali sucked in a sharp breath, not at all offended by his blunt comment. Quite the opposite in fact.

"But the way you're leaning on the bar puts it out there for everyone to enjoy, and trust me, they haven't missed it."

"And two?" she asked, a little breathless.

"That shirt's a torture all its own."

That took her aback a little.

What's wrong with my shirt?

Looking down, Ali saw the V-neck of her shirt gaping open to reveal her black push-up bra, giving her some kick-ass cleavage.

Nice!

A low growl rumbled up Kellen's throat, prompting her to smile up at him.

"You're killin' me." He leaned back and rubbed his bottom lip with his thumb.

"Sorry." Ali grinned, totally not sorry, as she straightened up, lowering her booted foot back to the ground. "Better?"

His teeth grazed his bottom lip as he stated, "Not in the least."

He had a sexy mouth. She'd love to feel his teeth on her neck.

Whoa! Where'd that come from?

She'd always enjoyed looking at him in an appreciative-bystander kind of way, but give her a little tequila, and apparently, her libido came out of hibernation.

Jesus. Maybe Joyce was right earlier.

Ali studied him then. Trying to decide if she wanted to smack him.

Nope.

The only thing her palm wanted to do was see if his abs did, in fact, feel like a washboard, like she suspected. Her eyes drifted down his torso, lingering on his defined pecs and flat stomach before dipping to the front of his jeans.

Aaand…now, I'm staring at his crotch.

Jerking her head back up, she met his laughing eyes.

While she tried to think of something witty to say to take the focus off of her wandering eyes, she noticed *his* eyes had circles under them, and his hair was a bit unstyled. Remembering he'd just finished a double shift, she now felt like a creeper. Funny how a few drinks could make her forget something that had seemed to take up the majority of her thoughts the last forty-eight hours. She opened her mouth, wanting to ask how his shift had gone but quickly shut it. It didn't feel like her place to ask.

In that moment, Ali was surprised to realize how much she wanted it to be her place. Startled by her wayward thoughts, she busied herself by picking up the drinks on the bar.

"You got a ride home?"

"You seem awfully worried about how I get myself home." She half-laughed while secretly hoping it meant something more. When all he did was stare her down, she relented with an eye roll. "Yes, Callie's our ride for the next few months."

"Okay. Call me if you need to." Kellen tapped the bar top and started to turn away.

"Why are you so worried about me?" The question fell out without her meaning it to and stopped him in his tracks.

Looking back at her, his eyes pinned her to the spot where she stood, holding the four drinks. "I need you safe." He said the words easily, like he was telling her the time.

It made her wonder why that was, and thanks to her slightly inebriated state, she had no trouble asking. As the saying went, *in for a penny, in for a pound.*

"Why is that?"

He studied her for a moment in that intense way he had without so much as a twitch to give away his thoughts. Just as she was about to give him an out and turn around, she watched his pupils dilate a split second before his hand reached out, catching her by the back of the neck. Ali gasped in surprise an instant before he crushed his mouth to hers in a firm kiss. It was hard and demanding and over before she had a chance to respond, but he didn't move away.

Keeping his face close, he spoke, "Go back to your table."

Without a backward glance, he turned and walked away for good this time, weaving his way to the front doors.

Stunned, Ali set the drinks back on the bar and touched the tips of her fingers to her lips.

What the hell just happened?

As soon as the bar door slammed behind Kellen, he drew in a deep breath of the cool night air, stuffing his hands into the front pockets of his jeans.

Fuck.

That was a mistake.

But he'd be damned if he regretted it.

She obviously wasn't firing on all cylinders, and he'd probably had one too many whiskeys, but she'd been standing there, looking too fucking tempting as she stared up at him with those dark brown eyes.

And that goddamn smile of hers. He had known when he finally got the full effect that it would be amazing, but he hadn't realized it'd be devastating.

Kellen let out another curse as he picked up his pace. The bar wasn't far from his apartment, and the walk would do him good. But, before he could get too far, he heard the noise from inside amplify as the door opened behind him.

"Hey!" Ali called to him.

Fuck.

He stopped but didn't turn around.

Ali came around to stand in front of him. "You can't do that!" Her dark eyes regarded him with annoyance. Kellen had an apology on the tip of his tongue, but she continued, "You don't get to just do that and walk away."

Before Kellen registered her words, she surprised him by launching herself at him, her hands going to the back of his neck as she sealed her mouth to his.

Kellen recovered quickly, sliding his hands around her waist. The kiss was just as hard and short as his had been, but he didn't let her go. Ali pulled back, her hands falling to his shoulders. In the confines of his arms, she sucked in an unsteady breath through her parted lips. She couldn't do this shit to him and expect him to stop at just one kiss again. He went in for a gentler taste before pulling back to gauge the look in her eyes. Both of their breaths were coming unsteady now, her chest rising and falling against his own. Reaching a hand up, he ran his thumb across her soft bottom lip.

"Damn it," he muttered under his breath.

This time, when he lowered his head, he took his time. His kiss was soft, just like her lips. He first kissed the top one, gently sucking on it, and then the bottom one. Grazing his teeth against the tender flesh, he could taste the fruity drink she'd been sipping on.

He'd jumped the gun inside. This girl deserved more than a single hard kiss. She deserved to be savored. She'd asked him why he needed her safe like it was the most ridiculous thing in the world. She honestly had no idea how often he thought about her. How many times he'd almost stopped by her place. How much he enjoyed being around her, claws and all. She'd held him at arm's length since day one, but tonight, when she'd smiled up at him, he was done. He hadn't planned on kissing her, but now that he had, there was no turning back.

Pulling away, he rested his forehead on hers. "Go back inside, Ali."

She shook her head and ran her nose up his neck, stopping to flick her tongue against his earlobe.

Jesus.

"Ali," he warned.

She left open-mouthed kisses along the edge of his jaw until she reached his lips again. He didn't hesitate opening his mouth to give her the access she wanted. She eagerly met his tongue, her hands sliding back up his neck to hold on, as he wrapped her up tight, one hand fisting her long hair.

A wolf whistle brought his head up. The passing car had its windows down, and the group of teenagers within hung their heads out, whooping and hollering at them. Timidly, Ali buried her head in his shoulder while he grinned.

A moment passed before she looked up at him, her eyes glossy. "I should go. They're going to wonder where I am."

Kellen thought that was a shitty idea but probably for the best.

"Go on." He cupped her cheek and brushed his thumb across her cold skin. "I'll see you later."

Placing her hand over his, she turned her head into his palm before giving a quick nod. Without another word, she walked away.

Letting out a deep breath into the cold night, Kellen watched her hips sway magnetically as she made her way back to the bar.

What'd we just do, Kitten?

7

"**M**mm-huh." That inhuman sound came from down the hall in Shelby's room.

Standing in their little kitchen, Ali smiled to herself as she filled her thermos with coffee. She'd given her last drink to Shelby after she went back inside and retrieved them from Karen, who'd set them back behind the bar. Shelby had today off and hadn't minded taking it off her hands. In the end, her roommate had ended up overindulging for the first time since Ali had known her.

Ali felt for her friend, she did, but drunk Shelby was a hoot. Not only had she gotten back up and sang all on her own last night, but she'd also gotten the whole place singing to an old drinking song by the time they left. And, although Shelby's performance was one to remember, that wasn't what had kept Ali up all night.

The feel of Kellen's kiss had been playing on a constant loop. The tender way his hands cradled her face and the leisurely way he kissed her that last time. Like they hadn't been standing in the middle of a sidewalk for the world to see. She both cursed and thanked those kids for making a spectacle of their spectacle. That was neither the place for that to happen nor the blood alcohol level with which it should have happened. Like it or not, she was a representative of this community now.

Ali snorted out a laugh.

Oh, if my mother could hear me now.

Listen to her, being all grown-up and reasonable about the whole thing. No parent wanted to run into their kid's teacher, making out with guys at bars. There was a time when she would have let him cop a feel against the wall and be damned who was there to witness it. But that was a long time ago and a different Ali. *This* Ali actually had a little bit of self-respect. *This* Ali hadn't so much as flirted with a guy since she'd been back home.

Did I ever flirt with Kellen?

Ali pursed her lips and mulled that over.

Maybe?

Has he been flirting with me this whole time?

That took her aback a little.

Has it really been so long since I've flirted with a guy that I'm not even sure what it looks like anymore?

Good Lord. Maybe I should take my vows and buy a habit.

Rolling her eyes, she pulled an extra mug from the shelf and filled it with the rest of the coffee. Down the hall, past her room, she gave a slight knock on the door before pushing it open. The shades were drawn tight, and the lump under the cloud comforter was curled up in a tight ball.

"Are you alive in here?" Ali called as she walked into the room.

"No." Shelby's voice was muffled.

"Does that mean I can have your curling iron?" she teased.

"Like you don't already use it every day." She threw the covers off her face and clapped her hand over her eyes. "Did I seriously sing 'Billy's Got His Beer Goggles On' last night?"

Ali choked back her snicker. "Do you want me to lie?"

"Please do."

"Then, no, you did not. You also never pulled that old man up onstage with you to line dance."

"Oh God." Shelby moaned and grabbed her other pillow to smother her groan.

Ali walked over to the bed and sat down before prying the pillow away. "Oh, don't be a drama queen. We all get on that stage and make a mockery of ourselves at some point. And, unlike you, we can't actually sing. Be thankful and drink this."

She held the steaming mug out to her friend. Sitting up against her headboard, Shelby took the coffee.

They sat in silence while she took a careful sip.

"Wait a minute." Shelby looked at her in surprise. "Is this you, up at dawn, with an actual *smile* on your face?"

Ali laughed at her friend.

"I just can't believe it. It's like finding a unicorn. I think a night out did your body good."

Ali thought so, too. She also thought it might have something to do with a kiss that had left her knees week. But she hadn't told the girls what had happened. She didn't know why. When they asked her what took so long, she lied and said she went to the restroom. Brooke and Shelby didn't even question it. Callie however, simply raised a questioning eyebrow at her. It didn't help her story that the restrooms were down the hall by the stage. Without calling her out on her lie, her sister-in-law had let it be. Ali was definitely racking up the lies and omissions these days.

Pushing that thought to the side, she checked the clock on the nightstand. "Doesn't that yoga class you wanted to go to start soon?"

Shelby picked up her phone and checked the time. "Crap! I gotta go!"

Throwing back her covers, she jumped out of bed, still holding the coffee mug. Ali shook her head as she smiled at her friend. Even hungover, she still had more energy than the normal person.

Ali's head was down as she sat at her desk, grading this week's spelling tests. She was so intent on getting them finished before she left that the throat being cleared startled her. Glancing up, she tried to paste a smile on her face when she saw Eric Bowman standing on the other side of her desk, but all she felt was annoyance.

Eric was a fifth grade teacher who'd been here a year longer than herself. He was in his mid- to late-twenties with large, bulging blue eyes and a leering smile that left her feeling like she needed a shower. He had unremarkable light-brown hair that he wore just a little too long to be considered stylish. Ali was pretty sure he thought it looked dangerous and sexy, but in reality, she thought it made him look like a slob. It brushed the top of his shoulders and frizzed out, so he was constantly tucking the thick mess behind his ears to contain it. By the end of the day, like today, it looked greasy at his temples. He had no reason for being here, but every few days, he found his way back. Ali was constantly trying to find new ways to politely send him on his way, but he didn't seem to take a hint.

"Hey, Eric," she greeted without emotion, folding her hands on top of the pile of tests. "What can I do for you?"

"Good afternoon, Alyssa." He took the liberty of using her full name.

She had never offered it and didn't encourage it, but he'd never used anything else. He probably thought it made him special, but it merely pissed her off. There were only a handful of people who used her full name, and Eric Bowman did not get to be counted in that category.

"Again, it's just Ali." She gave him a tight-lipped smile to keep from sneering.

He didn't even acknowledge her request.

"Did you get that email from Shawn about the staff meeting tomorrow morning?"

She thought, *Yes, you nitwit. I did get the email addressed to the whole staff about the meeting tomorrow.* But she only said, "I did."

"What do you think it's about?"

He came forward and sat one of his ass cheeks on the edge of her desk, knocking into her pencil jar. She moved the jar out of his way before he tipped it over, and then she rolled her chair over and back, trying to put as much distance between them as she could.

"The email said it was about the upcoming testing next week. So, my guess is that."

You fucking idiot.

He chuckled. "You're probably right." If he picked up on her annoyance, he didn't show it. "Pretty and smart. We should grab dinner tonight."

And there it is.

He'd been attempting to ask her out since she started last fall, but he never quite got around to making it an actual request. He'd suggested. He'd demanded. He'd even offered, but he'd never actually *asked.*

"I'm going to my brother's for dinner." It was a lie but not one she felt bad about.

"Another time then."

Not even if you paid me.

"I'd better finish these up." She scooted her chair back in and refocused on the tests in front of her, hoping he'd get the hint and leave. But when had her luck ever been that good?

Instead of leaving, he took the opportunity to lean in to snoop, scoffing at the misspelled *please* on the top test.

"Well, the world needs garbage men, too."

Ali blew out a steady breath that did nothing to calm her.

She was going to get fired. She was. She was going to punch him and lose her job.

"Hey, Miss Ali."

Oh, sweet angel babies.

That voice was her saving grace.

"Hello, Daryl." She looked up and smiled a grateful smile at the janitor as he rolled his cart into her room.

Eric stood up then. "I guess I'll catch you later, Alyssa."

The way he caressed his way through her name, like it was his to do so, made her cringe. She didn't answer him one way or the other and let him walk away.

Stopping side by side with Daryl, he said, "Could you actually make sure to clean the screen on my computer today? I swear, you miss it on purpose."

There was no *please* and no *thank you*. Eric simply strode out the door with one last leer back at her. As if he thought she was impressed by his asshole-ishness.

Daryl waited a beat before turning back to her with a grin. "Charmer."

Ali chuckled. "You know, if you want to superglue all of his items to his desk, I'll help you." Pushing back her chair, she got up and walked over to Daryl's cart.

His gray eyes twinkled. "I know you would."

Ali helped herself to a rag and some cleaner before walking back to her desk and spraying it off and then wiping down the area where Eric had sat.

Daryl was removing the full trash bag from her bin and chuckled. "Might want to give it one more pass." When Ali did just that, he let out a hearty laugh. "Attagirl."

Now that her desk was un-gross-ified, she handed Daryl back his supplies. "Got any plans this weekend?"

"The missus and I are driving down to Wyoming to see our grandbaby."

"Ah, little Kyle. Has he figured out how to ride his bike yet?"

"Not yet. They tried taking his training wheels off last week, but he crashed pretty hard. They're still tryin' to talk him into getting back on it after that."

"Is he okay?"

"Few bumps and bruises. It scared him more than anything."

"Poor kid. Maybe he'll get back on to show his Pappy how good he is."

"I'm countin' on it." Daryl grinned.

Ali would even bet that was the whole reason for the trip. Daryl and his wife, Bonnie, doted on their grandson. If Daryl thought a visit from Mami and Pappy would help Kyle get back on that bike, that was what he'd do.

"What about you? Eric ask you out again?"

Ali snorted. Daryl knew he had, just as he knew she'd turned him down.

"It's a quiet weekend for me."

"What about that policeman I saw you with last week? He seemed taken by you."

Ali almost snorted again. She hadn't heard from Kellen since their less than sober kiss. Now, twenty hours later, she'd officially overanalyzed things past the point of sanity.

"Who knows? Maybe he offers rides to every girl who almost passes out in front of him."

"Maybe," he mused as he wiped down the tables. "I asked around about him down at the club."

"You did not!" Ali exclaimed, although he officially had her full attention.

"Of course I did. Want to know what I found out?"

"Of course I do! Wait...no. Definitely not." She turned away, shaking her head.

Daryl patiently watched her as she warred with her conscience.

Turning back around, she asked, "Wait, what kind of info are we talkin'? Rap sheet or public opinion?"

"First of all, he's a cop, so I doubt he has a rap sheet. Second of all, what kind of club do you think I go to?"

"I dunno." Ali shrugged. "Maybe it's like a secret underground crime ring that has connections from here to Monaco."

"It's a Scrabble club."

"Scrabble? Well, that's a little disappointing. Any chance it's a front for an underground crime ring?"

"Not as far as you're concerned."

They eyed each other for a moment.

"Interesting."

"Do you want to know what I found out or not?"

"Well, yeah. But only the basics. No gritty details."

"Kellen O'Connell moved here four years ago with his brother from somewhere down south."

"Daryl...*everywhere* is south of here."

"I don't know. I think it was Arizona or New Mexico. Stop interrupting. Anyway, he's a good cop, but they didn't know much else. He's kept a low profile with his personal life."

"That's all you've got for me? He's been here for four years, he has a brother, and he's a good cop? Some crime ring you are. I could find out more with a Google search."

Except she couldn't because she'd already tried. The man had zero social media accounts that she could find.

Daryl mockingly shook his head at her. "So ungrateful."

Before she could retort to that nonsense, the sound of knuckles being rapped against her open door shut them both up.

"I don't mean to interrupt." Kellen walked into her room with confidence, like it was part of his everyday routine.

"Not interrupting anything." Daryl beamed. "Nice to see you again, Officer."

"Please, call me Kellen," he said, offering his hand.

"Daryl." They clasped hands in a firm shake. "Well, I was just leaving." He turned to her. "Ali, I'll see you in the morning."

"Bye."

Once Daryl was out of the room, she faced a grinning Kellen.

"Okay, so how much of that did you hear?"

"I'm from Texas actually, but I did move here from Arizona."

"Well, that's embarrassing."

"I kinda like that you were checking around about me. Although you could have just asked. I'll tell you anything you want to know."

"Noted." She thought about telling him that it was Daryl who had done the asking and not her, but she just wanted to change the subject at this point. "So, what are you doing here?"

"Have dinner with me."

Funny. Even though it was more of a statement than a question, she didn't feel like rolling her eyes like she had with

Eric. In fact, the jump in her stomach was far from an annoyance.

"Pick me up at six?"

"I'll be there."

"You know, pizza and beer aren't most guys' idea of a first date."

Kellen laughed as Ali took a sip from her bottle.

"First of all, calling Mike's a beer is an insult. That's not beer. And are you complaining or approving?"

"Oh, definitely approving. And don't knock my chick beer."

He could ignore the fact that she had shitty taste in drinks because this was the most relaxed he'd ever seen her. She'd changed into an off-the-shoulder ribbed sweater with tight jeans and sexy-as-fuck heels. He never thought shoulders could be erotic on their own, but the creamy skin was taking an obscene amount of his focus. Except when she smiled. It'd been hesitant at first, tight-lipped and not quite reaching her eyes, but as soon as he'd pulled up to the pizza joint, she'd looked over at him in the truck and smiled a full knock-him-on-his-ass smile that showed off the small dimple in her cheek.

"So, where was your last first date?"

He craved every little detail he could learn about her. Since that day at the station, he'd stopped looking into her. He wanted to hear it from her. Besides, the stuff from his search was just facts. He wanted to know about the other stuff. Stuff like her bad taste in drinks and sexy heels. He couldn't learn that from a database.

Just then, his phone silently rang against his leg from the pocket of his jacket sitting on the booth next to him. He could feel the vibration on the seat and ignored it.

"Um…" She tapped her finger against the side of her bottle while she thought about it. "It was to a frat party." The disbelief on her face was clear, like she didn't quite believe that was her answer.

"Classy."

"You have no idea." A look flashed across her face, but she tipped her bottle back, taking a long drink that hid her eyes from him.

He disregarded the vibrating phone again as he studied her. Deciding to fight his natural instinct to push, Kellen changed the subject.

"So, how did you find your roommate?"

"Shelby? She found me actually."

"How's that?"

"A few months ago, I walked into the coffee shop where she works, and I guess she overheard me complaining to Callie about not being able to find a place. Before I knew what was going on, she came over to our table, gave me the third degree, and informed me I was her new roommate. I moved in the next day." Ali smiled with a shrug across from him. "And here we are."

"She the one who sang last night?" He guessed it had to be the curly-haired blonde.

"The one and only."

For the third time, his phone went off beside him. Unable to ignore it again, Kellen pulled it out and saw it was his brother calling.

With a look of apology, he told Ali, "Sorry, I've got to take this."

"No problem."

He slid out of the booth and stepped around the corner near the restrooms before answering. "Hey, is everything okay?"

"Hey. Are you busy?"

He knew Finn better than he knew himself. It wasn't hard to hear the forced calmness in his brother's voice.

"Cut the bullshit. What's goin' on?"

"Connor called."

That son of a bitch.

"Are you okay?"

"Yeah, it's whatever. I just thought you should know."

"How bad was it?"

"Listen for yourself. I sent the audio to your email before I called."

"Do you want me to come down?"

"Nah, man. I'm good. Besides, I'll be home in a couple of weeks." Kellen waited a beat and let Finn continue. "Just sucks, ya know?"

"Yeah, I know, kid. But I'll take care of it. All right?"

"I know."

The confidence of Finn's statement humbled him. There wasn't anything he wouldn't do for his brother. He was all he had.

"I'll call you tomorrow."

"Sounds good. Talk to ya later."

"Later."

As soon as he pressed End, Kellen opened up his email and found the file from his brother. He listened to the first few minutes of the phone call before turning it off, already pissed off. He knew it was only a matter of time before that piece of shit went after Finn. But this time would be the last time. He'd make sure of it.

Ali looked up and smiled at him as he walked back to their booth. But it wasn't her happy smile. She was back to the tight-lipped version that didn't reach her eyes. He hated Connor for fucking this night up. Even from two states away, he'd found a way to screw with his world.

"Everything okay?" Ali asked as he slid in across from her.

"No. That was my brother. I'm going to have to take you home."

"Oh. Well, his timing was impeccable. I usually have Shelby call me about thirty minutes in, too. Your brother only beat her by a few seconds." Quickly gathering her purse and coat, she slid out of the booth.

What the hell is she talking about?

95

"Ali, wait," Kellen insisted, but she turned to walk toward the door.

"Don't worry. I'll get a different ride."

Kellen hastily pulled his wallet out and threw some bills on the table before rushing after her. He caught up to her just outside the main doors.

"Ali. *Stop*." Reaching out, he caught her upper arm with just enough force to spin her around. "What the fuck are you talking about?"

"The *emergency* call." Her eyes shot daggers at him. Kellen still didn't have the slightest idea what she was talking about, and it must have shown on his face. With an exasperated sigh, she explained, "The one you have someone make on a first date to give you an out if you need one."

Kellen tried not to smile. "Women actually do that?" That sounded vaguely familiar, but he hadn't thought it was a real thing.

"And guys, too, apparently." She flipped a hand in his direction.

"Is that why you're pissed? You think I'm trying to ditch you?"

"You're not?" For once, she looked unsure of herself.

Sometimes, he wasn't sure if he wanted to kiss her or shake her.

"Now, why the hell would I want to do that? You're smart. You're funny. Not to mention, you're gorgeous, and I finally got you all to myself. We went almost thirty minutes, you said, without you getting pissed at me. I think that's a new record. Why would I want to fuck with that?"

"So, you're not trying to ditch me?" Her hand flew to her mouth. "Is your brother okay?"

Kellen breathed a little easier now that they'd settled that nonsense. "He's fine, but I'm going to have to leave to take care of some stuff for a few days. The sooner I get it done, the better off we'll all be."

"I'm so sorry. I went evil Ali on you again."

Ah, Kitten.

"Let's get one thing straight. I like you. Claws and all. And I'd like nothing more than to finish our date, so I can finally get inside that head of yours."

"Oh, yeah?" Ali's voice went soft and flirty, sending a tug south of his belt.

Crowding her, he stepped into her personal space. "Yeah. So, what do you say?" He brushed her hair from her forehead. "Let me take care of my family stuff, and then you and I can try this again."

"Okay," she muttered, leaning into him. "And, next time, the claws will stay fully retracted. I promise."

Gripping her hips, he ran his nose against hers. "But I like your claws."

"Mmm."

Unable to resist, he leaned in and gently kissed her, savoring the warm feeling he got in his gut. He was reluctant to pull back but took solace in the fact that there would be another time.

"Come on. I'll take you home."

During the drive home, Kellen seemed preoccupied, so she left him to his thoughts.

When Shelby had called while Kellen was off, talking to his brother, she'd sent it straight to voice mail and sent her a message that all was good. That had been their long-standing signal to abandon any rescue missions.

She hadn't actually talked to Shelby yet today. She'd only texted her with the bare details from the car after they parked in front of the pizza place. Who, where, and what. Ali knew she would be expecting some explanation since, as far as Shelby knew, Kellen was just some cop who'd talked with the kids.

Admittedly, she'd jumped to conclusions when Kellen came back with the lame-ass excuse that he needed to leave.

She'd been pissed and hurt, but that had quickly been replaced by shame as soon as she realized her mistake.

Unable to stand the quiet any longer, she looked to Kellen and asked softly in the confines of the truck cab, "Do you want to talk about it?"

"Hmm?" he asked.

"Whatever it is, maybe it would help if you talked it through."

Awesome advice. Maybe you should try it.

Ali silenced her traitorous thoughts and angled her body toward Kellen. She could Dr. Phil herself later.

"My brother Finn got a phone call from someone we haven't heard from in a while, who's trying to start trouble," he vaguely answered.

"What kind of trouble?"

Kellen paused. Ali could see his grip tighten on the steering wheel and thought that maybe she was pushing too hard.

"My life's not pretty, Ali." He glanced over at her with those pale eyes. "I don't have a family like yours."

What is that supposed to mean?

She cautiously urged him on. "What kind of family do you have?"

It took a moment for him to answer, but when he did, it sent a shiver up her spine. "The kind that would give you nightmares."

He didn't offer any more, and she didn't push him again. How could she? She didn't understand what he meant by that, and honestly, she was kind of afraid to hear the details. Ali wasn't naive. She knew she'd gotten lucky in the family department, and she couldn't even begin to understand how Kellen had grown up, but that didn't mean she couldn't try.

Kellen turned on his blinker and took his next turn before stating, "My dad was an abusive junkie, and my mom was a passive shell of a human."

Ali sucked in an unsteady breath at his admission. It didn't go unnoticed that he'd used the past tense when talking about his parents.

"There were no family trips or little league games for us. When my dad wasn't beating on us, he was too high to give a damn. I've got two brothers. Connor is older than me by a year, but I was almost eleven when Finn came along. Connor didn't give a rat's ass about anything by that point, and here was this little baby who hadn't asked to be brought into our fucked up house. For years, I tried to shelter him from the worst of it, but I could only do so much. By his freshman year, Connor dropped out of school before ending up in juvie for the rest of his teenage years, and all I felt was relief." Kellen glanced at her with a self-deprecating look on his face. "How messed up is that?"

She didn't think any of this was anything other than horrible but didn't get a chance to say so because he continued, "I managed to graduate but just barely. Then, when I was twenty, my dad beat my mom into a coma. She never woke up, and he killed himself a week later."

"Jesus. Kellen..." She wasn't sure what shocked her more—his actual words or the complete detachment with which he'd said them.

"It was a long time ago."

But still...

Ali reached over and took his hand, sliding her fingers through his. "What happened to Finn?"

"I did." Kellen's voice softened, as did his features when he talked about Finn. "Initially, he went into the system, but I fought for custody and got it."

"That couldn't have been easy." She wasn't positive what that entailed, but she'd watched enough *Law & Order* to know they didn't just hand over custody of a child to a twenty-year-old sibling.

"No, it was not." Kellen didn't elaborate.

"And the person who called Finn, do you know them?"

"Yeah. It was Connor. He's lookin' for money. Threatened Finn. He's under the impression Finn got money when he turned eighteen."

"Why would he think that?"

"My mom took out a life insurance policy on herself a month before she died. Finn and I were the beneficiaries. Connor didn't get anything and thinks he's entitled to it."

"I'm so sorry, Kellen."

The difference in their worlds was bewildering. She also had two brothers, but while she considered them close, they definitely hadn't raised her. And, at the worst, she felt annoyance when they called. Kellen might have spoken with indifference when referring to his parents, but it was the opposite with his brothers. With Finn, Kellen's voice had softened, showing how much he meant to him, but when he'd mentioned Connor, his voice had taken on a hard edge that spoke of years of baggage and hurt.

"Don't be." Lifting their entwined hands, he kissed the back of hers. "I wouldn't change my life. I've resented it at times, but I'd never change raising Finn."

"He's lucky to have you." She was just beginning to realize how lucky.

Callie was right; Kellen was one of the good ones.

"I hope so." He turned the truck off, and Ali realized they were already at her apartment. Resting his arm across the steering wheel, Kellen turned to her. "Listen, I understand if you want to reconsider that rain check. My life's not easy. I don't want to pull you into the middle of it."

Ali forced a small smile, understanding that he was giving her an out, but she didn't want it. "You're not going to get rid of me that easy, O'Connell. We might have grown up differently, but so far, I like the man you've become, and I wouldn't mind getting to know you a little better."

His eyes did that plasma-ball thing again before he whispered in a gruff voice, "Come here."

Ali didn't need to be asked—or better yet, *told* twice. Unbuckling her seat belt, she leaned across the console. Kellen met her halfway as he glided his hand along her cheek until he was cupping the side of her head.

"You continue to surprise me." His breath whispered against her mouth.

"Back atcha."

With soft, lazy movements, he brushed his lips across hers, and she felt the zap go straight to her center. This man knew how to kiss. He'd perfected the slow-burn kiss. She didn't think she'd ever had anything like it. Most guys were in and out. They seemed to see kissing as an obstacle in their way to the good stuff. But the way Kellen did it made it seem like a victory all its own.

She felt his tongue sweep against her bottom lip, seeking entrance. Happy to oblige, she opened her mouth and met his tongue with her own. It wasn't long before she was cursing the leather console separating their bodies. The slow burn had definitely worked its way through her entire body, causing her to ache. Gripping the hair at the nape of his neck, she tried to pull him closer, but it was useless. They were as close as they were going to get in this position. Ali must have let out a grumble of frustration because Kellen chuckled.

"I know. I'm regretting not buying a truck with bench seats right about now."

With the moment broken, they rested their foreheads together.

"I should probably go anyway. You've got stuff to do."

"Kitten, I know this isn't how this night was supposed to go, but thank you for understanding." He skimmed his thumb across her bottom lip. "I promise, when this is taken care of, we'll try again."

"Kitten? No more Ali Cat?"

"God, I hope not." His lips pulled into a crooked smile. "They both have their appeal."

"Good to know." Smiling back, she ran her hand across the long stubble on his cheek.

She'd grown used to his asinine nickname for her, but she definitely liked the way he called her Kitten. No one had ever taken the time to nickname her before. She'd always just been Ali. She'd had one boyfriend in high school who had called her babe, and it had always pissed her off because he called every girl babe. The easier it was not to mix their names up, she'd guessed. But this felt different. Special.

"I hope everything goes okay with your brothers."

The fact that he seemed willing to go to war for one against the other was admirable, if not heartbreaking.

"It'll be fine. I'll call you when I get back."

She reached behind her and opened the door, but when he made a move to do the same, she stopped him. "You don't need to walk me up. I'm sure Shelby's been staring out the front window for the last five minutes. She'll have the door open before I can get my keys out."

Looking over her shoulder, he smiled, no doubt seeing her friend peeking through the curtains. "Okay then. I guess I'll see you later."

"Be safe."

"Always."

8

This was the last fucking place Kellen wanted to be. Not just today, but any day. He'd been on the road for almost twelve hours to get here. This nowhere, shithole of a town in Nevada. The dirt road had left a thick layer of dust all over his truck, and the air dried out his throat as soon as he stepped out onto the ground.

He'd seen very few trailer parks in his time that he considered nice, but this one looked like it was ready to be condemned. The rundown single-wide trailer was tilting just the slightest bit to the left. What was left of the siding was sun-bleached a piss yellow, and it had more trash in the yard than would fit in a single bin. And the smell? The smell made his eyes water. Kellen had seen homeless people live in better conditions than this. He wanted to feel sadness for his brother. He wanted to feel responsible for cleaning him up, but sentiments like that had faded a long time ago.

Kellen ran a finger down the thin scar that ran under his eyebrow, remembering the sound his face had made as it bounced off the coffee table.

It'd happened about a year after his parents died.

He'd finally been granted custody of Finn, and they were living on the south side of Chicago in a one-bedroom apartment. Kellen had just gotten off of a graveyard shift and walked in their door from taking Finn to school. He wanted nothing more than to crawl in bed when he was jumped from behind in his own place. Connor had come out of the back bedroom, tackling him to the ground before he knew what was going on. They wrestled for a few minutes, each of them trying to gain the upper hand.

Kellen vividly remembered a moment when their eyes had locked.

It had scared the shit out of him.

The person fighting him was no longer the brother he'd shared any kind of life with. Connor wasn't even seeing him. Hell, Kellen wasn't even sure his brother knew what he was doing. His eyes were bloodshot and dilated to the size of saucers. The frenzied state was one he'd seen multiple times on his father. It was one he'd learned to be scared of. It was hard to stop someone who felt nothing emotionally or physically.

He saw it coming. He felt the palm on the back of his head, and he watched in slow motion as his face cracked against the wood of the yard-sale coffee table. He didn't remember anything after that until he came to in a puddle of his own blood to find his place ransacked. He and Finn didn't have much, but everything that might be worth anything was gone.

The hospital asked questions he didn't answer, but explaining the stitches to Finn was different. After school, Finn took just one look at his face, and Kellen watched as the fear blossomed in his little brother's eyes.

He'd never forget the shaky words his brother had said.

"He's back?"

Kellen could hear him like it was yesterday. And it had broken his heart.

Of course, he hadn't been talking about Connor. No, his ten-year-old brother thought their father was back. It wasn't that he didn't know their father was dead, but fear could make you forget your reality. It could make you question things you'd thought you knew.

Staring into the terrified eyes of this kid who'd gotten the shaft his entire life made Kellen promise something he wasn't sure was right, but he did it anyway. Then and there, he decided that he wasn't going to lie to him. Ever. So, he told him the truth. That day and every day. It wasn't always easy, but he needed Finn to trust him. To know that he'd do everything he could to give them a life where he didn't have to be afraid all the time.

Connor had only shown up once more since that day, and it'd gone much like the first one, except Kellen wasn't a skinny twenty-one-year-old straight out of the academy anymore. That time, he was able to get the upper hand long enough for his partner at the time to arrive. Connor had done two years for assault.

It was always the same with him. Connor was a junkie, just like their father had been. Family didn't mean anything to him, and he'd hurt anyone he needed to in order to find his next fix.

Kellen had no problem fighting his own battles, but now that Connor was back, he had his sights set on Finn. That was where Kellen drew the line, and he was ready to do what needed to be done in order for his little brother to live his life in peace.

The crooked screen on the front door banged back in a quick move, and a shell of the man he used to know stepped out, wearing threadbare jeans and a dirty white undershirt. Connor was a spitting image of their father. From the long, stringy black hair to the track marks on both his arms.

"Well, look who it is." The nasty grin that spread across Connor's bony face made Kellen's stomach churn.

Leaning back against the door of his truck, Kellen crossed his arms as he impartially studied his older brother. They'd probably look a lot alike if Kellen lost eighty pounds, a few teeth, and all of his morals. He hated the fact that he shared anything in common with this piece of shit.

Without bothering with pleasantries, he cut to the chase. "Stay the fuck away from him."

Connor laughed. "Is that any way for you to talk to family?"

"You stopped being my family a long time ago. Same goes for Finn."

"Boy's legal now. That's his decision to make. Not yours. Not anymore."

"He's already made it. That's why I'm here. If you won't listen to him, you're sure as hell going to listen to me. Crawl back in your hole and stay the fuck away from us."

"Or what?" Connor puffed up his concave chest. "You think you can come to my house and make threats?"

Right on time, Kellen watched the car turn down the road behind the trailer.

Kellen squinted against the sun. "No threats. They're a waste of my time. See, you're a creature of habit, Connor. We knew you'd surface eventually, and Finn's a smart kid."

"What's that supposed to mean?"

"Do you remember that phone call you made a few days ago, trying to sweet-talk your way back into his life? And, when that didn't work, you started demanding that he give you the money you're owed. Remember doing that?"

"That little shit said there wasn't any money." Connor leveled a finger in his direction. "You'd better have brought me my cash, or you've wasted a trip."

Ignoring him, Kellen continued, "It wasn't a long phone call, but you managed to say a lot in five minutes."

"You don't know shit."

"But I do. Finn recorded your phone call."

Connor's face hardened at that news. His pale eyes shooting daggers at Kellen.

"That's extortion and criminal threats at the very least."

With impeccable timing, the white patrol car pulled to a stop next to Kellen's truck, and two uniformed police officers got out.

"That little cunt."

"Connor O'Connell?" the first officer asked. "You're going to need to come with us." He made the statement with calmness that was at odds with his hand on the butt of his pistol.

"This is bullshit! I ain't done nothin' wrong!" Connor roared from his elevated position.

"Sir, please step down and put your hands on the hood of the vehicle." The second officer was much younger than the first but seemed to have his shit tight.

"Fuck you!" His brother repeatedly poked himself in the chest, but Kellen could see the sweat starting to bead on his forehead. "I know my rights! I ain't goin' nowhere without a warrant."

The first officer produced the folded paper from his back pocket. "Then, we'll do it your way. We also have a warrant to search the premises."

Kellen thought he'd save them some time. "You'll want to check under his mattress." Looking at his brother, he asked, "You still hide your stash there, or have you become more inventive over the years?"

Connor looked murderous at his words.

"Yeah, didn't think so."

Seething, he slowly made his way down the steps of the rickety porch. "You're going to regret this. You and that little bitch."

Before he made it down to their position, a second police cruiser pulled in beside the first.

Without missing a beat, the first officer pushed Connor down until his cheek rested against the metal before patting him down and cuffing his wrists behind his back.

Kellen crouched down until he was eye-to-eye with his brother. "I regret a lot of things, but this isn't going to be one of them. You ever so much as contact Finn or me again, and I'll make sure they throw away the key."

"You'd really do this to your family?"

"Finn's my family. You? You're nothing to me."

As he stood up, the younger officer jerked Connor upright, marched him to the back of the patrol car, and put him inside.

The older one came up beside him, resting a hand on his shoulder. "You did the right thing by calling us in. Too many times, I've seen people make excuses for their family until it ruined everyone."

Kellen knew this well. He'd watched it happen firsthand, growing up, and he was determined to break the cycle.

As Kellen watched the cruiser drive away, he didn't regret anything even though this was the second time he was the reason for Connor going to prison.

Before long, the other officers came out of the run-down trailer with his brother's needles and supplies in an evidence bag. That should add a couple of more years onto the charges. He hoped his brother had fun detoxing from a cell.

Now, he could get back to his life and a certain kindergarten teacher without his past tainting his future.

At least, for now.

9

Ali took a long drink from her water bottle as she sat on the bench, watching Kellen. He was standing on the mats next to Max with his hands on his hips, wearing the same thing he'd had on that first night. His track pants sat low on trim hips, and his T-shirt was pulled tight in all the right places.

If she were honest with herself, she'd come here tonight, hoping to run into him.

He'd sent a text earlier this afternoon, saying he was back in town.

That was it.

She'd replied back, asking if he was okay, and got nothing. She was trying not to read too much into the fact that he hadn't responded. Maybe he *wasn't* okay. Maybe he was working. Maybe he was standing in the checkout line and had to go because it was his turn. *Maybe* he'd gotten into a horrible accident, and his phone was crushed into a useless heap.

And maybe you've officially lost it.

Ali rolled her eyes. Obviously, that wasn't the case because he was fifty feet away, looking completely healthy and virile.

But that didn't mean she didn't want to know how he was doing. Not that it was her place to know. They'd been on one date. Not even that. It was half a date. Maybe. She'd have to ask around, but she was pretty sure even half a date lasted longer than their non-dinner.

So, in her vain attempt at not stalking the man, she'd come to Hank's in the off chance that she'd run into him since it was the same day of the week that she'd seen him here the first time. She looked for him when she first got here and was disappointed when she didn't see him.

She hadn't planned on staying this long again, but close to two hours later, when he walked in, she was glad she'd stuck it out. When he pushed through the door, carrying his duffel bag, his eyes found her almost immediately. She paused, steadying the bag in front of her, but he only gave her a quick wink as he walked by on his way to the locker room. Ali smiled to herself as she set her feet and resumed her bag therapy. His wink alone was enough to weaken even the strongest resolve, but when paired with that little smirk, a girl didn't stand a chance.

Now, he was in the back on the mats with the self-defense class. It made sense. She knew Max had had volunteers from the police force as instructors in the past, and Kellen fit the bill. Nothing against Max, but he wasn't exactly spry enough to put the girls through some of the moves. Besides, the girls couldn't learn if they were afraid of breaking their instructors.

At the moment, Kellen was pinning the female instructor down by straddling her legs and holding her wrists down at the sides of her head while the other women watched.

Obviously, it wasn't sexual.

Ali knew this.

She did.

It was purely instructional.

A second later, the woman under him slowly slid her arm up while raising her opposite knee before she twisted her hips and rolled Kellen to his back, trading places with him. The woman wasted no time, hopping right off and addressing the women standing around as Kellen rolled to his knees, sitting back on his feet.

See, instructional.

After one more demonstration, the women paired off to practice the move with each other. There was a lot of laughing and fumbling going on, but they were getting it. Max, Kellen, and the other woman walked around, giving pointers as they were needed.

But it wasn't long before one of the other girls got on the mats, lying on her back, and Kellen straddled her just like he had the instructor. It took this girl a couple of tries before she flipped Kellen over, but unlike the other instructor, she didn't hop right off. This girl was one of the giggly ones Ali had pegged a few weeks ago. After the girl had Kellen pinned, she sat back and got comfortable, clapping her hands.

Ali took a deep breath and held it.

Okay, she was feeling jealous.

See, if she admitted it to herself, it lost its power over her. At least that was what Shelby had told her once.

"Own your feelings," she'd said. "If you own them, they can't own you."

Well, Ali was going to go home and tell Shelby that her advice was shit because she was owning her feelings just fine, and it didn't make her want to go over there and rip that chick off of him any less.

She tried to tell herself that it was stupid. She tried to tell herself that she didn't have any type of claim on him. She tried to tell herself that, up until a few days ago, she hadn't even been sure she liked the man. And, *surprise*, none of that diminished the jealousy she felt.

To make matters worse, that girl was only the first. As the girls got the hang of the move, they took turns in trying it on Kellen. He was like the final round apparently. If they could budge his tightly muscled ass, they passed. Most girls did the move and hopped out of the way as if to run, just like they had been taught. But not all of them, and each one seemed to stay on top of him longer than the last.

Ali gripped the edge of the bench she was sitting on and looked at her shoes.

What am I doing?

She'd been sitting here for who knew how long, watching the class.

It was pathetic.

Was she seriously just waiting for him to look up and notice her? It wasn't like he was going to stop what he was doing to walk over.

Blowing out a hard breath, Ali stood up and quickly gathered her stuff. She had better things to do than to sit here and torture herself.

Pausing at the door with both hands on the bar, she looked back at the class.

Kellen was in the process of getting flipped over as everyone else clapped and cheered the girl's victory. Ali smiled on the inside. He was doing good here…and she felt incredibly stupid for trying to make it about herself.

With a mental kick in the ass, she pushed out the door and got in her car.

It wasn't often she turned the radio off and drove in silence, but tonight, she did. Her head was loud enough; she didn't need the extra noise.

Addison held a hand down to Kellen and helped him up off the mat as Max addressed the class.

"All right, great job tonight, ladies." Max applauded the women. "We'll see you all back here next week. Remember, stay smart and stay together."

When the women scattered, Kellen turned, scanning the gym, but he already knew he wouldn't find Ali.

That woman was going to be the death of him. Through the first half of class, he could feel her watching him. She had made it impossible to concentrate on what he was supposed to be doing. The first time he pinned Addison down, he imagined it was Ali lying underneath him, and that was so fucking wrong, given the context of the situation. He struggled to focus and remember what he was here to do before Addy kneed him in the balls for real. After that, he'd refused to let himself look in her direction, so he could do his job. It was a personal lesson in self-control hell.

"Who ya lookin' for?" Addison came to stand next to him, looking toward the front of the gym with him.

Instead of answering her, he turned toward the small woman. "We need to talk."

"Okay." Addison folded her arms, looking wary at his tone.

He already felt like an ass for not thinking of this sooner, so he lowered his voice and stepped in closer. "Listen, I know you and Adam are trying to have a baby. I also know you've been having a hard time. And I also know you probably wouldn't say anything for a while even if it did happen, but I'm going to need you to tell me." Addison started to say something, but he cut her off, "I mean it. I won't say another word about it, but think about today." He pointed down at the worn gray mats. "I basically sat on top of you how many times? It didn't even occur to me until we were almost done. I'm not doing that shit if you're pregnant. What we do in here, we can still do it. I just need to know how to adjust it, so you're both safe."

Addison's eyes were glossy by the time he was done.

Ah, shit.

She swallowed hard and mouthed the word, *Okay.*

"We good?"

Composing herself, she smiled a little. "I promise."

"Good. Adam's still going to kick my ass for making you cry though."

"Pfft." She unfolded her arms and batted at the air with her right hand. "Who's crying? I'm not crying."

Kellen smiled down at her. He'd almost believe her if her nose wasn't all red.

"I must be seeing things."

"Damn straight."

"Grab your shit. I'll walk you out."

"Okay, just give me a second."

While Addison made a trip to the locker room, Kellen walked over to the back wall to gather his things. He just zipped up his bag when he heard the voice behind him.

"Hey, Kellen."

He turned to find Khloe standing there with her head cocked to the side, and her hand propped on her hip. She'd been coming to class the last month or so with two of her friends. All three of them were a pain in his ass. Kellen believed everyone should learn how to defend themselves, but he preferred to teach people who were here for the right reasons.

"What's up?" He kept his voice clipped in an attempt to keep the conversation short.

"We were wondering if you'd like to come out with us tonight."

She motioned to her friends standing across the mats with their heads bent together. They were pretending not to watch and failing horribly. Apparently, Khloe had been deemed their spokesperson. Lucky him.

"We're heading down to The Lighthouse for a couple of post-class drinks."

"Sorry, can't." His answer was the same as it was the last time they'd asked.

"Like can't or *can't?*"

What the fuck does that even mean?

His confusion must have shown on his face because she clarified, stepping in closer like she was sharing government secrets.

"Like, are you and Addison a thing?"

"She's married," he deadpanned, pointing out something they already knew.

Khloe rolled her eyes. "Duh. But you two are all over each other during class, so things are bound to happen."

Kellen clenched his jaw. This girl was trying the last of his nonexistent patience. As far as Kellen was concerned, class was over, and his job was done for the night.

"Are you actually saying that I'd hook up with my friend's wife just because we happen to have physical contact for our *job*?" His voice was deceptively calm.

"Well, yeah. But I totally get it. I swear, I won't say anything if you meet us tonight."

"Listen, Khloe, I think you've got the wrong impression here. I'm not here to find a date. I think it's best if I see you during class and leave it at that."

Khloe looked taken aback by his less than friendly tone, but he didn't stick around for her response.

Just then Addison walked up next to him, carrying her bag. "Hey, you ready?" Her timing was flawless.

Get me the fuck out of here.

"Let's go."

"What was that about?" she asked, motioning toward the trio behind them as they made their way across the gym.

"Nothing. Don't worry about it."

"She hit on you again, didn't she?" Kellen didn't respond, but Addison wasn't deterred. "Whatever happened with that girl Adam said you went out with? What was her name, Amber?"

"It's Ali," he said

"Amy?"

Kellen stopped walking and turned to her. "No, *Ali*."

He'd taken the bait, and she was standing there, looking smug. Gritting his teeth, he resumed walking, holding the door for her to walk through ahead of him.

"Little touchy there, aren't we?"

"What do you mean?"

"Nothing," Addison singsonged.

"Nothing is never *nothing*."

"I just think it's interesting that you haven't talked about her. I'm trying to figure out if you just don't care or if you *really* care. And, judging by the way you just snapped at me, I'd go with *really*, really. So, when do we get to meet her?"

"She was here tonight."

"Nuh-uh!" She stopped in her tracks. "In the *class*? Please tell me she isn't one of the giggle triplets!"

"For fuck's sake, Addy. You know there isn't an Ali in our class."

"I actually don't know that. I don't have time to learn all of their names. I give them nicknames. It's easier to keep track of."

"And you call them the giggle triplets?"

"Of course not. They're Bimbo One, Two, and Three. And it's not like you didn't know who I was talking about." She had him there. "Now, back on track. Which one was Ali?"

"No."

"What do you mean, *no*?"

"No, I'm not going to point her out, so you can make a new best friend."

"Why not? I'm an excellent best friend."

"Do you remember the last time?"

The last time he'd dated a woman, Addy had made it her personal mission to basically adopt the girl. They'd been on two, maybe three dates, and it'd fizzled out. Leaving everyone in an awkward position.

"I see your point."

It wasn't like he thought Ali was a one-time deal, but he wanted to at least have a chance to see where things went with her before siccing Addy on her.

"At least tell me how the date went." When he just looked at her, she whined, "Man, you're no fun."

When the knock sounded at her door, Ali put the spoon down on the ceramic rest next to the stove, but Shelby was coming down the hall already.

"I'll get it." With a little bounce in her step, Shelby crossed the living room and peeked out the peephole before swinging the door open. "Well, hello. Please tell me you're the mysterious Kellen."

Ali froze at her words.

"I am. And you must be Shelby."

No way!

Ali hurried to the door to stand behind Shelby and was met with piercing blue eyes. She'd missed those eyes. The one glimpse she'd gotten at the gym wasn't nearly enough.

"Hey." Kellen lazily looked at her with his hands tucked in the front pockets of his jeans.

"Hi. What are you doing here?"

Kellen glanced down at Shelby, who hadn't moved.

"Oh, don't mind me. Feeling the tension between you two right now is the most action I've had in a month."

"Okay, you're done." Horrified, Ali pushed her way past her friend, pulling the door with her until it was only open a foot. Hiding her face behind the door, she mouthed to Shelby, *Oh my God!*

All Shelby did was bite her lip while fanning herself, mouthing, *So hot!*

Go away!

Her friend walked over to the stove, grinning like the Cheshire cat. Praying she wasn't blushing, Ali moved her head back around the edge of the door where Kellen was waiting patiently with a gorgeous grin on his face.

"Sorry, she has no filter."

Without comment on the current uncomfortable situation, he simply asked, "Are you busy right now?"

Ali looked over to the stove where she'd been heating up last night's leftover tortilla soup. "Not really."

"Then, you should come with me. I think it's time we had a redo on our date. What do ya say?"

"Are you sure?" Ali looked over at the clock on the wall. It was already eight thirty. It wasn't going to earn her any cool points if she admitted to being in bed most nights by ten o'clock.

"All I'm asking for is two hours. I promise to have you back by ten thirty."

From the kitchen, Shelby hollered, "She'd love to!"

"What she said. Just let me change first."

"Don't. You look perfect."

Ali glanced down at her sweatpants and long-sleeved shirt. "Really? This doesn't exactly scream *date* to me."

"It's fine. Come on. Grab your coat."

"Okay, but I've got to tell you, this is a first." She turned around to grab her coat from the back of the kitchen chair and almost ran into Shelby, who was holding it out for her to take.

With a grateful smile for her friend, she put it on while Shelby whispered, "Have fun!"

Kellen called through the doorway, "It was nice to meet you, Shelby."

"You, too, handsome!" she called back, waggling her eyebrows at Ali.

Ali quickly slipped on her tennis shoes and pulled the door closed behind her.

As they walked to his truck, Kellen stated like it was an afterthought, "I like that."

Not following his thoughts, she asked, "Like what? Shelby?"

He grinned, not disagreeing, and she didn't blame him. It was hard not to like Shelby and all her crazy. "She's not exactly what I expected, but that wasn't what I was talking about. I like that this is a first for you. I like sharing firsts with you."

She liked that, too. A lot.

"You definitely don't disappoint, Officer O'Connell." Ali was lying next to Kellen in the back of his truck, looking up at the cloudless night sky.

He'd parked in the middle of an open field just outside of the city limits. Without the lights from town, every star was visible, including the hazy strip of the Milky Way that flowed across the sky before disappearing behind the mountain. They had pizza and a six-pack of Mike's Hard Lemonade, and he'd filled the bed with enough pillows and blankets to host a slumber party.

Turning her head, Ali looked at him with the moonlight reflecting in her eyes. "Thank you."

"Worth the redo?"

"I'll let you know," she teased.

He wanted to lean in and kiss that small smile but didn't just yet.

This hadn't been part of his plans tonight, but the few glimpses he'd stolen of Ali at the gym hadn't been enough. He hadn't wanted to go another day without hearing her voice, without touching her. He was beginning to crave her in a way that should scare him.

The trip down to see Connor had put him on edge. He'd contacted her as soon as he got back this morning, but when she asked if he was okay, he didn't know what to say. He'd just put his brother in jail. Again. Even though he was a piece of shit, they'd been brothers at one point. But, regardless, he had to choose, and there was no contest. Finn would win out every time. He hated Connor for making it that way. Kellen didn't hold any hope that prison would make Connor a better person or change who he was to the core. The most it could do was guarantee he'd be out of their lives for a few more years. They'd arrested him on possession, extortion, and criminal threats. Kellen had had to call in every favor he had, but he'd do it again in a heartbeat.

"What are you thinking about?" Ali was looking over at him again where he rested next to her with his hands clasped behind his head.

"About how much I prefer being here, in Montana, with you."

Hearing what he didn't say, she asked, "Did you accomplish what you wanted to?"

"For now."

"Well, I, for one, am glad you're back." She looked skyward again. "Do you see those stars there?" Ali pointed to a spot above them.

He scooted closer to her and followed her aim.

"That's Orion."

He didn't see shit. "Oh, yeah?"

"No idea." She smiled up at the sky and giggled. "It'd be cool if it was though. All I can remember is that he's got three stars that make up his belt."

"But, everywhere you look, there are three stars."

"*Exactly*! This is why I'd make a horrible astronomer. I don't want to pick them apart and make individual pictures like a Connect the Dots. I just want to enjoy them as a whole." With a sigh, she got quiet.

Scooting over another inch, she rested her head on his bent arm. He gladly unclasped his hands and folded his arm around her, pulling her closer. Turning into him, she placed her hand over the covers on his stomach, the scent of her hair invading his nose.

Closing his eyes, he breathed her in. If he wasn't careful, he was going to fall for this girl. She might not realize it yet, but he was already in this one hundred percent.

They lay there together in silence under the brilliant canopy of stars until he was sure she'd fallen asleep.

She surprised him when she whispered, as if not wanting to disturb the peacefulness, "Do you ever wonder why things happen?"

"What do you mean?"

"I don't know. Sometimes, I wonder if my life would have turned out differently if certain things hadn't happened. If I'd be a different person than I am today."

Kellen didn't think she was saying everything. Almost like she was tiptoeing around the actual words.

"What kinds of things?" he asked gently.

But she never answered, and he didn't ask again. If it had anything to do with whatever had broken her apart on her porch the other night, he didn't expect her to open up about it. Not yet anyway.

"Do you have a dog?"

He laughed a bit at her change of topic. "No, I don't. Do you?"

"No. I'd love to have one though. Did you ever meet Callie's dog?"

"I did." The first time he'd seen that dog, he'd been barking at the flames of a fire like he was going to take it on all by himself.

"If I got one, I'd want one just like Baxter. He's the best dog to ever dog."

"I don't know. Growing up, my friend had this little Chewbacca-looking dog that was pretty awesome. He was probably smaller than Baxter's head."

"Eh. Two kinds of people. We'd have to find a compromise."

Did she realize what she'd just said? If she didn't, he wasn't going to bring attention to it. He could see them picking out a dog together. Arguing over what breed to get or whether or not to adopt one from the shelter. Honestly, he'd only argue for the fun of it. He already knew he'd let her get whatever she wanted in the end.

The thought settled in his chest like a strong shot of whiskey. Warm and undeniable.

He'd always dreamed of having a traditional family one day. Something like what Adam and Addy had. He heard a lot of guys at the station complain about their wives and the fact that they bitched at them for leaving their socks lying around or the fact that they insisted on dragging them out to see the latest romantic comedy at the theater in Wellington. Kellen envied every last one of them. They didn't know how good they had it. God forbid they actually helped their wives pick up around the house or took them on a date. It didn't seem like a lot to ask, not if it meant they got to come home to a loving face every day. But what did he know?

Ali gasped. "Did you see it?"

"See what?" He'd been watching her hair run through his fingers.

"The shooting star over that tree." She lifted her hand off of his stomach and pointed.

"I must have missed it. Did you make a wish?"

"Of course, I did."

"What did you wish for?"

She pushed up a little to look down at him. "Can't say. But I'll let you know if it comes true."

Her long hair fell into her face, blocking his view of her eyes, so he reached up with a cold hand and dragged it back as he cupped the side of her head. "Deal."

Something changed when his fingers pushed into her hair. The teasing look she had was replaced by something far more sensual. He could feel it as the air around them became charged. Tipping her head into his hand, she closed her eyes.

"Look at me."

He didn't like that she'd shut him out, but she did what he'd asked, and he got a good look at the need swirling in her chocolate eyes. It was pure, undeniable desire.

"What do you want?" His voice came out in a gruff whisper, but he needed to hear her say it.

"You. I want you to kiss me."

With a groan, Kellen pulled her down and kissed her like he never had before. It was without restraint or apology. He poured every ounce of the need he felt for her into that kiss. He didn't worry about holding back or scaring her because she was right there with him, kissing him back with just as much longing. His other hand gripped her side as she twisted into him, running her fingers through his short hair, trying to find purchase.

Needing her closer, Kellen sat up and pulled her over his lap, so she was straddling him. Blindly, he found the blanket that had fallen down and wrapped it back around her shoulders, never once breaking the kiss.

122

Jesus, Mary, 'n' Joseph.

This was the slow-burn kiss cranked up to oh-my-God levels.

Ali felt Kellen wrap the blanket around them, but she didn't think she'd ever be cold again.

He'd been holding back before. She'd never been so happy to see someone break the way he just did. Now, she finally knew what all of those dirty romance novels that she'd been reading since she was fifteen were talking about. She'd always read about the type of kiss you felt throughout your entire body. Up until now, she'd always thought it was a bit of an exaggeration, but there wasn't a crevice or cranny in her entire body that wasn't on fire right now.

Straddling his lean hips, she pushed her hands inside his coat and gripped his sides. She could feel the tight muscles flex under her palms as he moved, wrapping his arms around her—one hand going to her ass, pulling her in tight, and the other to the back of her neck.

She wasn't able to stop herself from rocking into him, causing him to growl into her mouth. With a palm on her ass, he urged her to do it again, teasing them both.

"Tell me if this is too much."

"It's not enough."

"Kitten, you can have whatever you want. All you've got to do is ask."

This man. Ali didn't have the words to express everything she wanted, so she decided to show him instead.

With quick movements, she pushed the blanket from her shoulders and stripped off her coat and then her long-sleeved shirt before unhooking her bra and letting it fall from her shoulders. Once she was bare from the waist up, she wrapped the blanket back around her shoulders.

"Touch me."

Kellen's strong hands fell to her stomach, nearly spanning her waist, while his eyes drifted across her exposed skin, drinking her in. "Jesus, Ali."

Torturously slow, he stroked the skin at her sides, running them upward until his thumbs brushed along the underside of her breasts. Her nipples were pebbled as much from the cold as they were with need. And she *needed* him to touch them, suck on them. Whichever. It didn't matter.

"Please," she begged, hearing the husky sound of her voice.

"I'm getting there, Kitten. There's no rush."

She begged to differ. She felt the need to rush, but she let him keep his pace, knowing it would be more than worth it.

Leaning in, he left open-mouthed kisses across her collarbone and down her sternum. Basking in his caresses, she let her head fall back. The cold air hit the wet spots he'd left, sending goose bumps across her skin. He managed to lull her into such a submission that it surprised her when he took her nipple into his mouth. She let out a gasp, bringing her head back down. The sight of his lips latched around the tiny bud was incredibly erotic.

"Kellen."

He looked up at her from under his lashes, pinning her with a stare that instantly melted her insides. Unable to ask for more out loud, she rocked against him again, feeling his hard length through the material of her sweatpants. The sigh she let out was loud in the quiet of the night. She was sure there were some owls out there, getting more than they'd bargained for tonight.

Kellen palmed her breast and pulled away, rubbing his thumb across the tender bud before showing the other one the same treatment. His other hand moved around her back and slipped into the waistband of her pants. This time, when he rocked her, his hand was on her bare ass cheek.

With a groan, he pressed his lips to hers, snaking his tongue inside as his left hand abandoned her chest and joined the other. He caressed her cheeks, dipping his fingers low and hauling her closer. His hips jerked up into her when she pressed down, but the friction wasn't nearly enough. When

Kellen's fingertips ghosted across the flimsy fabric covering her center, she jolted in his hold.

More. I need more.

"Shh. I'll take care of you."

Ali realized she must have spoken out loud but didn't care. Not if he eased this ache she felt.

Ali was like liquid fire in his hands. Every time he thought he'd gone too far, she urged him further. Now, she was sitting half-naked in his lap, asking for more. He'd give her everything if she wanted it, but he couldn't tonight in the back of his truck with the wind picking up, making it even colder.

He'd been admiring this ass of hers since the first time he saw her in a pair of leggings at the gym. It was as tight and as supple as he had known it would be.

Slipping his hand under the strip of her thong, he ran his fingers back down, caressing her swollen mound from behind. He let out a growl of appreciation when he found her completely soaked. Slowly, he circled her opening as his other hand yanked down the front of her sweats, baring her bright yellow thong to his gaze. As soon as his thumb found her tight bundle of nerves, he pushed his middle finger roughly into her from behind.

With a long moan, Ali sank down on both of his hands.

"Are you still with me?"

She bit her lip and nodded her head, her eyes heavy on his. Leaning up, he took her lip from her with his own teeth before sucking the sting away. When her nose brushed along his, it was like ice. He needed to get her inside and warmed up. Adding another finger, he pushed them deeper still, over and over again, not letting up.

"Get there for me, Kitten. Find it."

She relentlessly rode his fingers as he played her like a well-tuned guitar. It wasn't long before she locked up tight and pulsed around him.

"There ya go. Ride it out."

When she loosened her hold, he slowly pulled out and righted her sweats. Pulling her in close, he continued whispering sweet words to her as she came down, rubbing her back over the blanket. She buried her face in his neck as she brought her breathing back to normal.

After a few minutes, he kissed her temple. "I think it's time to go."

She brought her head up, looking sleepy-eyed and satisfied. "But what about you?"

He couldn't help but chuckle. "Don't worry about me. Let's get you warm."

As if just now feeling the cold, she started to shiver. Together, they searched until they found her clothes, and he helped her back into them before hopping out of the bed of his truck and then lifting her down.

On the way back to her apartment, he rested his hand on Ali's thigh as she cradled his arm and laid her head on his shoulder. It wasn't long before she dozed off, cuddling close, and he let her sleep as he drove her home in silence.

Growing up the way he had, he didn't have a whole lot of peace in his life. Ali might be as feisty as they came, but tonight, he'd seen a different side of her. He wasn't thinking about the sensual, turn-to-fire-in-his-hands part, as fucking glorious as she was. No, he was thinking about the rest of the night where they'd simply lain there, basking in the peacefulness under the bright blanket of stars.

Maybe, just maybe, he'd finally found some peace.

10

"Ali, are you even listening to me?"
It was only then that she remembered she was sitting in the middle of her classroom at one of the miniature tables, eating fast food. Snapping her head up, she told Callie, "Of course I am. Baby stuff."

"You know, that would almost be believable if I wasn't telling you about my current bridezilla."

Callie was a phenomenal baker and ran an amazingly successful business out of her home. While the majority of her clients were wonderful, she did have to deal with some difficult brides every now and then.

"What's up with you today?"

Oh, you know, just reliving the amazing date—not to mention, the remarkable orgasm—that I had last night.

"It's nothing." Ali waved her off and sat up straight.

Callie had a slow day today and had been nice enough to bring her a hamburger. The least she could do was pay attention.

Clasping her hands on the table, she leaned in. "So, another bridezilla, huh? Is she worse than the last one?"

"Nope, too late." Callie laughed and popped a fry in her mouth. "Now, we talk about you. Last time I saw you, you were acting weird at karaoke, and now, you're doing it again. What gives? Are you still not sleeping?"

Actually, the past week, she'd slept great.

"No, that's not it. I mean, it was bad for a couple of weeks, but I think it's getting better."

"Hon, you know you can talk to me, right? No judgments here."

"I know." And she did. But there were some things she just didn't talk about. Not to anyone. "Do you remember when you told me Kellen was one of the good ones and that I should apologize?"

"Of course." Callie uncapped her water bottle and took a drink.

"Well, I did."

An approving grin spread across Callie's face. "And it felt good, didn't it?"

"Oh. It felt *very good.*"

It took Callie a second to hear what she'd just said. "Oh. *OH!*"

"Shush!" Ali looked over at the open door.

"Are you and Kellen ..." Her hands fluttered around in front of her as she looked for the right words.

"Kinda. Yeah. Well, just barely."

"Aw, you two would be perfect together! Is he perfect? He seems a little perfect. Please tell me he has a flaw somewhere. I mean, besides that whole answering-your-questions-without-really-answering-them thing that he does."

Ali thought about that. "He *does* do that, doesn't he?"

"It's aggravating, right?"

"He does have that effect on me, yes."

"But you like him?"

"Definitely." She didn't even have to think about that one.

"Aw, sweetie. I'm so happy for you." Callie reached over and squeezed her hand. "So, tell me when it happened. I want the details, missy. When, how, where? Don't leave anything out."

Ali gave her the speed-round version during the last fifteen minutes of her lunch break. From the day he had been here, talking with the kids, to the night on her porch, all the way through last night.

When she finally stopped to take a breath, Callie only had one thing to say. "Damn."

Ali was feeling the same way, hearing it all back like that.

Then, Callie suddenly said, "Bring him over."

"I'm sorry, what?"

"We'll do a big dinner at our house. You can bring him over."

"So, my brother can glare at him all night? No, thank you."

"Mason is *not* going to glare."

"Oh, he'll glare. I don't think he's ever smiled or held a polite conversation with any guy who's so much as looked at me."

"Point taken. But he actually likes Kellen."

"He won't once he realizes his lips have been anywhere near me."

"Leave your brother to me. Just come over. When's a good night?"

Ali thought about it. It would be fun. "I'm free Thursday, but I don't know when he's off again. I'll ask him and let you know."

"Perfect!"

They wrapped up just in time for her kids to come bounding through the doorway.

"Mrs. Callie!"

Most of the kids came running over to where her sister-in-law sat.

"Did you have your baby yet?" Little Tyler looked around the room.

"No, Tyler. Look, her belly is still big," Autumn helpfully chimed in, pointing at Callie's small baby bump.

Eli walked right over and placed a hand on her stomach. "Can I feel him kick?"

Not to be outdone, Vincent leaned on the table next to her. "I think you should name him after me."

Callie was just looking between the kids, grinning at their antics, if not a bit overwhelmed.

"All right, kids. Let's give Mrs. Callie some space."

The kids backed up but just barely.

"Well, I've still got a long way to go before I have the baby, and we don't know if it's going to be a boy or a girl, so we haven't picked out a name yet. I also can't feel the kicking yet. I'm sure he's doing flips and turns in there, but he's just too small for me to feel it."

Morgan raised his hand, standing over by the reading nook.

"Yes?"

"When my mom was pregnant with my little sister, she farted *a lot.*"

That was all it took. Every kid lost it in a fit of giggles. Callie took the opportunity to escape her fan club and walk over to Ali.

"And, on that note, I'm outta here. Let me know if we're on for Thursday."

"Thank you for lunch."

"Anytime, hon." Callie waved over her head as she walked into the hall.

Once Callie was gone, Ali got her class back under control and attempted to distract them with amazing facts about butterflies, so they could go home and tell their parents about something other than pregnant women's bodily functions.

Kellen stepped out of the shower and grabbed a towel, wrapping it around his waist before wiping the fog away from the mirror with his hand. His phone vibrated on the counter just as he finished brushing his teeth.

> *Ali Cat: I really hope this doesn't wake you up, but I wanted to give you a heads-up. Callie was here today, and she wants us to come over for dinner. Are you free Thursday? I completely understand if you're not or if you don't want to. I know we haven't even talked*

about anything with us, and it's a lot. No hard feelings if you don't want to go. Maybe we could do something, just the two of us, if you're free. I mean, if you want to. Do you want to?

That was probably the most information he'd ever read in a single text before, but damn if he didn't find it cute. Turning around, he leaned against the counter and sent her a reply.

Kellen: Dinner at Callie's sounds great.

Ali Cat: Are you sure?

Kellen: Yes. I want to.

She was right; they hadn't talked about what they were to each other, but the fact that she wanted to share him with some of her family meant something. Sure, he'd already met Mason and Callie, but he'd met them as a cop. This was different.

Ali Cat: Okay. :) I'll let her know.

Ali Cat: Is there any way you could send me a picture? I need something to go with your contact info.

Kellen liked that she wanted a picture of him. Actually, he fucking loved it. Giving the lady what she wanted, he held the phone out and snapped a picture. His hair was still wet, and he was sitting half-naked on the bathroom counter, but it'd have to do. As soon as it sent, he watched the three little dots pop up and then disappear, only to come back a few seconds later. They did this a few more times before her reply came through.

Ali Cat: Did you just take that?

Kellen: Yeah. And I'm pretty sure that's the only selfie I've ever taken. The things I do for you...

Ali Cat: That is so unfair.

Kellen: What do you mean?

*Ali Cat: Seriously? Never mind. It's a great picture.
Thank you.*

Kellen: Do I get one?

The picture she sent was adorable. She had her dark hair pulled up with some of it falling around her face as she held her hand under her chin while she blew him a kiss. She was fucking perfect. Those plump lips of hers were painted a dark pink, and he'd love nothing more than to have that lipstick smeared all over his body.

And, now, he was hard again.

Jesus Christ.

He'd spent the better part of the last twenty-four hours hard as steel.

*Kellen: Thanks, Kitten. I've got to head into
the station. I can't wait to see you again.*

Ali Cat: Same. Be safe out there.

Kellen: Always.

Their parting had become a routine that he looked forward to. Mainly because it was never a good-bye. He liked that she worried about him. Putting his phone down, he finished getting ready for work.

Kellen's thoughts were on a certain sexy teacher when he walked into the station. It'd been like that for a while now. He was trying not to get ahead of himself, but it was useless. The last few days, he'd started picturing his future. He'd never done that before.

His life had been one giant struggle just to get from day to day. The women he'd been with were only ever a blip on his radar. When he was younger, he was embarrassed of his life, so he never let a girl close enough to see it. Then, as he got older, he never felt comfortable with bringing anyone home with his little brother sleeping on the other side of the hall. And he sure as hell had never sent a girl a picture of himself or lay with her under the stars.

Shaking his head at his ridiculous thoughts, he pushed through the doors.

West Grove Police Department was small compared to some of the larger cities he'd worked in. The single-story building was located on Main Street, just a two-minute drive from his apartment. The entire building only had about twenty employees, and they all worked three different shifts, so there was only ever a handful of them on at once. Less so during the graveyard shift. Tonight wasn't any different.

He nodded at Amelia, who was sitting behind the front desk as he passed by. She'd been doing a lot better these last few weeks. Besides her, there were only three other people here. Travis Brooks stood by the coffeemaker, poking around, probably trying to get the ancient thing to work. Aaron Jones and James Holdren sat stoic at their desks, no doubt wrapping up their paperwork before they headed home.

Kellen's desk was along the right side of the room, butted up against Holdren's.

When he pulled out his chair, Holdren looked up. "Hey, man. How's it going?"

The only complaint he had was that he wouldn't be talking to Ali until tomorrow. It hadn't escaped his attention that, as soon as he went on shift, she went radio silence. Even if he texted her, she wouldn't answer until the next day. He'd like to think that it was because she was sleeping well all night, but he didn't think she'd mysteriously gotten over whatever it was that kept her awake. But Holdren didn't need to know any of that.

"No complaints. How'd it go today?"

"Oh, you know, couple traffic stops, two domestic calls, and one pissed off Chihuahua on the loose."

Kellen chuckled at the visual. "Everyone make it out alive?"

"Barely. Jones almost lost his ear." He motioned over to the other man sitting on the other side of the room, his fingers flying over the keyboard.

"Dude, it's not funny." Jones shook his head, his eyes never leaving his screen.

"Come on. Show him."

Reluctantly, Jones turned his head toward them, and Kellen saw the white bandage covering his left ear.

"Little fucker would not let go. If I wanted a pierced ear, I'd have one."

Amelia snorted from her position up front, trying desperately to keep her laughs at bay and failing miserably.

"I had to get a goddamn rabies shot!"

Officially losing her battle, Amelia broke out laughing, causing Jones's cheeks to turn a deep shade of red as he stole glances at her.

Kellen watched the younger man watch Amelia. Even as pissed off as he was, his lips started to twitch into an affectionate grin. Looked like someone had a thing for the young single mom. Kellen just hoped the kid got off his ass and did something about it.

It wasn't long before Jones and Holdren finished up and headed home for the night. With Brooks headed out on patrol, that left him to catch up on a mountain of paperwork.

He was going through his desk, looking for the report he'd typed up before he left for Nevada, when the front door banged open, and in walked the owner of the Ponderosa Grill. Kellen had met him once during a charity auction the station had a few years ago. Kellen tried to recall his name but came up empty. The older gentleman was carrying what looked like a flash drive clasped in his hand.

Stopping at Amelia's desk, he stated, "I'd like to make a report, but I'm not sure how to do that."

Kellen was already walking across the room when Amelia pointed in his direction. "Officer O'Connell can help you with that."

"Yes, yes." He met him halfway with his hand outstretched. "I believe we've met before."

"Yes, sir. Briefly."

"The name's Charles Rafferty. I do believe one of my employees has been stealing from me. I've got the security footage here." He held up the flash drive he'd been carrying.

"All right, let's start from the beginning."

Kellen led the old man to his desk and pulled up a chair for him to sit on at the end. While the man took his time sitting down, Kellen's phone vibrated on the desktop. After a quick look, he sent it to voice mail and flipped it over. The only reason he'd be getting a call from a Nevada area code would involve Connor, and right now, he didn't have time to deal with that headache.

Mr. Rafferty pulled a bulging file folder out of his leather satchel and placed it on his desk. Kellen pulled his chair out and sat down. They'd better get comfortable because this looked like it was going to take a while.

11

Kellen drove up to the single-story ranch house with the wraparound porch and parked next to the detached garage. Looking up at the new structure, he huffed out a laugh. Mason didn't dick around. Their old garage had been burned down, and this was the first time Kellen had seen the new one. It was easily double the size of the old one. He assumed Mason had more to do with that than Callie. He'd be lying right now if he said he didn't have a bit of garage envy going on.

Ali hopped out of the truck ahead of him, and they made their way up the steps. They didn't even have a chance to knock before the door swung open. Callie greeted them with a smile and then stumbled to the side when her dog pushed past her legs and out the door. The large dog went straight for Ali in a frenzy of wiggling limbs and high-pitched whines.

"Someone's happy to see you." Callie laughed.

"Well, of course he is." Ali's voice morphed into a high-pitched tone that only seemed to egg the dog on as she rubbed and scratched at any available surface. "Can't you see he's starved for attention? No one ever pets you, do they? No, they don't."

Baxter flopped to the ground, unable to contain his excitement as he rolled and rubbed himself all over the deck.

That was, until he saw Kellen. Registering the unfamiliar guest, Baxter got on all fours again, going into total watchdog mode as he eyed him with a wary stare.

Kellen crouched down and held his hand out to the dog. "Hey, boy. Do you remember me?"

Baxter stretched his nose out to sniff at Kellen's hand. Apparently gaining his approval, the dog pushed into him for more loves.

"Yeah, you know me. It's been a while, huh?" Kellen stroked down the short black fur on his back before standing back up.

"Hey, Callie."

"Hey, Kellen. Please, come in." She stepped back and motioned them inside. Grabbing his arm as he walked by, she whispered, "I am *so* sorry."

He didn't have to wonder what she was talking about for long.

Ali saw them the same time he did. "Oh, you've got to be fucking kidding me. Really, guys?"

Mason, Kade, and who he could only guess was her other brother Jase stood inside the living room over to the left of the front door.

"Man, listen to that mouth. When did you become so crass, Ali?" Kade grinned, crossing his arms across his chest.

"Oh, I don't know. When did you start ambushing my dates? Oh, that's right! You've never stopped." She planted her fists on her hips and disappointedly shook her head. "You should all be ashamed."

"I have no idea what you're talking about." Jase sat down on the sofa and propped his feet up on the coffee table. "We heard Callie was making dinner and didn't see the problem with coming over for a nice family meal."

"Yeah, huh."

Kellen stepped forward, resting his hand on Ali's lower back in a show of support. All three men's gazes swung to his with the move, and Kellen met them stare for stare. He understood exactly why they were all here. If he had a sister, he'd probably act the same way.

Addressing Mason first, he met his eyes head-on. "Thanks for having us over."

Mason didn't react, so Kellen turned his eyes on Kade. Last time he'd seen him, he'd had his foot in a walking cast. Months before that, he'd been in a pretty serious car wreck that left him more than a little banged up. He seemed to be all healed up now.

"Kade. Good to see you again."

"Hey, O'Connell. How's it goin'?"

"No complaints." Turning toward the one he hadn't met, he stepped forward and held out his hand. "You must be Jase. I'm Kellen."

The other man stood from the couch and took his hand. "Nice to meet you."

"Likewise."

Mason still stood motionless with his arms crossed, watching the scene. He was the older brother, the protector. Kellen could relate to that. When he was just a cop, they'd been fine with each other. But, now that he was here with his little sister, he could see they were going to have problems. That was okay. Because the only way he could actually have a problem with him was if he ended up hurting Ali, and Kellen had absolutely no intention of ever doing that.

The two of them had a silent stare-down in the middle of the living room with everyone watching. Kellen stepped back next to Ali and returned his hand to her back. That only caused Mason's glare to deepen, but when Ali leaned into him, Mason's face softened just the slightest bit.

"Don't make me give you the *I'll rip you apart if you ever hurt her* speech. Just know that it's a given, okay?"

"Understood."

"All right," Callie chimed in a little too eagerly, "what can I get you guys to drink?"

"What the hell, Callie?" Ali was hot on Callie's heels as they walked into the kitchen.

The guys had all headed out back to do whatever it was that guys did around a grill.

"I know. I know. I know." Callie was obviously frustrated as she flitted around with the containers on the counter.

"I thought I'd, I don't know, ease him into the whole family thing. Not ambush him with over half of them after only two dates!"

Or was it one date? One and a half?

She was still unclear about that.

Whatever. It didn't matter.

The end result was still the same.

"No shit!" Her sister-in-law spun around. "That's why I suggested dinner here. You might as well have just brought him to your parents' next week!"

Over the last couple of years, Ali's mom made sure they all got together for dinner at least once a month. Ali hadn't always been able to make it while she was at school but hadn't missed one yet since she'd been back home. The dinners were bigger than ever now that Callie had joined the family because her father joined them when he could, and here in a few months, there was going to be a little baby. Even Kade had started coming about a year ago. She wasn't sure what had prompted that, but it felt right. He'd been family for as long as she could remember. Ali had loved the days when it was just her parents, Mason, Jase, and herself, but she wouldn't change what it had become for the world. When Mason had added Callie, it had changed their entire world for the better.

She couldn't help the image that Callie's words had created. The one where Kellen sat next to her at her mother's worn dining room table, surrounded by her family. It felt right. But she quickly brushed the image aside. It was too soon to go there.

Leaning her elbows on the counter, Ali dropped her head in her hands with a whine. "How did this happen?"

"Oh, stop. I don't think it went that bad. Give Kellen some credit. He held his own just fine."

She thought about the death glares he had been met with and then remembered the comforting feeling of his hand on her back. When she'd glanced up at him, he hadn't look intimidated at all. He'd looked confident. And, damn it, she'd found that sexy.

"He did, didn't he?"

"See? It's going to be fine. Now, help me carry these outside."

Callie handed her two bowls, and they carried them out back onto the new deck Mason and Kade had added on last summer. Their house sat on a couple acres near the edge of town and had a killer view of the mountains from the backyard.

After setting the bowls down on the patio table, she walked over to Kellen, who was leaning against the railing, talking with Kade. Without missing a beat, he raised his arm, welcoming her over, and she happily curled under it. Mason was busy building a fire in the tabletop fire pit while Jase manned the grill.

She didn't know what they'd been talking about before she came out here, but out of nowhere, Kade asked Kellen, "So, did Ali ever tell you about that time she ran through the house naked, screaming like a banshee?"

Jase barked out a laugh as he flipped the burgers.

Pointing a finger at Kade, she clarified, "I was THREE! Mr. I Cried Because I Got My Finger Stuck In The Barrel Of A Gun."

"Toy gun," he corrected. "And it was scary, okay? I feared for my life."

Laughing, she looked up at Kellen and found him smiling down at her with affection. It was a good look on him. His eyes crinkled up at the corners while his talented mouth pulled up just the slightest bit on one side.

"Kellen, tell us about yourself." Jase turned around, asking from his spot by the grill, "Where're you from? What's your family like?"

And, now, that look was gone.

"Back off, Jase," she ordered with a pointed look at her brother.

This was nothing new. Every time she'd ever made the mistake of bringing a boy around, her brothers would interrogate him until he cracked and was never heard from again. But, this time, it was different. This wasn't just some boy who wanted to take her to a dance.

Kellen squeezed her shoulder and said under his breath, "It's okay." Louder, he answered the question, "I'm originally from Texas, but I spent some time in Chicago before moving to Arizona for a spell. Then, about four years ago, we ended up here."

"We?" Mason asked suspiciously.

"Me and my younger brother. He's going to school down at MSU."

"That's where Ali and I went. Callie, too." Jase approved with a nod.

"He seems to like it."

"What about your parents?" Mason pushed as he wrapped a blanket around Callie who sat cross-legged in one of the Adirondack chairs around the fire.

Kellen simply stated, "Not in the picture."

Ali was the only one here who knew what a colossal understatement that was, but Mason picked up on the undercurrent.

"I'm sorry."

Turning to Mason, Kellen put him at ease. "Don't be. I'm not."

She could tell that her brother was taken aback by that, but he didn't say anything more. Like her, Mason and Jase had grown up with two loving parents. The thought of not being sorry they were gone was foreign to them. Same went for Kade. He'd been raised by a single mom, but they were still close.

Wanting to change the subject, she asked Mason, "So, how's business? Whittle any wood lately?"

After that, the questions backed off a little bit. It seemed less like an interrogation and a little more like friendly conversation. Kellen still had to field a lot of questions, but he was handling it like a champ. It seemed that even her brothers understood that this time was different.

By the end of dinner, everyone sat, cozied up around the fire, talking. Mason sat on the bench with Callie snuggled up next to him. Ali loved how happy her brother was with Callie. He seemed so attuned to her. Attentive and loving. Ali would even go as far as to say that he'd lost his glare completely. She wanted that for Jase and Kade, too. If anyone had asked her two years ago if the three of them would ever settle down, she wouldn't have been so sure, but now? When Mason had fallen in love with Callie, it seemed to set a lot of things in motion. Mason wasn't the only one to change. Jase and Kade changed, too. If Ali didn't know any better, she'd think Callie had magical powers.

"Hey, friends!" The back door slid open, and Brooke and Marc stepped through onto the deck.

Marc walked right over to the extra chairs stacked against the side of the house and grabbed two for them.

"Hey, guys! What are you doing here?" Callie asked as she reached up and hugged Brooke.

"My mom stole Gracie to do some birthday shopping, so we figured we'd come hang out here."

Gracie was their adorable little girl who was going to be turning five this weekend. She'd be starting kindergarten in the fall, and Ali already had plans to snatch her up for her class when they figured out the roster in a few months.

"What the hell, Cal? Were we the only ones you didn't invite?" Marc shook his head, sadly looking around the fire.

"Ha! Hardly. I didn't invite these bozos either." Callie pointed an accusatory finger at Jase and Kade.

Laughing, Marc looked over at Ali and winked. "Hey, Ali." Then, he turned his attention to Kellen. "O'Connell, right?"

"That's right." Kellen reached up and shook his hand. "Marc?"

With a nod of affirmation, Marc sat down next to his wife.

Brooke's husband was her opposite in every way. Where she was loud and opinionated, Marc was more of the strong, silent type. He was tall to her short and dark to her blonde.

Ali had always had a bit of a crush on the handsome Italian construction worker. And, unfortunately, he knew it. Of course, he did because Callie had a big mouth, and she was a lousy drunk.

They'd all been playing an asinine game of Truth or Dare one night at her and Shelby's apartment, and Ali *might* have admitted to having a teeny, tiny crush on him, which was not the craziest thing in the world because Lord knew he was hot. And Brooke, thankfully, just thought it was adorable. No, the problem came when Marc showed up to drive Brooke and Callie home. It took Callie five-point-two seconds to spill the beans. Everyone had found it sweet, except for Ali. She'd been mortified.

But, looking at him tonight, she didn't feel any of the same embarrassment that she usually did when he was around. Tonight, he was just another pretty face. Something she could admire without any of the normal butterflies. Kinda like Kade. Lord knew he was gorgeous, too, but she didn't feel anything for him. She never had.

But Kellen was a different story. Ali looked over at him now. He sat in one of the Adirondack chairs to her left, leaning forward, resting his elbows on his knees with a beer dangling loosely in one hand. As if he could sense her eyes on him, he looked over, pinning her with his pale stare. And that was all it took. One look from him had her stomach tightening as she sucked in an unsteady breath.

Now that she'd finally stopped fighting her attraction to him, there was no denying what he did to her. She squirmed in her chair, remembering that night under the stars, and he definitely noticed. Quirking a brow at her, he reached over with his right hand and tucked her hair behind her ear, letting his fingers linger as they ran down the side of her neck. Those eyes of his grew heated when she shivered under his touch.

"Fifteen more minutes," Kellen leaned over and whispered while Brooke laughed at something on the other side of the fire. "Then, I get you all to myself."

Ali nodded, agreeing wholeheartedly.

The ten minutes it took to drive to his apartment from Callie's place felt like a lifetime.

By the time they'd made it out of there, the fifteen minutes he'd promised Ali turned into more like forty-five. It seemed every time either one of them went to stand up, someone would ask them another question. After the fourth time, he was pretty sure they were doing it on purpose. Especially Mason and Jase. All he wanted to do was throw Ali over his shoulder and hightail it for the truck, but what could he do? Instead, he politely sat there and answered all of their questions. Ali was the one who broke first.

The last time, when Kade asked her whether she preferred ruffle chips to original, she snapped.

Standing up, she leveled a finger at Kade. "I know what you're doing." He busted out laughing, and she turned on the rest of the group. "You're all shameless. It's been fun, but we're leaving." She reached down and grabbed his hand, pulling him toward the back door.

He was glad she'd been the one to do it because he was two seconds from dragging her out of there himself.

They'd walked across the deck with everyone laughing in their wake. Everyone, except for Mason. He'd stared Kellen down until they were out of sight.

Kellen drove them straight to his apartment and parked along the curb out front.

"When were you going to tell me that you only lived a block away from me?"

"Now seems like a good time," he teased with a grin, making her smile back.

Getting out, he walked around the truck, and she met him there as she hopped down onto the sidewalk.

Looking up at him with her big brown eyes, she smiled a sweet smile. "Thank you for coming tonight."

"I wouldn't have missed it."

"Even though you were ambushed?"

"Especially because of that. You're lucky to have them, Ali. They're only looking out for you."

"You are one of a kind, Kellen O'Connell."

He wasn't sure what to say to that. Kellen didn't think there had ever been a girl in his life who saw him the way Ali seemed to. It was a heady feeling to know that a girl like her saw something in him that was worth anything. He'd done a whole lot of surviving over the last couple of decades. But he didn't want to just survive anymore. With Finn at school and Connor taken care of, he felt like he finally had a chance to focus on himself and what he wanted. And, right now, he wanted Ali Crawford more than he'd ever wanted anything.

Reaching out, he laced his fingers with hers and led her up the stairs to his second-floor apartment. The building was quiet for once. He didn't hear anything other than their footsteps on the wooden stairs. When they got to his door, he had to let go of her hand to retrieve his keys from his pocket. He almost had the key in the lock when he felt her warm breath against his neck a split second before her lips left a lingering kiss just below his ear.

That was it.

That was all it took to snap the patience he'd held on to the past hour. With a quick flick of his wrist, he unlocked the door and pocketed the keys. In one quick move, he spun around and pulled Ali against his chest. Her eyes were wicked as she looked up at him through the thickest lashes he'd ever seen.

"You want me to lose control, don't you?"

"In the worst way."

A growl of approval made its way up his throat as he ran his thumb across her bottom lip before drawing her mouth to his. Like a drug, the taste of her hit his tongue, lighting up every cell in his body. They sank into each other, neither one able to get close enough. With a fumbling hand, Kellen reached behind his back and found the doorknob.

The front door thumped against the wall as they practically fell through it in their frenzied state. After kicking the door closed, Kellen backed her up until she hit the wall, never letting their lips lose contact. Running his hand through her hair, he tugged it backward, so he could taste the silky skin at her neck. Her sigh was needy as she arched into him, pressing her chest against his own. Her responsiveness drove him insane. He needed more of her.

In one swift move, he had her sweater off, throwing it to the side. Her bra quickly followed. Frantically, she tugged at the hem of his shirt, and they worked together until it joined hers somewhere on the floor.

Her delicate fingers explored his body, sending currents of heat everywhere she touched. He couldn't take any more of her gentle caresses. She'd wanted him to lose control, and he was dangerously close. Crashing his mouth down on hers again, he pinned her hands above her head before roughly tugging the button open on her jeans and slipping his hand inside her underwear. Ali sucked in a sharp breath that went straight to his cock when he found her soaked.

He loosened his hold on her hands, letting them fall to his shoulders. Bringing his other hand down, he gently cradled her head as he slowly sank his middle finger into her slick heat.

Ali moaned long and low when he pulled back out, dragging his palm across her clit, only to add another finger.

Fuck, she's tight.

Kellen broke their kiss to rest his forehead on hers. Their lips only brushing against each other, both of them breathing hard.

He could tell she was getting closer, but before she came, she started desperately tugging at his belt. As soon as she got it undone, she slid to her knees, sliding off of his hand in the process.

Those glossy dark eyes of hers stared up at him through long lashes as she pushed his pants down and freed him from the confines of his boxers. Almost timidly, she ran her hand down his length before flicking her tongue along the slit.

"Ah, Kitten."

She was going to be the death of him.

Just when he couldn't take any more of her teasing touches, she took his length between her full lips, sucking hard.

Slamming his hand on the wall, he braced himself. "Jesus."

She worked him over hard, taking him right to the edge before he forced himself to pull out of that talented mouth of hers. He didn't waste any time. Hooking his hands under her arms, he stood her back up and claimed her mouth again.

"But I wasn't done," she complained when he broke the kiss.

"I want to be inside you when I come."

Flirting with the razor's edge of control, he spun her around to face the wall.

That was when he saw the delicate, beaded tattoo that ran down the center of her back. Starting between her shoulder blades and ending just above the two dimples at the base of her spine.

It was sexy as hell.

With an arm around her waist, he pulled her to his chest and nipped her ear before whispering, "What other surprises do you have for me?"

"Why don't you keep going and find out?"

With a dark chuckle, he did just that. Kneeling behind her, he tugged her jeans down her legs and helped her step out of them after slipping off her shoes. She wasn't wearing a thong tonight but some satiny thing that left the bottom half of her ass cheeks hanging out. On his way back up her body, he sank his teeth into that very spot, taking pleasure in her sharp inhale.

"I like these, but they've got to go, too."

She shimmied out of those sexy-as-fuck panties, kicking them to the side.

"Better?" She looked coyly over her shoulder.

The bedroom was too far away at this point. Fishing a condom out of his pants pocket, he rolled it on before guiding himself to her entrance. Ali leaned forward and braced her palms on the wall in front of her, pushing back the same time he gripped her hips and pushed inside.

Wet heat seized him as he sank in to the hilt.

Time stood still in that moment.

They fit together like they'd been made for each other. Her body holding his perfectly.

But she still wasn't close enough.

Wrapping his arms around her, he stood her up, snaking one arm between her breasts to grip her throat while the other anchored across her hips.

Ali was on fire. An aching mess. And begging was not beneath her. "Please."

Seeming to know exactly what she wanted, he pulled out, leaving a trail of raw nerves in his path, only to sink roughly back in. Her head fell to his shoulder in defeat. Nothing had ever felt this good. Reaching her hands back, she gripped his hips and held on. He took it slow and hard at first, building her up with a relentlessness that was devastating. She didn't stand a chance. She was putty in his exceedingly capable hands.

"You feel so fucking good, Kitten." Kellen sucked the lobe of her ear between his lips as he squeezed her throat just a little tighter. It wasn't enough to hinder her air supply but just enough to make her soar. "It's never…tell me you feel it."

Oh, she felt it, but all she could do was give a small nod in response because her orgasm was barreling down on her fast. His other hand found her hard bundle of nerves and pressed down, working her clit in tight circles.

He must have felt it happening because he whispered in her ear, "I got you. Let go."

Kellen started losing control, too. Slamming into her with enough force to split her in two as his grip tightened on her throat. While that might scare some people, she'd always been a little unconventional. Everything Kellen was doing to her was exactly what she needed to send her spiraling over the edge, taking him with her.

When she came back down, Kellen was talking her through it like he'd done the first time in his truck. She didn't comprehend most of what he said, but the low timbre of his voice soothed something deep inside her. It honestly didn't matter what he said as long as he kept talking to her.

"You okay?" Kellen wrapped his arms around her and nuzzled her neck.

"More than." She felt sated and blissfully happy.

He trailed light kisses over her throat. "Are you sure? None of that bothered you?"

Realizing he was talking about grabbing her throat, she still wouldn't change her answer. He'd applied the perfect amount of pressure. There wouldn't be any bruises or marks. She understood that some people wanted to be choked to the point of passing out, but that wasn't her thing. Rougher sex might turn her on, but pain was definitely not what she was looking for.

Turning her head to look at him, she tried for a shaky smile, her nerves getting the better of her. "I loved it," she whispered softly. "Just don't think less of me for it, okay?"

She could feel the rumble of his chuckle against her back more than she could hear it.

"Never. You have no idea how perfect you are for me." With gentle fingers, he caught her chin and brought her lips to his for a slow, deep kiss that started to reignite her need. By the time he broke the kiss, they were both breathing heavy again.

"Stay with me tonight." His request was gravelly, his pale eyes heavy-lidded as they raked across her face.

"Yes, please."

Ever so slowly, he pulled out of her, making her gasp. She immediately missed the feel of him. After disposing of the condom in the small trash can next to his couch, he took her hand and led her to his bedroom down the hall.

12

Ali blinked her eyes open, wondering where she was for just the smallest of seconds before it all came rushing back. The dinner, the sex. The other sex. And then there was more sex. By the time they'd finally fallen asleep, there wasn't an inch of skin unexplored between them.

The room was still dark, and Kellen lay next to her on his stomach with his arm slung over her bare back. His dark sheets were rumpled around them, barely covering their lower halves. Turning her head to the other side, she looked for a clock of any kind and found one on the nightstand. It was only four thirty. Ali didn't think she'd ever been up this early without a reason in her whole life.

Now that she was wide awake, she had to pee. Carefully, she slid out from under Kellen's arm and off the bed, wincing a little. She was deliciously sore in all the right places. Walking naked, she searched for the bathroom and found it across the hall.

When she was done, she picked her way through the dark house, trying to find her clothes. Kellen's apartment had a simple layout with the front door opening into a modest living room with a connecting kitchen. Kellen's room was at the end of a short hallway off the back of the living room, and on the other side of the hall were two doors, one of which was the bathroom and the other she assumed was probably Finn's room. Searching for her clothes took longer in the dark, but she didn't want to turn on any lights. She only found her jeans and one shoe when the overhead light turned on, startling her. Standing up with a start, she held the jeans in front of her to cover her nakedness.

Kellen stood in a pair of black boxer briefs with a finger on the light switch. The longer hair on the top of his head was a total mess, and his hard body was on full display. She'd spent hours learning every inch of that body, and looking at it now, she wanted to do it all over again.

"Your actions say you're getting ready to leave, but your eyes are telling me to take you back to bed."

"Gotta say, I'm not sure what the right choice is here."

He practically stalked her across the expanse of the room, his eyes never leaving hers. When he reached her, he took the pants and shoe out of her hands and tossed them onto the couch before pulling her naked chest against his. The light dusting of dark chest hair was soft against her skin and only emphasized that he was *all* man.

Tangling her arms around his neck, she leaned up and pressed her lips to his. "As much as I want to stay, I should probably go home."

"It's not even five yet." His short beard scratched tantalizingly against her skin as he kissed his way down her neck, stopping to nip at the nape.

He'd learned quickly that, that spot turned her to mush, and he was using it to his advantage right now. When his hands slid down and cupped her ass, she wanted to give in.

Vainly, she tried to talk some sense into herself, even as she pushed harder against him. "We can't. We don't have time."

"That sounds like a challenge." He lifted her then, her legs automatically locking around his waist as he carried her back to bed.

They had had time. At least they would have if he'd been able to let her go after her first orgasm, but he'd been greedy.

Now, she was running up to her door with only thirty minutes to go before the bell rang. Luckily for her, that last round in the shower had been productive *and* fun.

After her door shut behind her, he pulled away and headed for Wellington.

Thirty minutes later, he pulled up to the curb in front of Addison and Adam's house. The neighborhood was bustling this morning. He'd passed a few kids on their bikes, wearing backpacks, and three or four more groups walking to school, but most families were piling into their cars, headed out for the day.

When Kellen stepped out of his truck, he raised his hand to the older lady who was backing out of her driveway in front of him. She waved back with a big smile and rolled down the passenger window, stopping the car halfway across the sidewalk and into the street.

"Good morning, Kellen," she hollered across the car.

"Morning, Mrs. Barker." He stepped around the front of his truck and ducked down, so he could see her.

"You got the day off?"

"Yes, ma'am. I don't work until tonight."

"Graveyards…oy." She shook her head. "I don't know how you do it. Well, I'd better get going. You tell Addy I said hi, okay?"

"Will do. Have a good day."

"You, too, sweetie."

As she drove off, Kellen made his way up the front steps and rapped on the door. The deep barking was immediate, and he could hear Sam, their golden retriever, rushing closer. He could also hear Adam telling the dog to shut up before the door swung open.

Adam opened the door, wearing only a pair of basketball shorts, and dropped his head with a grumble when he saw it was him. "I can't believe I just lost five bucks."

"What did Addy bet you now?" Kellen asked as Adam stepped back and let him in.

"That you would show up for breakfast."

Kellen had to laugh at that. Addy was a smart woman. She also happened to be a dirty little con artist. "You know I woke up with a text from her this morning, telling me to come over, right?"

"Kellen!" Addy yelled from down the hall in the kitchen where the smell of bacon wafted, making his stomach growl. "Where's the loyalty?"

"You little liar!" Adam marched toward his wife, and Kellen followed with Sam weaving between his legs the whole way. "You don't win the money if you rig the game, sweetheart."

Kellen crouched down to pet the dog while Adam advanced on his wife in mock anger. With a squeal, she tried to get around the island in the center of the kitchen, but Adam caught her around the waist before hefting her onto his shoulder, giving her a solid smack on the ass that rang throughout the room. Addison wasn't even fazed. The woman was laughing so hard; she was barely breathing.

"It's not my fault you didn't think of it first," Addison called out, still laughing from her upside-down position.

Lowering his wife to the ground, he held her close as he disbelievingly shook his head at her. "I had no idea I'd married such a devious woman."

Yes, he did. This was not a rare display at their house.

"You know you love me." Addison cupped her husband's face as she smiled sweetly up at him.

"I'm a sick, sick man." Closing the distance, he gave her a lingering kiss.

They'd been this way since he'd known them. The two of them always had this easy way about them. They fought, they teased, they played. It wasn't hard to see the love between them.

"Does this mean you're not going to feed me?" Kellen joked as he stood back up from petting the dog.

"And force you to fend for yourself? Never." Addy unwound herself from Adam as she waved him in and went back to the stove.

Kellen leaned down and gave her a kiss on the cheek as he passed.

Addy was also wearing her sweatpants and a worn T-shirt. She was lucky enough to have every other Friday off from her job at the hospital where she worked as a trauma nurse. She hadn't always had a set schedule, but the hospital had implemented a new system a few years ago, a lot like the shifts they worked at the station. Since Adam owned his own mechanic shop here in town, he was able to put someone else in charge on the Fridays Addison had off, allowing them to spend the day together.

"So, what's new?" Adam asked as he handed him a cup of coffee.

"Screw the small talk." Addy walked over and set a plate of bacon and a plate of pancakes on the table before turning to where they stood against the island. "I want to know about Ali."

"Is that the only reason you invited me over?" Kellen asked suspiciously.

"The answer to that isn't going to change the fact that you're already here." She shrugged and walked over to the fridge to grab a pitcher of orange juice.

Kellen looked at Adam, who was used to his wife's antics, and found him grinning at him over his coffee mug, happy to have someone else in her crosshairs.

He relented. "Things with Ali are good."

She simply looked over her shoulder at him and raised her eyebrow.

"Better than good. She's great."

"I *knew* it! Does that mean I get to meet her now?"

Kellen thought about it. Ali had shared her family with him, and he wanted to do the same.

"Yeah, if she's okay with it. Maybe we can all do something while Finn's here."

"I didn't know Finn was coming home." Addy cracked an egg over the pan on the stove.

"Yeah. He texted me a couple of days ago. Said he'll be home tomorrow."

Adam was hesitant at first but finally asked, "Does your girl know about Finn? About your whole situation?"

"She does." He watched a look pass between his friends. "What?"

"It's nothing." Addy grabbed the spatula from the counter and looked over at him. "It's just…that's not something you usually share."

"It's not," Kellen agreed. And it wasn't. "I was out with her the night Finn called about Connor. I had to tell her something."

"That's not true," Adam said with conviction before taking a sip of his coffee.

"What do you mean?"

"I mean, you didn't have to tell her anything. I've seen you date plenty of girls who you never said a thing to."

"How did she take it?"

"She actually took it pretty well. She didn't run for the hills or anything."

"Answer this: would you have told her if she wasn't there that night?"

Leaning back, Kellen crossed his ankles and contemplated, staring at the brown liquid steaming from his cup, but came up with the same answer. "Yeah, I would have. Maybe not that night, but I wanted her to know."

Because things were different with Ali. *She* was different. Again, that look passed between his friends.

"Now what?"

Addy's eyes lit up as she looked back at him. "I definitely want to meet this girl."

"You can't keep her to yourself forever." Adam shrugged one burly shoulder.

Kellen narrowed his eyes at his friends. "Don't you two have better things to do than worry about who I'm dating?"

"I'm a great multitasker." Addy grinned as she dumped the eggs out of the pan and onto a waiting plate.

"Lovely." Outwardly, Kellen sighed, but on the inside, he was smiling.

He would expect nothing less from his friends. They had truly become a part of his family, and their opinion mattered to him. He just hoped Addison kept her opinions to herself for a little while. Not that he thought she wouldn't approve, but because he knew she would, and he didn't want her to pressure Ali into anything she wasn't ready for.

On the way back to West Grove, Kellen called Ali, fully intending for her voice mail to pick up, and was surprised when she picked up on the third ring.

"Hey, you," she greeted with a smile in her voice.

"Hey, beautiful. Got a sec?"

"Sure. Is everything okay?"

"The only thing that could've made today any better was if you'd never left my bed. I'm not nearly done with you, Kitten."

Her hum of agreement went straight south of his belt. He pushed those thoughts aside but not without effort.

"But that's not why I called. Finn's coming into town for the weekend. I want you to meet him."

"Really?"

"Yeah, if that's something you'd be interested in."

"I would love that, but tomorrow, I'm working the Spring Festival. Maybe tomorrow night?"

Kellen parked in the grocery store parking lot and ran his hand through his hair in frustration. "I've got to work the next few nights." Lately, the graveyard shifts he'd been working for the last decade were starting to lose their appeal. He'd started them, so he'd be home around Finn's school schedule, but he didn't know anymore. At this rate, they wouldn't ever see each other. "Maybe I can drag him out to the festival."

"Are you sure Finn wants to do that?" She sounded doubtful.

Definitely not.

"Of course," he lied. Finn hated that festival. They had gone a couple of years ago, and the only thing Finn liked about it was the food. But he'd go if he asked him to. "We'll see you tomorrow."

"Can't wait." He loved hearing the smile in her voice. "Stay safe tonight."

"Always."

Kellen hung up without saying good-bye. He didn't need to.

Turning off the truck, he headed into the store. Kellen wasn't much of a cook, but he could grill a mean steak with some baked potatoes, which just happened to be Finn's favorites. It had been almost two months since he saw his brother, and he'd be lying if he said he didn't miss him.

13

West Grove held the Spring Festival a few weeks before Easter every year. The city put together a massive egg hunt for the kids and a few of those giant bouncy houses. Live music was one of their biggest draws and played all day long from local bands. People came to sit and listen while eating copious amounts of fried food from the venders set up around the park. There were silly races and three-on-three basketball games as well as a pie toss and hot-dog-eating contests.

Ali remembered coming here year after year since she was a child. More than a handful of those years had been in the snow, but it didn't stop the town from showing up. Come rain or shine, the show went on.

Today, the grass under Ali's feet had finally started to turn more green than brown, and it was warm enough outside that she got away with wearing her favorite jean jacket with a pair of red leggings and a T-shirt. She'd initially put on a cute summer dress but taken one step out her door and turned right around to change when her legs turned into Popsicles.

Right now, she sat on a stool in front of a little girl who couldn't be older than three, attempting to paint a butterfly on her cheek.

"Sweetie, I need you to hold still for me, or you might end up with an Easter egg instead of a butterfly." Ali tried to coax the girl who'd obviously had her fair share of cotton candy, judging by the sticky blue crust that had formed in the corners of her mouth.

"Butterfly!" She clapped and bounced in her seat.

Ali shushed her while trying to finish her up as quickly as possible. The music was constant from their small booth, and the smells were a little overwhelming, but it was all part of the experience.

How her mother had talked her into this, she'd never know. But that was Maggie Crawford. She always had a foot in everything around here. If it wasn't the *Nutcracker* production in the winter, it was the fair in the summer and everything in between. Her mom was not above begging and flat-out guilt-tripping her into helping where needed. And, today, that meant face painting. Luckily, Ali had been able to talk Shelby into coming with her.

Ali looked over her shoulder to check if her roommate was having better luck with her wiggly boy and his Ninja Turtle mask.

"Hey." Shelby leaned backward with a whisper, "Which one's Donatello again? The red one or the purple one?"

"No idea. Maybe the yellow one?"

"Is there a yellow one?"

"Um…" Ali trailed off, trying to remember the posters she'd seen of the show. There could be a turquoise one for all she knew.

"Never mind. He's gettin' blue."

"Solid choice." There was definitely a blue one.

Shelby went back to her mask, humming along with the music drifting over from the stage, while Ali finished up her would-be butterfly. In the end, it turned out more like a deformed Easter egg, just like she'd feared, but the little girl seemed happy with it.

As the girl bounced off with her mom, Ali spun around on her stool as she called up the next person in line.

"All right, who's next?"

"That would be me," the deep voice answered behind her.

Ali stopped short with her spin, knowing she was grinning like a schoolgirl. Kellen stood at the front of her line, looking like he'd just walked out of a photo shoot for sexy country boys. He had on a red-and-black flannel shirt over a long-sleeved gray henley, both of which were rolled up, showing his thick forearms. She wanted to jump up and throw herself at him but played it cool, gluing her ass to the stool.

"Hi." Although she couldn't do anything about the dreamy quality to her voice.

"Hey, Kitten."

"Hey, handsome," Shelby piped up with a quick look over her shoulder.

"Hey, Shelby." Kellen grinned good-naturedly at her flirting.

Just the sight of him flooded her with the memories from the night they'd shared together. It had been...intense. The romantic in her wanted to say it had been life-altering, but the realist in her settled on mutually satisfying.

And her romantic half wanted to hog-tie the realist and send it down the river.

She'd been almost desperate to see him since then, but that was where her realistic side had raised its ugly head. They always seemed to be going in two different directions. By the time she was sitting down to dinner, he was just starting a shift, and when he was getting home, she was walking out the door.

She'd been avoiding the question in the back of her mind that asked, *If we only have a handful of nights a month, can we even make this work?*

But it was something she was going to have to accept if she wanted to be with him. She knew there were plenty of people who did it.

But it's not enough.

Ali wanted to shut that voice in her head up. She wanted to throw caution to the wind and accept whatever she could get, but that damn realist kept popping in, trying to ruin her rosy filter.

She was so caught up, looking at Kellen, that she almost missed the guy standing next to him. This must be Finn, but he was nothing like she'd pictured. He was quite a bit smaller than Kellen in both height and build with a curly mop of strawberry-blond hair. If it wasn't for the pale blue eyes behind his square-rimmed glasses, she wouldn't have recognized him.

"Ali, this is my brother Finn. Finn, this is my Ali."

My Ali.

That short phrase held so much meaning, but she tried not to get too giddy at its implications.

"It's nice to meet you."

Finn had his hands stuck firmly in his jeans pockets, so she just gave him a small wave from her stool.

"Yeah, you, too." His smile was shy if not a little awkward.

"So, do you guys really want to pick out a picture?" She held up the laminated sheet with their options on it. "You're never too old for a shark on your cheek."

"No, thanks. I saw that mouse you drew on your last victim." Finn grimaced, causing her mouth to fall open in mock outrage.

"Excuse me. That was a butterfly, thank you very much."

"If you say so."

What a little punk.

"Do you think you can do better?" She got up from her stool and handed him the paintbrush with a challenging stare.

He grinned boyishly and took the brush from her. "You so owe me a corn dog when I nail this."

"Deal." Ali could tell she was going to like this kid.

He called the next kid over, who enthusiastically picked out the full tiger face. Ali snorted under her breath. She'd had a little girl choose that one earlier, but she'd been a chicken and *known* she'd turn it into some kind of deformed jack-o'-lantern, so she'd talked her into a delicate vine of flowers around her eye and down her cheek. There was no way he was going to be able to do this.

Kellen wrapped his arm around her shoulders and pulled her into his side. "You are so screwed."

"Yeah, he is." Ali turned into him and placed her hand on his flat stomach.

"I was talking to you."

"Wait, what?" She looked up into his smiling face.

"You'll see." Kellen watched his brother as he sat on the stool across from the boy.

It wasn't long before she understood exactly what Kellen had been talking about. Not only did Finn rock that tiger face, but he also did it quickly and better than the sample picture.

But he didn't stop there.

As the next three kids hopped up, one right after the other, Finn proceeded to crank out a pirate, a princess, and the best damn butterfly she'd ever seen as they watched in awe. Even Shelby had stopped painting to look.

When the final kid in line hopped off the stool, Ali conceded, "So, does that count as one corn dog or four?"

"I'll settle for a corn dog and a turkey leg."

"You totally played me." Ali shook her head, more proud than anything.

"I'm not the one who handed me the brush." He shyly looked away but was unable to contain his smile.

"Touché." She turned to Kellen. "You could have at least warned me."

"Where's the fun in that? Kid's got talent. Always has."

She saw it then. The pride in Kellen's eyes wasn't that of a brother, but instead, it was more fatherly. That shouldn't have been surprising, given everything he'd told her, but she was still taken aback by it. The responsibility he had taken on was nothing short of amazing. And Finn seemed like a great kid with talent and a sense of humor. Kellen had done that. He had given him a life where he could thrive instead of simply survive.

Her thoughts choked her up a little, and she dropped her eyes to the ground to hide the emotion she was being bombarded with.

"Any chance we could steal you away for a bit?" Kellen placed a kiss on the side of her head.

Ali checked her watch with disappointment. She still had another hour left here before she had to relieve the person at the pie toss.

But, before she could apologize, Shelby, who'd been abnormally quiet this whole time, waved them off with a smile. "Go get this kid some food. I've got this."

"You sure?"

Her friend called the next kid up onto the stool before turning her royal-blue eyes on her. "Positive. Go have fun." She turned back around but then spun back, pointing the paintbrush in her direction. "But bring me back a funnel cake!"

"One funnel cake coming right up." As they started to walk away, Ali mouthed a sincere, *Thank you*, to her friend and got a wink in return.

Kellen reached out and gripped her hand as they fell into step together and headed for the food vendors.

After they collected their abundant pile of provisions, they found a spot at one of the picnic tables in the area around the stage. Kellen and Finn both took the end seats across from one another while she sat next to Kellen.

Finn ate in silence while Kellen squeezed her knee under the table. The band was playing, so it wasn't exactly quiet, but she quickly realized the men around her were not going to be carrying the conversation, so she stepped up to the plate.

"So, Finn, how do you like school?"

He paused to swallow. "It's good. Keeps me busy, ya know."

"Do you know what you're going to study yet?" Ali took a bite of her pulled pork sandwich.

"Graphic design."

Ali could picture him doing that. He definitely seemed creative enough.

"Finn's an artist." Kellen elaborated, "Drawing, paint, sculpture. All of it."

"I saw that. You're definitely talented."

Clearly uncomfortable with the compliment, Finn redirected the conversation. "Kellen said you're a kindergarten teacher?"

"I am. I actually graduated from MSU last spring."

"No shit?"

"No shit."

"You look like you were in a sorority." He suspiciously eyed her. "You were, weren't you?"

That made Ali laugh, unsure if that was a compliment or an insult. "You would be wrong." She didn't have anything against them. That just hadn't been her focus. "The political aspects of college never interested me." No, her focus had definitely been elsewhere. Ali suddenly became awfully interested in her sandwich.

"Huh." Finn pondered her for a second. "I do think I like you, Ali Crawford. Even if you do paint deformed butterflies."

Kellen huffed out a laugh at her side as she snapped her head back up, looking at the grinning teenager.

"It was *not* that bad!"

"Whatever you say, Ali Cat." Kellen laughed, pressing his lips to her temple.

"Yeah, whose call was it for you to work the face-painting booth anyway?" Finn's good-natured teasing had her grinning.

"My mom volunteered me because there was a cancellation, okay? It's not like I do this every day."

"Obviously."

"You know what? I don't have to sit here and take this," Ali said jokingly and got up to leave, only to have Kellen grab her around the waist and tug her into his lap.

Her squeal of surprise ended in a fit of giggles, but Kellen held her firmly in place with one arm around her waist and his other hand on her thigh.

His mouth was right over her ear when he spoke, so only she could hear, "I love your laugh." Funnily enough, that statement made her laugh die out and her heart go into overtime. "I thought it was your smile that did me in, but it was definitely your laugh."

Okay, she was done. Utterly and completely done for. Turning her head to look at him, she focused on his lips, wanting so badly to kiss them. She didn't have time to want very long because he lifted his chin and pressed his lips to hers with devastating tenderness.

But the moment was broken when Finn cleared his throat. "Come on, guys. I'm trying to eat here."

They pulled apart and locked eyes. There was something different about the way he was looking at her. She didn't understand it, but she liked it. She liked it a whole hell of a lot.

"What's up, O'Connell clan?"

Ali twisted in Kellen's lap, so she could see the newcomers at the end of the table. The woman was the other instructor she'd seen at Hank's. Her brown hair was cut in a short, sassy pixie style that complemented her heart-shaped face. Standing next to her was a burly man who stood head and shoulders above her. He had a full dark beard and not a single strand of hair on his head. And his dark eyes were currently locked on her, but they were twinkling warmly.

"And you must be Ali."

"That's me." She smiled cautiously.

"Ali, this is Addison. You've probably seen her at the gym, and this is her husband, Adam." Kellen rested his chin on her shoulder as he introduced them.

"Is that what I've been reduced to, 'her husband'?" Adam glared at Kellen before turning his grin back to her. "Don't let him fool you, doll. We're besties."

"Ignore him." Addison stepped forward. "Hi. I *have* seen you at Hank's a few times, but I didn't know your name. I've been dying to meet you. I finally wore Kellen down."

Ali looked back at Kellen. Accusation clear on her face.

"Guilty. Sorry to ambush you like this, but it was only fair after the night at your brother's."

"True." She turned back to the couple. "Hi. I'm glad you wore him down. It's wonderful to meet you both."

"Ditto, toots." Addison beamed at her before she and her husband sat down on either side of Finn, effectively trapping him in.

Ali took the opportunity to slide off Kellen's lap. But she didn't get very far. He held her fast, not wanting her to move. But, with a quick pinch to his ribs, he let her go with a huff. She was not going to be perched on his lap while they all sat around to talk.

"Hey, kid." Adam reached over and stole one of Finn's nachos. "You don't write. You don't call. I'm hurt."

"Sorry, man." Finn smiled boyishly at the mountain of a man sitting next to him.

"Sorry, my ass. Who else is supposed to help me keep this jackhole in line?" Adam jerked his head in Kellen's direction, making him laugh. "Addy's totally on his side. I'm all on my own here."

"Wait a minute," Kellen broke in. "Since when is Addy on my side?"

Addison leaned across the table and whispered as the guys continued to argue, "Just accept the crazy. It's easier if you don't fight it."

"I'm starting to get that." Ali smiled, loving these people already.

"So, do you like shopping and/or getting mani-pedis?"

"Both."

Addison reached over and patted her hand. "You and I are going to get along just fine."

Kellen held Ali's hand as they walked slowly across the park. Everyone else had stayed behind to give them a few minutes alone. His time with her was almost up, and he wasn't ready to walk away just yet. Something had changed for her when she was sitting across his lap. It wasn't that he'd so much as seen it, but he'd *felt* it.

"Thank you for coming by today." Ali looked up at him. "I'm sorry I'm so busy."

"You've got nothin' to apologize for." He wished their schedules were different, but he'd take what he could get. Even if it was an hour-long lunch. "They all wanted to meet you, so it worked out."

They passed by a crowd cheering on a heated three-legged race. The winning couple, who looked like sisters, fell into a laughing heap as soon as they crossed the finish line.

"Finn wasn't what I expected."

Kellen was pretty sure he knew what she meant but asked anyway, "How's that?"

"If it wasn't for the eyes, I wouldn't have realized he was your brother."

"He looks a lot like our mother. She had curly red hair, too. I look like my dad."

It had always been a point of contention with his father that Finn looked nothing like him. Kellen remembered his father accusing his mother of cheating on him more than once. There had never been any question that he and Connor were his blood, but he couldn't see it with Finn, and that had pissed him off.

"Who did the eyes come from?"

"That's all our mother."

She squeezed his hand a little tighter.

"So, where are we headed?"

"The pie toss." She pointed at a booth down the row.

It had a line of people waiting behind a low table that was full of pie tins filled with what looked like whipped cream. About fifteen feet away from the table sat a large plywood board standing on end, painted red and white to look like a target with the center cut out for someone's face. There was currently an older man sitting on a stool behind the board and a woman taking tickets and handing out pies.

"I hope you're taking over for her and not him." He knew it was all in the spirit of fun, but he didn't like the thought of people throwing stuff at her. In fact, it kind of pissed him off.

"Ha! There's not a chance in hell I'm sticking my face through that hole. I'll be the one handing out the pies."

"Good."

The woman behind the table greeted them when they walked up, "Well, hey there."

Despite the friendly tone, Kellen didn't like her. It was immediate and unequivocal. It had a lot to do with the way her smile changed when she looked from Ali and then over to him. It went from fake to damn near predatory.

"Who's this?" She eyed him up and down like he wasn't holding another girl's hand. *His girl's* hand.

"Sarah, this is Kellen. Kellen, meet Sarah. We work together."

Ali was pretty easy to read by now, and it was clear she didn't like this Sarah person either. Her tone was one of forced politeness that he'd only heard her use once before—the first time he'd met her outside of the diner. She hadn't liked him then either.

"Well, hello, Kellen. You must be new around here," Sarah practically purred.

"Been here some years now."

"Then, how have we never run into one another?"

"We must run in different circles."

"Well, that's something we must change."

"I don't think so." He stepped into Ali, pulling her closer. "I'm perfectly happy where I'm at."

She gave a haughty little huff, getting his meaning perfectly clear.

He felt Ali laugh next to him before she smiled at Sarah. "I'm here now, so you're free to go."

"Where's your partner? I can't leave until you're both here." She'd lost all sense of politeness, turning downright bitchy.

"I'm right here." Kade ran up and draped an arm around Ali's shoulders.

Sarah's mouth got tight as she untied her small waitress apron where she'd been collecting the tickets. Handing it over

171

to Ali, she walked away without another word. They all waited a beat before Kade looked down at Ali.

"You ready to do this?"

"Watch you take multiple pies to the face? Hell yeah. I've even got a ticket with your name on it."

"Of course you do." Kade turned to him. "Hey, man. How's it goin'?"

"Hey."

"You going to throw a pie at me, too? You kinda look like you want to."

Kellen couldn't say that he wasn't thinking about it. And, as much as he wished Kade would move his arm, he couldn't help but like the guy.

"Maybe."

When Kade walked over to switch places with the man behind the board, Kellen turned to Ali as she crisscrossed the apron strings behind her back and tied them around front. He'd been wondering something for a while now, and he figured he'd just get it out of the way.

"So, there's not really a right time to ask this, but have you and Kade ever hooked up?"

Ali's lips briefly pressed together over her teeth before she snickered. "Why?"

"It's just a question."

"Because that's what's supposed to happen, right? The girl falls for her brother's best friend. The one who's always around, so it's inevitable? You've watched too many chick flicks."

"That's a no then?"

"That's a hard no. He's my family. My incredibly *platonic* family."

"Good to know." He liked that answer. "And the deal with that Sarah chick?"

"Oh, complete bitch."

"Got it." Kellen placed a kiss on her forehead, fighting a smile. This girl never failed to amuse him.

"Hey! Alyssa June!" They looked over to see Kade's face resting in the center cutout. "Let's get this thing going!"

"Duty calls." She reached out and touched the center of his stomach, sending a little jolt through his body. "Will I see you again this weekend?"

"I don't think so, Kitten. After I get off in the morning, I'm taking Finn fishing before he heads back to school, and then I've got to work again. Except for the class at Hank's, I'm off Monday night. You free then?"

She was trying hard to hide her disappointment, but she kinda sucked at it. But he understood it because he felt it, too. Their schedules were awful.

"Yeah. Meet you at the gym?"

"It's a date." He gave her a quick kiss, lingering a second or two longer than he'd meant to. When he raised his head, he forced himself to take a step back. "Go on. Go throw one for me. Yeah?"

She nodded her agreement, and he walked back to find Finn, so they could leave. He'd never get used to walking away from her.

In fact, he hated it.

14

Ali practically ran to her car in the teachers' parking lot. She was already behind schedule to meet Kellen at Hank's for their evening date. The plan was for her to drive over after her meeting and get in a workout while Kellen taught his class before they went to dinner.

That plan had started to slip away the second she stepped into her meeting and found the superintendent of their school district in front of the room with a presentation ready. The short meeting that their principal had promised had turned into a two-hour snooze show, talking about statewide test scores. Complete with more bar graphs, line graphs, pie charts, and scatter plots than anyone ever needed to see. And the big reveal at the end? They were right on track and had fantastic numbers. The whole thing was a painstakingly, mind-numbing, dragged-out attaboy. She could practically hear the eye rolls from her fellow teachers at the end. It was Monday, and *everyone* wanted to go home.

Finally free, everyone rushed to their cars. Ali quickly hopped into her Mustang and pressed the start button, but instead of hearing her baby roar to life, the only sound that answered her was that telltale click of a dead battery.

"Oh, you've got to be kidding me." She tried a few more times just in case without any progress.

The knock on her window startled her as Eric's all-too-happy face filled her side window.

She briefly entertained the idea of sending him away, but she had places to be and a sexy policeman to see, so she opened her door and got out.

"Looks like you need a jump." Eric eyed her with his buggy eyes.

Ali studiously ignored the innuendo dripping from his words and soldiered through.

"If you wouldn't mind, that'd be great." She even managed a tight smile of thanks for him.

More than happy to help her, he rushed back to his car and positioned it in front of hers. Ali popped her hood and propped it open while he rummaged around in his trunk before producing some red and black jumper cables. He took his sweet time in getting his own hood up, and Ali was trying not to get antsy. But it soon became obvious that Eric had no idea what he was doing as he held the clamps, merely staring at the engine.

"Do you want me to do it?" she offered carefully.

"I know what I'm doing," he snapped over his shoulder.

Ali highly doubted that but tried to calm her nerves long enough for him to figure it out.

Her father had taught her how to jump a car when she was fifteen. She thought everyone knew how, but watching Eric as he actually Googled *how to attach jumper cables* was just sad. She could have been finished by now.

Checking her phone, she watched the time slowly drift away as her anxiety rose to new heights.

But, just when she didn't think she could take it any longer, she heard the blessed words, "Try it now."

She wasted no time climbing back into her car and listened to the engine turn over with a rumble. Before she was able to enjoy the sound, Eric was filling the space in her open car door as he crouched down to her level.

"We should probably let it charge for a few minutes."

She knew he was trying, but his creepy eyes wandered down to her bare knees. It was then she noticed the skirt she wore had ridden up her thighs when she slid into the seat.

Silently nodding her head, she angled her legs into the car, further away from him. "I appreciate the help."

"Anytime, Alyssa. Anytime."

Ali didn't bother correcting him with her name again. He never listened anyway.

"You could thank me by letting me buy you dinner."

All right, enough is enough.

"While I am grateful for your help tonight, I won't be going out with you."

"Well, if tonight's no good, I'm free tomorr—"

"Ever, Eric," she cut him off. "I'm just not interested."

He rocked back a little as if she'd actually hit him. The shock on his face apparent. "Oh. Okay then."

She felt prompted to apologize, although she had no reason to. "I'm sorry."

"No, don't be." He stood up and stepped back. "I guess I should have caught on a little sooner, huh?" His small laugh was without humor. "You can only have so many dinners with your brother." Shaking his head, he walked around front to unhook the cables.

Getting out, she followed him. She wished there were something she could say to fix the wounded look in his eyes he was trying to hide, but she was at a loss. It wasn't her fault the man couldn't take a hint.

By then, they were the only two left in the lot. It was quiet now as she lowered her hood, and he wadded up the cables, tossing them back in his trunk.

The awkwardness was crippling as they stood next to their cars, so she put them both out of their misery. "Thank you for the help. I appreciate it. I'll see you at school."

He gave her a stiff nod before she got back in her car and pulled out of the lot.

After a quick trip home to change out of her work clothes and into something more gym-worthy, she was finally headed in the right direction.

She was already running ridiculously late and could feel a migraine starting behind her left eye, but she was determined to follow through with their plans. Who knew when she'd get to see him again?

Scanning through the three radio stations that came in clearly, she managed to find a tolerable song and turned it on low. She easily maneuvered around the other cars on the road as she made her way out of town. She was only two blocks away from the town limits when she saw them. The blue and red lights flashing in her rearview mirror. Quickly glancing down at her speedometer, she saw she was going well over the speed limit.

Oh, fuck me.

At this point, Ali honestly didn't think her day could get any worse, and she started laughing hysterically as she pulled over to the side of the road. The only upside to this was that she knew Kellen was thirty minutes in the other direction, so there was no way it was him in the car behind her. The cop took a few minutes to get out of his SUV, and thankfully, that was enough time for her to get her shit together. She knew she was about to get a ticket, and she didn't need to make it worse by acting like a crazy person.

Reaching into her glove box, she pulled out her papers and got her license from her purse before rolling down her window.

"Good evening, miss. License and registration, please."

She obediently handed them over to the young cop who was probably only a few years younger than herself. The vest he wore over his uniform had the name Jones stitched into it, but she didn't recognize him.

"Do you know why I pulled you over?"

"I'm going to go out on a limb and say speeding." Cringing at her smart-ass reply, she tried to remind herself that A), it was true, and B), it wasn't this guy's fault her day had turned to shit.

"You'd be right. I got you doing forty-four in a thirty-five."

"Sounds about right."

"I'm going to have to write you a ticket, Ms. Crawford."

That wasn't a surprise. She'd gotten tickets for less.

"I understand."

While he went back to his car, she checked her phone. There was no way she was going to have time to work out before Kellen finished his class, but with just a little luck, they could still make their date. Although she wasn't holding out any hope at this point. Resting her head on the steering wheel, she closed her eyes. She was pretty sure they'd made a movie about horrible, no good, very bad days, and this one was shaping up to be a doozy.

Officer Jones wasn't gone long before he came back to hand her the ticket. It was then she noticed the bandage on his left ear. Maybe she wasn't the only one having a little bad luck lately.

"Injured in the line of duty?" She pointed to the white gauze.

The grin that graced his face was adorably boyish. "Something like that. Have a good night, Ms. Crawford. And slow down."

"You got it. Have a good night, too."

She waited for Officer Jones to get back in his car before pulling back out onto the street. This time, she took it slower—at least until she got on the highway.

Now, after a forty-minute drive that usually only took her thirty, Ali pulled up to the gym and parked in the nearly empty lot. Before she could get out, her phone chimed in the cupholder.

> *Callie: You got pulled over?*

> *Ali: How the hell do you know that?*

> *Callie: Apparently, Marc saw you and told Brooke, and she just told me.*

Of course. Because why not?

> *Callie: Did you get another ticket?*

Ali: Yes. I'll call you later. I'm running late.

Callie: Fine. FYI, your mom knows, too. She and Brooke were here when Marc called.

Ali just hung her head. She'd have to deal with that lecture later.

One thing at a time.

After shoving her purse under the seat, she pocketed her phone and keys before walking into Hank's.

As she pushed through the doors, she almost ran into one of the girls she recognized from the self-defense class. It was one of the giggly ones who'd spent far too much time sitting on Kellen last week.

"Hey! Watch it." The girl scowled as she sidestepped to avoid running into her.

"Sorry," Ali uttered a quick apology, only to have the other girl roll her eyes before moving to stand against the wall by the door, her attention already on her phone.

Okay...

Ali quickly recovered and located Kellen standing on the mats in the back of the gym. From the looks of it, class was already over. Pulling out her phone, she checked the time. They should still have at least ten minutes left.

"No, no, no, no."

She hurried over to Kellen, who had his back turned as he shoved giant pads into a mesh sack. As she approached, he turned, a small, tired smile on his handsome face.

"I know I'm late, but I'm not *this* late. What happened?" Ali indicated the nearly empty gym.

"Addison got stuck at work and couldn't make it tonight. Then, Max got sick and had to bail. I decided to call it early. Half the girls weren't here anyway." Kellen stretched his neck from side to side, obviously feeling tense.

"What is going on today? Is it a full moon or something?"

"Somethin'," Kellen said absently before looking at her. "Rough day?"

"I've had better. You?"

"It's better now." Grabbing the front of her shirt, he pulled her in close and wrapped his arms around her.

Feeling calm for the first time today, she pushed closer and pressed her lips to his for a brief kiss before he wrapped her up tight in a hug that promised to cure all of her problems.

"Agreed."

Ali was content to stay there the rest of the night, but then she looked over his shoulder and saw that same girl still standing by the door. Only this time, she was mentally shooting laser beams out of her eyes in their direction.

Maybe I spoke too soon.

Pulling back, Ali looked at Kellen and stated nonchalantly, "You know, my day has been pretty craptastic up to this point, so if there's something I should be preparing myself for, I'd like a heads-up. You know, murder...mayhem...mean-girl texts. Stuff like that."

"What are you talking about?" he asked, confusion making two lines appear between his eyebrows.

Nodding in the direction of the girl who was now angrily texting on her phone, she asked, "Is she your ex or something?"

Ali would never admit how that thought twisted up her insides. This girl wasn't ugly, and she'd like very much to keep on pretending that all of his exes were nasty little trolls.

After a quick look over his shoulder, he turned back to her with a grin. "No. That's Khloe from class. Ignore her. She's just pissed that she's not you."

"Is that all?"

"In a nutshell."

Choosing to heed his advice, she refocused her attention on Kellen. "Sorry I'm late. Did you still want to grab dinner?"

Her words seemed to catch him off guard. He'd definitely forgotten about dinner.

"Shit. I can't. When Max left, I told him I'd close up."

Ali slightly pulled back, trying not to be hurt that he hadn't remembered.

"Oh, that's okay." Ali relented, having lost some of her calmness from a few moments ago.

She couldn't help but chastise herself for being so determined to come tonight when he, apparently, hadn't even remembered.

"No, it's not okay." He crouched down until he was level with her eyes. "I'm sorry. Do you want to stay and keep me company? This place is pretty empty, but I've got to keep it open until nine."

She wanted to be pissed off, but she just didn't have it in her tonight. And she was just pathetic enough to take what she could get from him. "Yeah. Sure."

Kellen smiled down at her before he kissed her temple, hugging her just a little bit tighter, and she remembered how tense he'd seemed when she got here. Obviously, she wasn't the only one having a bad day. They both just needed to de-stress a little bit.

Kellen let her go and walked over to where he'd been picking up the pads from class. Gathering up three of the stuffed bags, he headed for the storage room next to the office beyond the gray mats. She grabbed the last one with an unattractive grunt and followed.

Cripes. That's heavier than it looks.

"How did class go today?"

"It went all right." He took the bag from her and easily tossed it in with the others. "There were only three girls, so we did a lot of review."

She knew for a fact that one of those girls was Khloe, aka mean girl by the door, aka one of the girls who wouldn't get off his lap last week.

Ali didn't know why she said what she said next. Maybe it was Shelby's whole own-your-feelings shtick, but whatever the reason, she found herself admitting, "You know, I actually got jealous last week." When Kellen only looked at her in confusion, she reminded him, "Here, at the gym. You were doing that move where you straddled the girls, and they flipped you over. There were a few of them who seemed to enjoy having you underneath them." And could she even blame them?

Kellen laughed. Actually *laughed*. "You didn't have anything to be jealous of." It was a great laugh, but she could only imagine what her admission sounded like to him.

"I know. We weren't even…anything. I felt ridiculous." *Kinda like now.* "You were just doing your job. I get that." Toeing a scuffmark on the floor, she lowered her eyes, feeling awkward.

Wow. Probably should have kept that to myself. Freaking Shelby!

Kellen's tone went soft as he interrupted her inner tirade, "That's not true."

Wait. What?

"You weren't just doing your job?"

"We were something. Even that day, we were already something."

She laughed a little to hide how much his admission affected her. "You mean, you don't have non-dinners with just anyone?"

Could he actually feel this, too? This overwhelming pull she felt to be near him. To trust him.

"Our non-dinner was unfortunate. But the stuff I told you about me and my family, not a lot of people know that. And you're still here. That's somethin' to me."

Ali turned around and busied herself, restacking the clean pile of towels on the shelf by the office. She didn't say anything because she felt tears burning behind her eyes. Though she wasn't sure why. No, that was a lie. He'd opened up to her on their first non-date. Laid it all out in the open and given her the option to walk away. She'd never even considered walking away. So what? He had a past, and it was ugly. But he'd trusted her with it, and more than anything, she wanted to trust him with hers.

"Show me."

Startled, she looked up at him, thinking he was reading her mind.

"What did you say?"

"I said, show me your moves." He started walking backward onto the mat.

"What?" Ali was surprised at Kellen's change of subject. "Seriously?"

"Yeah, I called class early. Maybe I could teach you something instead. Besides, you said you were jealous. Now's your chance to get on top of me." He waggled his eyebrows at her, making her smile.

"I've already been on top of you…and underneath you." And, *good God*, did she want to be there again.

"Mmm, careful, Kitten." His eyes went hot at her reminder.

Ali looked around the gym at the handful of people using the equipment, wishing they had the place to themselves. Pushing those thoughts aside, she relented and followed him onto the mat. "Do your worst."

I've so got this.

They circled each other a few times before Kellen reached out, quick as a snake, and grabbed her around the shoulders from behind, slamming her back against him.

"What should you do now?" his hot breath whispered in her ear.

Ali smirked to herself. It was almost too easy. Reaching up, she grabbed his forearms before abruptly dropping her center of gravity. From there, she simulated stomping on the arch of his foot before throwing her head back into his face.

Kellen let her go, looking impressed. "Something tells me, this isn't your first time."

"Self-defense three years ago at college. I was a star student," she bragged with a grin.

"I have no doubt. All right, let's see what else you remember." He backed her up against the wall and pinned her there with his large body pressed into hers. His hands on the wall by her head.

For the briefest of moments, she let herself enjoy the feel of his body on hers and the warm smell of his skin before she remembered she wasn't supposed to want him there. Using her fingertips, she hooked them into the base of his neck, where his throat met his sternum, and pushed, causing him to back away. Once his weight lifted off of hers, she simulated kneeing him in the groin, which he expected and caught gently with his hands.

The pride shining in his eyes made her feel all sorts of amazing. Those blue depths were also swirling with something far more carnal.

"Do you think I'll go to hell if I admit that you're completely turning me on right now?"

Laughing, she replied, "At least I'll be there with you." Because she felt it, too. Good Lord, did she ever.

"Lie down," Kellen ordered, his voice going husky.

That deep voice of his ordering her to lie down sent a jolt straight to her center, and she quickly obeyed.

Yep, definitely going to hell.

Once she was on her back, Kellen slowly straddled her, pinning her wrists next to her head, putting her in the exact position she'd been jealous of last week.

"I know you know this one. Show me what you got."

But she genuinely didn't want to move. His black hair was disheveled, hanging down over his forehead, and his breathing was slightly labored. Whether it was from exertion or desire, she didn't know, but he was beautiful. His light eyes were like two beacons showing her the way home. It was then she realized she was losing herself to him. Every aggravating, beautiful, damaged part of him.

The urge to touch him was overwhelming. She went to lift her hand up to his face, but her arm barely twitched in his hold. She tried again with the same results, causing her breathing to come faster. The fluttering of butterflies she'd been feeling were now a raging swarm inside her. She tried to sit up, but Kellen held her pinned to the mat. He was waiting for something, but she couldn't remember what. She was supposed to be doing something. Her legs were useless, trapped between his, while the majority of his weight rested on her hips, holding them down. Sweat started to break out across her brow when she tried to slow her breathing and failed.

She was no longer seeing Kellen above her.

She was looking into a black abyss that there was no escape from.

Kellen sat above Ali, smiling down at her. She wiggled and tried to move, unable to budge him. He thought he'd finally stumped her when she looked up at him, but it was like she was looking right through him. The color draining from her face.

What the hell?

"Ali?"

She didn't even acknowledge him. She was on the verge of hyperventilating, her dark eyes wide with panic. Immediately loosening his grip on her wrists, he cupped her face, finding it cold and clammy.

"Kitten, talk to me. What's goin' on?"

His touch seemed to snap her out of wherever she had gone as she refocused on him, her wide eyes blinking rapidly.

"Get off." She pushed at his chest, the flatness of her voice surprising him. "Get off of me."

Kellen promptly got up, letting her roll to her feet. She wouldn't make eye contact as she turned her back to him, adjusting her top.

"What just happened?" he asked gently.

Every cell in his body wanted to go to her, but he didn't. He let her have her space even though it took everything he had to stay where he was.

"Ali, talk to me."

She still didn't acknowledge him.

Then, a sickening thought occurred to him. "Did I hurt you?"

She turned around to look at him then, and the change in her face knocked him back a step. "You didn't hurt me. I'm fine."

Any trace of panic or whatever that had been was gone. If he hadn't seen it for himself, he wouldn't have known anything happened at all. And that pissed him off. It was something his mother had perfected. And it was complete bullshit.

"Don't lie to me." He flexed his jaw. "Not right now. You know I'd never do anything to hurt you, right?"

"You didn't do anything wrong." She let just a hint of emotion into her voice, but it didn't show on her face. She was locked down tight.

"Will you just talk to me?" he begged. "What the fuck just happened?"

"There's nothing to talk about. I'm fine. But I think I'm going to head home." She casually walked over to the bench and gathered her phone and keys.

She was shutting him out. After everything he'd shared with her, she was shutting him out. And it fucking hurt.

Placing his hands on his hips, he looked down and shook his head. "Don't leave like this."

"Like what?" she asked as she came back, keys in hand.

Kellen clenched his jaw in his frustration. This wasn't his Ali Cat or his Kitten. He didn't know this Ali. This Ali wasn't hot or cold; she was completely indifferent. And, as long as she was, he knew there was nothing he could do or say to make it past the walls she'd put up this time.

"Will you at least let me know when you make it home?"

"Sure."

She smiled at him, and it was almost genuine. She was good. But not that good. When his Ali *really* smiled, her eyes were the first to show it. Apparently, she couldn't fake that part. Walking up to him, she kissed him on the cheek before turning to leave.

And he let her go.

What else could he do?

15

Kellen's phone vibrated in his pocket as he sat at a small two-person table by the window at the diner. Pulling it out, he saw an unfamiliar number and sent it straight to voice mail as his waitress brought his food over. He had come off another shift and didn't have a scrap of food in his house, so he'd stopped in for some breakfast. Over the last few days, he'd picked up extra shifts and worked until he couldn't keep his eyes open anymore. It was easier to keep busy. Because, if he didn't, he was going to put his fist through a wall.

He was giving Ali space to work out whatever it was that she needed to work out, and it was fucking torture. He wanted to help her, but she'd resisted every damn time he tried. And, even though he admired her fierce independence, he also found it frustrating.

"Here ya go." Amy set his plate of bacon, eggs, and toast in front of him with a warm smile.

He'd been a regular here for a while now, and Amy had been here the whole time.

"Thank you."

"Anytime. Let me know if I can get you anything else."

He nodded, and she went off to see to her other tables.

Just as he picked up his fork, his phone rang again with the same number. This time, he picked up.

"O'Connell."

"Well, it's about damn time. We need to talk."

"Shelby?" She'd never called before, and it made him sit up and take notice. "What's wrong?"

"Where are you right now?"

"I'm at the diner."

"Perfect! I'll be right there."

Shelby hung up without a good-bye, and Kellen was left staring at his phone.

What the fuck was that?

He didn't have to wonder long because not three minutes later did the little blonde plop into the chair across from him.

"Where did you come from?"

No way had she driven here that fast.

"The coffeehouse around the corner. Now, listen up. I've only got ten minutes left on my break, and we need to talk." Her tone worried him.

"Is Ali okay?"

"That depends on your definition of okay. Is she alive? Yes. Is she sick? No. Is she being a world-class bitch? Oh, yeah."

Okay. Not what he'd thought she was going to say.

"What the hell happened between you two?"

"Nothing happened."

If Ali hadn't told her, he wasn't about to.

"Bullshit. A week ago, she was running out the door to meet you and then nothing. Not one mention of you. Every time I ask, she shuts me down. I'm done asking her. Now, I'm asking you."

"She's not sleeping again, is she?" Although he was certain he already knew the answer. He'd done his fair share of drive-bys since that day in the gym, and there were lights on every damn time; it didn't matter the hour.

Shelby scoffed at his question. "No, she's not. I got up to pee the other night—sorry, TMI—and she was awake, reading in bed, at three in the morning. And she has been up before me every day this week. I'm pretty sure that's like the first sign of the apocalypse or something. Lord knows I love her, and Ali has always been a little short-tempered and a bit snarky, but she's crossed over into full-on bitch mode. She actually snapped at our new barista the other day because we were out of cinnamon rolls. She doesn't even *like* cinnamon rolls. So, I repeat, what the hell happened between you two?"

Kellen ran a hand down his beard that he still hadn't gotten around to shaving. "I wish I knew. But trust me when I say, I'll figure it out."

"Well, you'd better hurry up because I might have to kill her before someone else does."

Shelby pointedly looked at him and got up, leaving as quickly as she'd come. At least, now, Kellen had a clearer picture of what was going on.

He might not have seen Ali in a few days, but they'd been texting off and on, although their texts had been lifeless. Just fluff about their days. She hadn't given any indication that she wanted anything from him since that day in the gym. He'd been waiting for some sign that she still wanted him around.

And he was done.

He tried giving her space.

He tried playing things her way.

She thought she had everything locked up so tight that nothing affected her. But, if that were true, she wouldn't be taking it out on everyone she knew.

Everyone, except for him. He didn't even get that.

He was finished with this indifferent shit. He was going to get a reaction out of her if it broke both of them. Because, sometimes, you had to break in order to heal.

Kellen spent the afternoon sleeping as he waited for Ali to finish up at the school. By now, she should just be getting home. He'd given her enough space. Now, it was time to go it his way.

Making his way up the walk, he knocked on her front door.

No one answered.

If anything, it fueled his decision even more. Her Mustang was parked out front, so he knew she was home.

Knocking again, he called out, "I can do this all damn night, Ali Cat."

This time, the door swung open. Ali stood there, already in a pair of sleep shorts and a T-shirt. She looked exhausted. The shadows under her eyes that had disappeared a few weeks ago were now back, and they were more pronounced than ever.

"What are you doing here?" she asked, holding on to the open door.

He didn't ask for permission as he walked directly into the room. "We need to talk."

"Okay," she said, her tone completely emotionless.

Pointing a finger at her, he seethed. "See, that, right there. Why are you doing that?"

"I have no idea what you're talking about."

Bullshit.

"Are you ready to talk about what happened last week?"

"There's nothing to talk about." She defensively crossed her arms. "Nothing happened."

So, that's how she wants to play this? Fine.

"You're seriously going to stand there and pretend like you didn't lose your shit for a split second and then bail?"

"Kellen, I'm fine." She smiled at him like she was convincing a child.

Exasperated, he dug his heels in. "Ali, you can't fix things by pretending they don't exist. I should know. My mom was a master at it."

It was a low blow, and he knew it, but it hit its mark as he watched her eyes flash with anger.

"That's not what I'm doing."

For the first time, he saw a crack in her composure, so he pushed harder.

"Bullshit. That's exactly what you're doing. You're hoping that, by ignoring whatever it is, it will magically go away, like it never happened. You think I didn't have to watch my mom do that every time my dad threw one of us against the wall or backhanded us so hard that it gave us a black eye? She'd look right through us and then ask us to come sit down for dinner or some shit. Like it never even happened. Do you think that stopped him from doing it again the next day? Or the next?"

"Stop."

Ignoring her, he kept going. "Fuck no. Not once did her ignoring it *ever help us*. Not once did she say a word or lift a finger to help us."

"Why are you doing this?" She paced to the other side of the couch.

"Because you need to help yourself."

She spun on him. "Don't act like you know what I need."

There it is.

There was that spark back in her eyes. She was getting pissed, and he'd take that over indifferent any day.

"I know you need sleep." He arched an eyebrow at her, daring her to disagree.

"How would you even know that?"

"Not from you. That's for damn sure."

"Shelby." Ali shook her head, annoyed at her friend.

"Is that so bad? She cares about you. *I care about you.* And, if you're not going to take care of yourself, I'm going to be here to help you."

"I didn't ask you for that."

"No shit. You don't ask for anything." Now, he was starting to get pretty pissed off, too. "After everything I've told you about my fucked up life, you still haven't given me *anything!*"

"That's *not* true!" she yelled back at him. "Just because I don't have a fucked up past doesn't mean I haven't opened up to you! I'm not going to stand here and apologize for having loving parents and a happy childhood."

"If your life has been so perfect, then why are you at Hank's, beating your fists until they bleed?"

"What does that have to do with anything?"

Everything.

"What are you so afraid of?"

"I am not afraid."

"Yes, you are, and you're letting whatever it is tear you apart."

She sneered at him. "Like you said, you don't know anything about me."

"That's not what I said, Kitten. I said, you haven't *given* me anything. Everything I've learned about you, I've had to fight for it. You don't make it easy, but I know you. I know you like chick beer and pizza. I know you don't know shit about constellations. I know you worry about me every night I go to work. I know you'd do anything to help out those closest to you. I know you have the biggest heart of anyone I've ever met. And you are going to make an amazing mother someday because of it. I also know you feel powerful when you're in the gym, and I know the reason you push yourself so hard is because you're afraid of being weak."

"I am *not* weak." Tears filled her eyes, one spilling over, running unchecked down her cheek.

Now, we're getting somewhere.

"No, you're not." He softened his voice in agreement. "You're one of the strongest people I know. But that doesn't mean you've never *felt* weak."

Ali was shaking her head in denial as she bit her bottom lip to try to stop it from trembling.

"What made you feel so weak? Tell me what happened."

Throwing her arms out to the sides, she finally broke. "*I don't remember!*" she screamed at him before a sob escaped, and she crumpled in on herself.

Kellen immediately pulled her into his arms, soothing her as she fell apart. All of her pent-up emotions coming out at once. Picking her up, he carried her over to the couch and sat down with her in his lap.

He couldn't make sense of what she'd said. She was the only one who could do that. So, Kellen waited. He waited for her to finally let it all out, to get rid of it all now that she'd finally popped the cork.

Her sobs slowly quieted to gentle shakes. And, eventually, her breathing evened out. When she was ready, she sat up, wiping under her eyes.

Kellen tucked her hair back away from her face as her red-rimmed eyes traveled up to meet his. "Help me understand."

She nodded.

The indifference was long gone, her face now showing every single thing running through her mind. Scooting back, she sat cross-legged, facing him on the couch. Taking a deep breath, she began, "I have this memory, but it's not complete. My dreams are like fragments. Just bits and pieces of something I can't fully remember. And I've tried. God, I am so tired of trying. It's why I have trouble sleeping."

"When did it start?"

"About a year and a half ago. I remember coming home for one of our monthly dinners just days after the dreams started."

"Does it happen every night?"

"It depends." She shrugged, pulling a pillow into her lap. "Sometimes, I'll go weeks without one, but then I'll have them back-to-back for a while."

"Have you talked to anyone about them?" He was pretty sure he knew the answer.

"No."

"Will you tell me?"

God, for once, he just wanted her to let him in.

She looked at him, searching his face for something, and he patiently waited while she came to a decision. Hugging the pillow tighter to her chest, she looked at a spot over his shoulder.

"They're always the same. It never changes. Night after night, the same damn thing. But it's more of a feeling than anything tangible. I remember feeling disconnected, fuzzy even. From everything. People. Voices. Even my own body. My thoughts. My limbs. Everything. And there's this weight on top of me. It's like an elephant is sitting on my chest. I try to move, but I can't. No matter how hard I try, nothing works.

My arms, my legs. Nothing. I feel like I'm dying. Whatever I'm under is crushing me, and there is nothing I can do about it. I can't breathe. All I feel is panic. I'm completely helpless. I can't do anything. That's when I wake up."

"That's a scary feeling. Being helpless."

"Yeah, it is."

He had been well accustomed to being helpless when he was younger. It wasn't something he wished on anyone. Especially not Ali.

But things were finally starting to make sense.

"Can you remember anything else that can tell you what your dream is about?"

"I know what it's about." She looked at him then with anger simmering in her eyes. "I might not *remember*, but I know exactly what happened."

"You're going to have to give me more, Kitten." He didn't understand.

"There's something you need to understand about me first." She paused, tears gathering in her eyes again.

"Hey, listen to me." He cupped her cheeks, brushing his thumbs under her eyes, catching a tear that spilled over. "There is nothing you could tell me that would change the way I feel about you. Do you understand me?"

Her sad smile frustrated him. She didn't believe him.

"You met the Ali I am today. The responsible, educated kindergarten teacher. You like her. But that is a very new version of me. Before, I was always a bit of a wild child. My parents were great parents, but I pushed and pushed every chance I got. It's a miracle they let me survive until adulthood. I've embarrassed them and pissed them off more times than I can count.

"When I went away to college, I was finally free to do whatever I wanted. And I took advantage of that. I was a walking cliché. Parties every weekend, sometimes even during the week. Drinking, drugs, boys. All of it. I didn't hold back. I wish I had. Thankfully, I was able to keep my grades up. That part's always come easy for me. If you need advice on how to get through finals while still a little buzzed, I'm your girl. The first three years of college were a little crazy and a bit of a blur. That tattoo on my back you like so much? Courtesy of a dare after a little too much pot. Such a meaningful experience, I know.

"I never stopped long enough to realize what I was doing to myself. And, when I finally did step back, it was almost too late."

Kellen thought he could see where this was headed, and he hoped to God he was wrong.

"It happened the night of my last first date. The one you asked me about, remember?"

"The frat party."

"Yeah. This guy I'd gone out with a couple times before asked me to go. It was his friend's brother's party or something like that. It started out like any other party. I remember the house was dirty and beyond loud, but the music was tolerable, and the drinks were free. You couldn't even see the kitchen counter, for all of the liquor bottles. People were handing out drinks left and right, but I only remember drinking two of them. They were awful. My date didn't seem to think so because he got well and truly plastered.

"He started to get a little handsy after that, but he was cute, so why not?" She shrugged, looking disgusted with herself. "I remember we were dancing, but then things started to get a little fuzzy. Next thing I know, I woke up in my own dorm room with this." Ali pushed the hair on her forehead aside to reveal a thin scar at the edge of her hairline. "I don't remember getting this either."

Kellen reached out and ran a finger over the inch-long scar. Even drunk, she would have remembered getting that. Ali closed her eyes at his touch and leaned into his hand.

"Kitten." He paused, not knowing how to ask what needed to be asked. He'd been a cop for almost a decade. And a lot of that was spent in bigger cities where the crime rate was out of control. Unfortunately, he'd seen this more than a few times. He'd done the interviews, he'd testified in court, but right now, he couldn't find the words to ask her.

"It's okay." She reached up and took his hand, squeezing it between both of hers. "I know what it sounds like. Trust me. But, along with a bloody head, I woke up fully clothed."

"That doesn't mean—"

"I know it doesn't," she cut him off. "But that's not what happened."

"Okay." He hoped to God she was right. But just because she hadn't been raped didn't mean that what had happened to her was not all kinds of fucked up. "It sounds like you were definitely drugged though. You know that, right?"

"That's what I figured. I've done the research. Weak, confused, memory loss. Fun stuff." She laughed scornfully. "My roommate was with me when I woke up. She filled in most of the blanks for me."

As much as he needed to hear the rest of the story, he gave her an out. "You don't have to tell me if you don't want to." She'd already opened up to him more than she ever had before.

"No, it's okay. I want to."

She looked up at him, her dark eyes still sad. He wanted so badly to pull her back into his lap and hold her, but she seemed content to play with his fingers of the hand she still held on top of the pillow in her lap.

"Her name was Jess. We were friends, but we weren't super close. I didn't even know she was there that night, but apparently, she was there with her boyfriend. I think he was part of the band or something. Jess told me that she'd been worried about me because of how drunk I was. Or at least, she thought I was drunk. So, when I disappeared, she grabbed her boyfriend, and they went looking for me." She flattened out his hand, running her fingers along every crease, every vein. "They found me in an upstairs bedroom. My date was in there, on top of me. Not really doing anything, but I guess her boyfriend pulled him off of me, and they started fighting. They ended up knocking over a lamp, and it hit me in the head." She pointed to her scar. "I never even felt it. Apparently, my date insisted that nothing was going on, that he'd only brought me up there to lie down. But my friends took me home anyway. Bandaged me up."

Ali got quiet then, still holding his hand.

Kellen didn't know what to say.

"And it *pisses me off*. Everything about that night pisses me off. I know the facts. I don't remember them, but I know them. I'm pissed off at how stupid I was. I'm pissed off about how careless I used to be. And that stupid dream that I keep having? It pisses me off more than anything because I don't even know if it's real or if it's just something my mind made up, knowing what *could have* happened if Jess hadn't gotten there in time. Because the only thing that night left me with besides this scar was panic. Pure, breath-stealing panic."

Kellen understood now. "That day in the gym."

"You didn't do anything wrong, but when I couldn't move, that panicked feeling came at me out of nowhere. I didn't even know it was happening until it was too late. I'm so sorry for the way I acted." Her eyes pleaded with him to understand.

"You have nothing to apologize for." He leaned forward and pressed his lips to her forehead. "Thank you."

"For what?" She scoffed. "For walking away from you? For shutting you out?"

"For trusting me."

Tears filled her eyes again. "I do. I do trust you. And you were right before. I felt weak. And stupid. And, every time I dream about it, it makes me feel weak and stupid all over again."

Kellen took both of her hands in his. Bending his head down, he waited for her chocolate eyes to meet his.

"You. Are. Not. Weak." He believed that unequivocally, and he needed her to believe that, too. "There is not a single bone inside of you that is weak. Physically or mentally."

"But I *was* stupid." When he opened his mouth to disagree again, she held up her hand, halting him. "Don't. It's true. I had zero self-respect, and I treated my body like an amusement park. I'm under no illusions about the part I played in what happened that night. I know no one *asks* for those kinds of things to happen to them but that doesn't mean that we aren't responsible for our own actions. And I was ashamed of the person I'd turned into. So, I decided I needed to grow up. Take accountability for my life. And I did, to the extreme. Even now, I'm still trying to find a balance I can live with." Ali shrugged. Then she smiled at him, looking more settled than she had in a while. "Did you know you're the first guy I've even looked at twice since that night?"

"Is that so?"

"Mmhmm."

"I'm honored. Lord knows, you made me work for it."

Her mouth quirked up on one side. "Damn straight."

"There's my Ali Cat."

He brushed his knuckles along her jaw. She was tougher than she gave herself credit for.

A blush stole across her cheeks at his touch. "Am I? Yours?"

He echoed her words back at her, "Damn straight." If he was sure of anything in this world, it was that.

"I'd really like that."

"Kitten, you've had me since the beginning."

"I'm sorry I've been such a bitch."

"Bitch I can handle. Just don't shut me out. Not again. If we're going to do this, we have to do it together."

Ali gave him a small nod. "Together."

Ali looked at the man sitting in front of her. After all that he'd been through, he was still everything that was right in this world. And she'd almost ruined this.

She'd held on to this…this shame over everything that had happened. Today was the first time she'd ever spoken about it.

That next day, Jess had offered to go with her to the police station to report it, if Ali wanted to. But the more she thought about it, the more she wondered what the point would be. Who would she have pressed charges against? She couldn't prove she had been drugged, and even if she could, anyone at that party could have done it. The guys pouring the drinks, her date, or just some random person walking by. Anyone. It didn't even have to be a guy.

So, instead, she'd chosen to lock down the memory, determined to move on with her life. Until recently, she hadn't realized how much anger and shame still existed inside of her. The idea that she should have known better. That she should have kept a better eye on her drink or realized something was off. The idea that she should have been able to stop it.

Ali knew she'd still have her moments, but right now, she felt lighter somehow. Like some of that anger and shame was gone. And she had Kellen to thank for that. Only he would have barged in here and pushed at her until he found a way around the walls she'd built up. She'd never been able to keep him out before, and she was glad he'd shown up this time.

"Thank you for not giving up on me. And for understanding."

"Come here."

Gladly.

Kellen cupped her cheeks and brought her mouth to his. It'd been days since she was able to touch him, to kiss him. And, when he kissed her, she felt whole, like a small piece of her that had been missing this week was finally back.

"I missed you," she admitted against his lips.

"I'm not going anywhere. This"—he pressed his hand over her heart—"is worth fighting for. You are this beautiful ball of attitude wrapped around this compassionate, soft center, and I can't get enough of you."

If it was possible to pinpoint the moment she lost her heart to someone, this was it. This was that moment.

She couldn't seem to get the words past the lump in her throat, so she showed him.

Tossing the pillow aside, she climbed into his lap, straddling his lean hips. He easily welcomed her, tightly wrapping his arms around her. Their kiss started slow and sensual but quickly became desperate.

"Where's Shelby?" Kellen asked as he kissed across her collarbone.

"At yoga and then her parents' for dinner. When do you need to be at work?"

His eyes darted up to the clock on the wall. "I've got about ninety minutes."

"I'll take it."

Kellen stood up, taking her with him. His hands gripping her ass. "Bedroom?"

Wrapping her arms and legs around him, she took his earlobe between her teeth before whispering, "Second door on the left."

Quickly making his way down the hall, he found her room and took her straight to her full-sized bed. Her back hit the mattress, and he followed her down, kneeling between her open knees. The rough material of his jeans rubbed delightfully against her bare legs as she entangled them with his.

Kellen's callous hands slipped under the hem of her shirt, sending tingles across her stomach. Skating his fingers across her skin, he brought the material up and over her head, exposing her bare breasts.

The appreciative growl that made its way up his throat said more than any words could have as he bent his head and took her pebbled nub into his mouth. His hands automatically went to her elbows that were above her head and slowly slid up to her wrists, holding them firmly against the pillow. Ali's body arched, pushing her breast closer to his mouth. The fire was burning through her body, and she needed more.

That was when she felt it.

The change in him.

His grip on her wrists immediately gentled before letting go entirely, his hands falling to the bed on either side of her head. The powerful suction of his mouth also became a soft lick.

"Don't do that," Ali demanded. "Don't treat me like I'm going to break."

"I'm not."

"Yes, you are. I've never wanted you to treat me like a doll. I can take whatever you want to do to me, and you know it."

"I know you can. I just thought—"

"You're wrong." She knew exactly what he'd thought. And she adored him all the more for it, but the panic she'd felt when he held her down on the mats at the gym was completely different. That reminded her of her dream. The dream of something that *could have* happened. This was real. And this was her choice.

Ali crossed her wrists above her head and gave him a challenging stare. "I want all of you. Got it?"

A beautiful smile touched his lips. "Yes, ma'am." His hand slid lovingly back up her arm until his fingers closed over her wrists, pinning them down.

Leaning in, he roughly took her mouth, and she met him as an equal.

In that moment, they understood each other. And they came together with the force of a tidal wave. Powerful. Demanding. But with effortless grace.

Ali had never been more certain of anything in her life than she was at that very moment. This was home. Here, with Kellen. This was where she belonged.

16

"And there's nothing more you can do?" Kellen sat at his desk, fighting the frustration building up inside him.

After the evening he'd spent with Ali, he didn't think that would be possible. That girl made his chest feel tight in all the best kinds of ways.

"I'm sorry, son."

Sergeant Gentry was a friend of his old commander's out of Chicago and one who currently ran things down in Nevada. Kellen had first contacted him to help handle things with his brother, and they'd been going back and forth for over a week now. There was only one reason he would be trying to get ahold of him personally, and it was nothing good.

Kellen had known things were going sideways after he listened to that first voice mail Gentry left the night Charles Rafferty had him looking through hours of security footage from his restaurant. When he tried calling him back the next day, he was told that he'd be out of the office until the following Monday. And, honestly, Kellen had forgotten about calling him back until Gentry woke him up out of a dead sleep only an hour before he had to leave for Hank's to teach the class. He'd thrown around phrases like "mishandled evidence" and "incomplete paperwork." Because of a few minor mistakes by some rookie, his brother had grounds to get the charges against him dropped.

Beyond pissed off, Kellen had driven to the gym in a haze, thinking there was no way his night could get any worse. His mind had been in such a jumble that he even forgot about the plans he'd made with Ali that night. The hurt look on her face had felt like a well-deserved slap to the face. He didn't forget shit like that. And they both knew how that night had ended.

He'd just walked in the station tonight when he got the call. It was one he had known was probably coming, but it still pissed him off. Leave it to Connor to get a competent public defender. His lawyer had officially gotten all of the charges dropped as of this afternoon. His brother was a free man again, and Kellen was completely out of cards to play. Barring Connor fucking up again, there was nothing Sergeant Gentry could do.

"We'll keep an eye on him, and if he so much as sets a toe outside the law, you'll be the first to know."

And, knowing Connor, it was only a matter of time.

"I appreciate that, Sergeant."

"I'm sorry we couldn't do more."

"Shit happens. We all know that."

"Unfortunately. Take care of yourself."

"Same to you."

Kellen hung up the phone and sat back in his chair.

Fuck.

He knew better than anyone that the justice system was flawed. There were times when they couldn't intervene, no matter how wrong they knew something was. Like with Ali. She'd most likely been drugged, except there was no way to prove it, so there was absolutely nothing he could do about it. But with Connor? They had all the proof they needed. Those charges had been solid, but because of an explainable mistake, his brother was now a free man. And, as much as that pissed him off and as much as he sometimes questioned whether or not it was worth it, he *knew* the system worked. He believed in it, heart and soul. Was it perfect? No. But then again, show him a system that was.

Now, he just had to tell Finn.

"Goddamn it." Kellen snatched the phone from its cradle again and tapped in Finn's cell number.

"Hello?" Finn's voice sounded wary.

Kellen didn't blame him; he never called from the station.

"Hey, kid." Picking up his pen, he absently twirled it around his fingers.

"What happened?"

Kellen sighed. Guess they were going to cut through the shit.

"Connor's out."

"What?" Finn all but shouted. "How? I thought you said it was a done deal."

"I know. One of the officers down there left the evidence from the trailer in his car when he ran into the store to get his wife some formula for their two-month-old baby before driving thirty minutes out of his way to take it to her."

"So, what?"

"I know it's bullshit, but Connor's attorney got the evidence thrown out because it broke the chain of custody."

"What about that file I sent you?"

"Apparently, part of the paperwork was incomplete when it was submitted into evidence."

"So, it got thrown out, too. Got it." Finn was pissed, and he couldn't blame him. He felt the exact same way. "Now, what do we do?"

"We do the same thing we've always done. We live our lives, and if Connor shows back up, we deal."

"Do you think getting arrested scared him into backing off?"

No, Kellen didn't think that for a second.

"Maybe we'll get lucky, and he'll just lie down in a ditch and die," Finn added.

"Maybe." But they'd never been that lucky. "Sergeant Gentry is going to keep an eye on him. He'll fuck up eventually. We both know that. For now, you stay smart and call me if he contacts you again. You got it?"

"I got it."

When Finn got quiet, Kellen propped his elbows on his desk and waited him out. Finn did this a lot when he had something that needed processing, whether it was big or small. There were times when Kellen would give anything to know what he was thinking, but he'd learned to just let him be.

After a minute or two, Finn spoke again, "Thanks for trying."

"I'm sorry things went down this way."

"It's not your fault." Then, he asked something Kellen hadn't expected. "Does Ali know about all of this?"

"She does. She's known for a while." His answer was cautious. There were only a handful of people who knew, and neither of them had ever told a girl they were seeing. Kellen wasn't sure how Finn would feel about that. It hadn't been just his story to tell.

"You told her everything? And she stuck around?"

"Yeah. She did. I think she'd surprise you."

"Nah, man. That doesn't surprise me at all. I like her. I think she's good for you." Kellen could hear the smile in his brother's voice, and he couldn't help but grin in return.

"I *know* she is." And he kinda liked her, too. In fact, he more than liked her. Way more.

"Don't fuck it up."

Kellen barked out a laugh, causing Amelia to look his way. "Watch your mouth."

"Whatever. She'd better still be around when I come home for spring break."

"That's the plan."

After that, they said their good-byes, and Kellen headed out on patrol.

Shelby held Ali in a hug so fierce that it was cutting off her air supply, but Ali didn't want her to let go. They both needed this.

She'd waited up for Shelby to get home from her parents' because, for the first time in over a year, she felt lighter.

After that night, she'd shut down part of herself. She didn't miss that person, but she wasn't going to keep pretending like she never existed. Not even her parents knew how bad it'd gotten. No one in her family did.

The first time she'd woken up mid–panic attack after she moved in with Shelby, her new roommate had rushed into her room, brandishing a two-inch-thick psychology book, ready to take on Satan himself. In that moment, Ali almost told her everything. But, instead, she played it off like any old nightmare, not ready for her to know about the person she used to be. Their friendship had been too new and too fragile, and Ali had been afraid of what Shelby would think of her.

She'd been doing exactly what Kellen accused her of. Hoping that, if she pretended like it never happened, then it would magically go away. She'd been so naive.

Shelby deserved to know exactly who her roommate was. Because chances were, she wouldn't be the same person she was today without that girl she used to be. Wisdom came with experience after all.

"Oh my God, I am so stupid." Shelby finally released her stranglehold and pulled back, her eyes glossy with unshed tears. That was, until a horrified expression took over her face. "I tried to shrink you! Here I was, going on and on about what your dream meant, and I never took the time to actually listen to you. Some psychologist I am."

"Don't do that. It's not your fault. I wasn't ready to talk."

Shelby nodded in understanding. "I'm really glad you told me though. Who knows? Maybe, now that you're talking about it, it will help you work through it."

"I think I've heard that somewhere before."

"It is a tried and true method stemming back to the beginning of time."

"Huh." Ali tapped her chin. "I think I've read that on a fortune cookie before."

Her friend grew serious. "All joking aside, nothing you've done in the past could make me think less of you. You know that, right?"

"I do. It just took a long time for *me* not to think less of myself. I'm still not quite there yet, but someone tall and handsome told me that I needed to pull my head out of my ass and move on."

The shocked amusement on Shelby's face was instant. "He did *not*."

"Okay, so maybe those weren't his exact words, but the sentiment was still the same. And it worked. So, if I haven't said it yet, thanks for sending him over."

She winced. "Yeah, that could have gone either way, but I can't regret it if it got me my Ali back. Because bitchy Ali was about to get throat-punched."

Rolling her eyes, she disagreed, "I was not that bad."

Shelby arched a perfectly manicured brow. "The sixteen-year-old barista and I beg to differ. Lack of sleep makes you a little scary."

Ali relented because she knew this to be the truth. "I know. I didn't say anything too irredeemable, did I?"

Shelby sighed dramatically. "Nothing a week's worth of cooking can't fix."

"Does takeout count?"

"As long as I don't have to thaw it, cook it, or nuke it, I'll take it."

"Deal."

"Now, can we please talk about your sexy policeman? I'm assuming you two are good now, judging by that beard burn all over your neck."

Ali's hand automatically went to the side of her neck to cover the redness she'd seen in the mirror earlier, making Shelby laugh.

"Uh, honey, too little, too late."

"Yes, we are more than good. At least, I hope we are because I think I'm in love with him."

"Really?" Shelby gasped happily.

Ali's nod was as goofy as her smile.

"Have you told him?"

"Not yet. What am I going to do if he doesn't feel the same way?"

"Oh, please." Shelby rolled her eyes. "That man is so far gone for you."

"How would you even know? You've seen him, like, twice."

"Three times, thank you very much. But you didn't see his face this morning. He's miserable without you. As drop-dead gorgeous as that hunk of man is, he was looking more than a little haggard. You clearly weren't the only one losing sleep over all of this. I watched him go from exhausted to concerned to determined, all in the space of about two minutes. And it was sexy as hell. I'd give anything to have a man that focused on me."

Ali had seen the fatigue around his eyes today, too, but she'd been too busy trying to hold up her walls to acknowledge it. Maybe Shelby was right. Maybe it was possible that Kellen felt something for her, too.

"I guess there's only one way to find out." She took a deep breath, determination rising inside of her.

"You go get him, girl." Shelby slapped her on the thigh.

"But it's going to have to wait until tomorrow. He's working tonight."

Shelby sighed. "That boy really needs to get a day job."

Sometimes, Ali wished that he would, but she understood the reasoning behind it. Everything Kellen had done was for Finn. This was what worked for them.

"That's okay. I've kind of had a lot of revelations today, so I don't mind waiting. Tonight, I'm going to *sleep*."

And she truly believed she would. For the first time in almost two years, she'd actually told not one, but *two people* the entire story about what had happened. What used to be this shameful story didn't seem quite so big now. It'd happened, and it was done. What was it that monkey from *The Lion King* said? The past could hurt, but she could either run from it or learn from it. And she was so very tired of running.

Kellen parked his truck along the curb and cut the engine. Sunrise was still about an hour away, and his neighborhood was dark and quiet. The only glow came from a few streetlamps that shone down on the sidewalks.

It was one of those perfect mornings. The wind was calm, and only a few clouds hung over the mountains, but other than that, the sky was clear. If he wasn't so fucking tired, he'd have half a mind to change out of his uniform and grab his fly pole. A few quiet hours on the river was all the therapy he ever needed. The sound of the water and the whip of his line soothed something deep inside him. It was a peacefulness that he hadn't been able to find until he and Finn moved up here, away from the noise of the cities. It was the best thing he could have ever done for them.

It was funny how life worked sometimes. If it hadn't been for all the shit in their lives, they never would have found their way to Montana. And that meant that Kellen never would have met Ali. He wasn't one to believe in fate or grand design, but he believed Ali was the one he'd been looking for. People could call it whatever they wanted. He was just thankful things had worked out the way they did.

Pulling out his phone, he sent Ali a text. He'd driven by her apartment last night, and he'd smiled because, for the first time in days, every light was switched off. By now, she'd be awake and getting ready for work.

Kellen: Morning, Kitten.

> *Ali Cat: Good morning. :) Although it'd be a lot better if you actually got out of your truck.*

Kellen grinned at her reply. There was only one way she knew where he was. Looking out his passenger window, he couldn't see anything but darkness.

Kellen: Stalker.

Ali Cat: Slowpoke.

Feeling a lot less tired than he had been a few minutes ago, Kellen hopped out of his truck and heard an instant, "Marco," called out, making him chuckle.

He hadn't played that game since Finn was a little boy, but his reply was second nature. "Polo."

"Marco."

He followed her sultry voice and saw her sitting at the top of the wooden stairs by his door. The soft glow of his porch light shining a halo of light down around her.

"'Bout time," she called to him as he started to climb.

She stood as he neared the top, and he stopped one stair below her, so they were eye-to-eye. She was already put together for the day, wearing a white dress with pink and gray flowers that hit just above her knees, showing off her long legs. The long-sleeved sweater she wore over the top was almost as long as the dress, and her hair was down in loose waves.

"Hey, gorgeous. What are you doing up so early?"

"It might be early, but ya see"—her arms wound around his neck she playfully tilted her head—"I'm running on a full eight and a half hours of sleep."

"Is that so?" His hands found her waist and pulled her closer. The scent of her light perfume invaded his senses as he nuzzled her neck. He liked seeing her first thing in the morning.

With a hum of approval, she tipped her head further to the side. "It's amazing what a pent-up confession can do for the soul *and* the REM cycle. I think Catholics could really be on to something."

"I'll be sure to mention it to Father Tom next time I see him."

She pulled back, forcing him to stop kissing her neck, so she could look him in the eye. "I didn't know you were Catholic."

"I'm not. But every guy likes to fish. Even a man of the cloth."

He'd shared a river with Father Tom on more than one occasion. The man had given him some tips on how to tie some of his best flies.

"Figures, you fish, too. I think my dad would adopt you on that knowledge alone. By the way, my parents want to meet you. Like, yesterday."

"Okay."

"That's it? Okay?"

"Yeah. Okay."

"You do remember what happened at Callie's house, right? You really want to go through that again?"

"I figure I should probably meet the parents of the girl I love sooner rather than later, don't you?" He smiled when Ali's whole face froze.

"I'm sorry, could you repeat that?"

"Which part?" he teased.

"You love me?"

"You didn't pick up on that?"

"Well, it's not like you *said* it! You need to *say* these things! You can't just leave them up for interpretation. I need the actual words; otherwise, it's just my imagination, and she can be a tricky little minx."

Kellen laughed at her rambling before cupping her face between his hands, his fingers tangling in her hair. "I love you. I love *everything* about you. Every frustrating, stubborn bone in your body."

"Really?"

"Really."

Ali's smile was radiant. Her small dimple creasing her cheek. "I love you, too. Every infuriating, amazing part of you."

He didn't think he'd ever been happier than he was in this moment. That was the first time he'd ever uttered those three words to anyone besides Finn. The fact that she felt the same was...was staggering. This was it for him. Plain and simple. He physically had to stop himself from dropping down to one knee on these stairs. Ali Crawford might not know it yet, but he was going to get her down that aisle before the year was out. Just watch. The thought of getting to keep her forever made his heart damn near fly out of his chest.

Leaning forward, he nipped at the end of her nose, making her squeal before tilting his head, slowly kissing her. Her hands hooked under his arms and over his shoulders, pressing her body against his, her pillowy lips molding perfectly to his. The taste of her flowed over his lips, and he kissed her harder, needing more. Always needing more.

There was a time in his life when he didn't think he was capable of loving another person. Finn didn't count because he was family. He was talking about the kick-in-the-gut feeling he got when he looked at this girl. That kind of love had always seemed like a myth that songwriters and poets made up to give people hope. But they were all wrong because there were no words to accurately describe how he felt for the woman in his arms.

He finally pulled back, smoothing her hair away from her face, noticing for the first time how cold her cheeks were.

"Let's go inside."

"Okay."

Stepping past her, he unlocked the door and let her in, turning on a lamp as he followed her into the living room.

"How long before you've got to be at the school?"

"I've got about an hour."

"Seems like all we get most days."

"We'll make it work."

Kellen had a thought then. Walking over to the kitchen drawer, he rummaged around until he found what he was looking for and went back to Ali.

"Take this." He placed the key in her open palm and closed her fingers over it.

Ali studied the object in her hand. Nervously, she licked her lips as she looked back up at him. "Is this…are you…what is this?"

"It's just a key. And I want you to use it. Sleep here. Leave your shit all over my bathroom. Put your chick beer in my fridge. Just be here. As much or as little as you like. Just no more sitting on my step, waiting for me to get home."

"Are you sure? That's a big step."

"I have never been more sure of anything before. You don't have to move in if you don't want to, but I want you here as much as I can get you. I'd love nothing more than for you to grade papers on my couch and clog up my DVR."

"You'd better be careful what you ask for," she quipped, looking down at her shoes.

Realizing she was freaking out a little bit, he gently nudged her chin up with the edge of his finger.

"Look at me." He waited until her watery eyes met his. "We can take it as slow or as fast as you want to. I'll let you set the pace. Just know, you're it for me. The grow-old-together kind of it for me."

Ali didn't know what to say. This man should come with some sort of warning label. Taking a deep breath, she tried to settle the shaking in her hands. Right now, with those striking eyes on her, she felt like she could believe in happily ever after. This man loved her, until *death do us part* loved her. She was still waiting for that part to sink in.

"I'm not an easy person to love," she blurted, figuring he should know exactly what he was getting himself into.

Kellen laughed. Freaking *laughed*! It might have been deep and gravelly, turning her insides to mush, but that was beside the point.

"Stop laughing! You know it's true."

"Ah, my little Ali Cat. You're wrong. You might be stubborn and quick to blow a fuse, and we both know that your first instinct is to fight rather than talk—"

"Not making me feel better here," she mumbled, interrupting him.

But he kept on talking anyway, "But loving you is the easiest thing I've ever done. I don't love you in spite of all of those things. They are part of the reason I was drawn to you in the first place. We work. I know you feel it, too."

Okay. That was a great response.

"I feel it." She *so* felt it.

Over the last month, even when things hadn't been great between them, she'd begun to realize that this time was different. That *he* was different from anyone she'd ever known. The first time she'd met him, she'd felt something so profound that she immediately threw up her walls.

Was it love at first sight? No, she wouldn't call it that. That was for fairy tales and Hallmark movies. But she did feel like a part of herself recognized something in him. He'd made her feel vulnerable, like she was scared of what he might see when he looked at her the way he did. But she was finally beginning to understand what a rarity that kind of connection was. To have someone so attuned to you that all it took was a look or a touch to understand things that couldn't be put into words.

Like right now, he was looking at her so lovingly that it made her heart ache. Reaching up, she cupped his cheek, his short beard scratchy on her palm. He leaned into her hand and closed his eyes, but when he opened them again, there was no mistaking the desire swirling in their blue depths. When her body reacted with an answering clench low in her stomach, she knew he saw the same want reflected back at him.

Kellen reached out and ran his fingertips across her exposed collarbone as he brushed her hair back over her shoulder. That one little touch sent sparks flying over her skin.

"If you keep looking at me like that, you're never going to make it to class on time."

Damn it! He's right.

Reluctantly, she dropped her head to his chest with a groan, gripping his sides above the gear on his belt. She felt his chuckle more than she heard it.

"This is not funny."

His hands soothed up and down her back, totally not helping the situation when he traced the exact line of her tattoo with a single finger, like he could see it through the two layers of fabric. "Of course not."

"Whatever," she grumbled. "You get to go to bed and do something about it while *I* have to go to work."

"Do something about it?"

She actually heard his laugh this time and pulled back to glare at him.

"You know." She waved a hand toward the obvious bulge in the front of his uniform pants.

"Ah, Kitten. You're just jealous because you won't be here to watch." The teasing edge to his voice was completely overshadowed by the hot look he was giving her.

He was right. She'd give anything to stay here and watch that.

He crowded her, backing her up against the back of the couch, caging her in as he leaned down, bracing his arms on the gray cushions on either side of her. His nose skimmed her cheek as he whispered in her ear, "When I'm stroking my dick, do you know what I'm going to be thinking about?"

A shiver raced down her spine at his crass words, and she gave a subtle shake of her head.

"I'm going to think about you on the edge of my bed with your knees tucked up to your chest, pushing that perfect ass of yours up in the air. Prone and waiting for whatever I want to do to you. You're so ready for me; your thighs are wet. Fucking. Dripping. You can't help the needy little moan that rolls its way up your throat when I grab a handful of that sweet ass."

She did moan then. His erotic words painting an incredibly clear picture.

"Yeah, just like that." He tongued her earlobe then, sharply nipping it with his teeth, and she saw stars, but he wasn't done yet. "You'll have your arms stretched out in front of you, gripping the comforter, as I trace that sexy little tattoo of yours with my tongue."

Her breath was coming fast. She swore, she could feel everything he was describing, and he wasn't even touching her. His lips brushing against her ear was their only contact.

"Just as you beg me to put us both out of our misery, I'll grip your hips and bury myself so deep inside your tight little body that you'll be able to feel me in the back of your throat."

Her body clenched around nothing, making her whimper.

Holy shit.

She freaking whimpered.

This was torture. But she wasn't the only one affected.

Kellen's voice was rough with need. "Your body feels like fucking heaven." His hand left the couch and brushed up against her knee. The light touch felt like an iron brand. "Are you wet for me, Kitten?"

She couldn't have stopped herself from spreading her feet wider if she tried. And she didn't try. Not even a little bit.

"Why don't you check for me?"

His growl was a low rumble at the back of his throat as his hand slid up the inside of her thigh, brushing lightly against the satin of her underwear.

"Soaked." He cupped her then, pressing the heel of his hand against her tight bundle of nerves, making her squirm. "You liked me telling you about the things I'm going to do to you, didn't you?"

"I loved it. I love everything you do to me."

"Sinful and sweet. You're absolutely perfect."

"Kiss me."

Almost desperately, Ali reached up, guiding his mouth to hers. Their lips met in a rough, lewd kiss while his hand worked between her thighs, his fingers slipping under the thin material, driving deep inside. Ali broke the kiss on a gasp.

With a gentle hand on her sternum and a look that sent tremors all the way to her toes, he pushed her upper body backward until her head hit the cushion on the couch. Keeping a grip on her hips, he tucked a large pillow behind her back.

Before she could contemplate the strange position, he flipped her dress up over her hips and hooked her panties to the side. The cold air hitting her wet center sent goose bumps chasing across her thighs seconds before his warm mouth covered her. He was a man on a mission, and the only thing she could do was hang on for the ride. Her hands struggled to find purchase as she clawed at the couch. He never let up and never slowed down, racing her toward her orgasm with a power that should scare her, but all she felt was absolute ecstasy as every cell in her body exploded with a flash of white light.

Absently, she heard a clatter as she came back down and looked up to see Kellen ridding himself of his belt and vest. Next went his uniform shirt, tugging it over his head instead of dealing with all of the buttons, throwing it off to the side. The tight black T-shirt that he wore followed quickly, and she couldn't help but stare. She'd never tire of looking at him. His body was hard and powerful and undeniably beautiful.

She reached up, her hands itching to touch him. He smiled down at her as he grabbed her wrists and easily sat her up, her legs bracketing his hips. Without wasting time, she flicked her tongue over his small, pebbled nipple. Looking up at him through her lashes, she smiled at his sharp intake of breath.

"We've got to hurry." His eyes were blue fire.

Totally in agreement, she raked her nails down the ridges of his abdomen, stopping to fumble with the closure on his cargo pants.

As soon as she had him freed, she leaned forward, running her tongue over the broad head. He gripped a handful of her hair, pulling her mouth off of him. The desire in his eyes had turned almost feral.

"I want inside you."

She couldn't agree more.

His hand reached between her legs and gave a harsh tug. The bite of her underwear was a sharp sting before it snapped. Fisting his length with his other hand, he guided himself through her slick folds, and then with one long thrust, he was buried to the hilt.

The pressure and fullness were incredible, but nothing could compare to the feeling when he hooked a hand under her knee and started to move.

Ali anchored herself to his shoulders as her other foot hooked around his calf.

The long moan that tore from her throat had her teeth clamping down on his shoulder as he mercilessly plunged into her with short, deep thrusts. Heat radiated off of his bare chest, and she snuggled closer, but it was never close enough. His devastating pace was pushing her to that cliff at record speeds, and she chased after it. Desperate for it. Within minutes, she was locking up tight as she tumbled over the edge. It wasn't long before he joined her with one last thrust as he embedded himself as deep as he could possibly go.

They stayed locked together as they both rode out the aftershocks. His hand was gentle on the back of her head as he held her to his chest.

His lips were pressed in her hair as he whispered those three life-changing words, "I love you."

Her lips found his chest. Kissing him over his heart. "I love you, too."

With one last kiss to the top of her head, he pulled out of her with a groan.

Gently, he lowered her to the ground before tucking himself back inside his pants.

It was then she realized they hadn't used a condom. She waited for the panic to hit, but it never came. She'd been careless with her body in the past, but since then, she'd had tests done. Twice. Because she was paranoid like that, but she was totally clean and on birth control.

Kellen, obviously thinking about the same thing, looked at her and cradled her jaw between his hands. "We probably should have talked about that first, but I'm more than okay with it if you are. If you're not, just say the word."

"No, it's okay."

He nodded and kissed her forehead. "Come on. I'll walk you home."

Ali righted her dress and grabbed her ruined underwear off the floor. Realizing she was going to be walking home commando, she tossed the tattered garment into the trash can next to the fridge.

Kellen grinned at her as he shrugged his T-shirt back on and grabbed two jackets off the hook by the door.

"Wish I could say I was sorry about that, but I'm not."

He handed her the smaller one that had to be one of Finn's. She put it on, grateful for the extra layer because her sweater definitely hadn't cut it on the walk over.

"Do I look mad?" They were just underwear. It wasn't like she didn't have an entire drawer full.

"No." He gave her a quick kiss. "You look satisfied, and that is a damn good look on you. But you'd better PG that look up before you get to school, or every teacher there is going to know exactly how you spent your morning."

"And, to think, I just came over here to see if you'd have breakfast with me."

Kellen's eyes closed for a brief second, as he no doubt chastised himself. "And I'm the ass who didn't feed you. You should have said something."

She placed both of her hands on his chest. "You know, I'm walking out of here with a key to your apartment and two pretty great orgasms. I can grab a granola bar when I grab some more panties."

He looked awfully offended. "Pretty great?"

"Above average?" She arched her brow, teasing him.

"Nope. Try harder."

"*Mind-blowing.*"

"Now, you're talkin'." He gave her a smacking kiss on her cheek as he opened the door for her. "Speaking of that key, I want you to use it. I meant that."

"I promise, all the chick beer and counter clutter your heart can handle."

"That's my girl." Kellen slapped her on the ass on the way out the door, making her squeal.

By now, the sun was up, and the streets were busy. The block-and-a-half walk felt a little bit like the walk of shame, especially when the breeze blew across her bare ass. However, with the protective arm of the man she loved over her shoulders, she was finding it difficult to wipe the smile from her face.

17

During lunch, Ali was eating her yogurt while contemplating how many shows she could set up to record on Kellen's DVR before he revoked her key privileges. She figured she could get at least a dozen or so on there before he even started to notice. If she pushed it past twenty, she would be risking termination.

The brisk knock on the doorframe snapped her out of her plans, and she looked up to see Principal Sherlock—yes, as in no shit—poking his head around the corner.

"Ali, do you have a minute?"

"Of course. Come on in."

Because he wasn't really asking so much as he was going to barge in, no matter what she said. But he was a good guy to work for, and thankfully, he insisted that they all call him Shawn.

Setting down her spoon, she got up from her desk and walked around to meet him as he came in. Shawn was about forty, she'd guess, and fairly personable for a principal. At least, the kids always responded to him well.

Ali was a little surprised when a young boy followed Shawn into the room, clinging tightly to a woman who looked to be in her mid- to late-twenties. Both newcomers had the same dark mahogany hair that glinted red under the fluorescent lights. Ali would kill to have natural hair that color. And, unless the woman colored the little boy's hair, too, which she highly doubted, that was one hundred percent all them. They also shared the same amber-colored eyes. There would never be any denying these two were related.

"Ali, I'd like to introduce you to Harper and Greyson Davenport. They will be joining us for the rest of the year. And, Greyson, this is Ms. Crawford. She is going to be your new teacher."

Ali kept the shock off of her face as she knelt down to smile at the boy. She'd had no idea she'd be getting a new student this late in the year.

"Hello, Greyson." She pointed to the picture on his shirt of Iron Man and Captain America. "Do you like The Avengers?"

He gave her a shy nod, angling his body away from his mother just a tiny bit.

"Do you want to know a secret?" She lowered her voice. "I like The Avengers, too. Thor is my favorite. Who's yours?"

Greyson looked up at his mom, and she gave him an encouraging nod. Carefully, he leaned toward her and whispered back, "Spider-Man."

"Nice choice." Ali nodded her approval. "Funny, heroic, and he's got a cool suit. Am I right?"

Greyson began to smile, showing off his two missing bottom teeth, and nodded back enthusiastically. Ali held her fist out and was surprised when he bumped it back with only the slightest hesitation. They were going to get along just fine.

Standing, she held her hand out to his mother. "Mrs. Davenport, it's nice to meet you."

"Please, call me Harper. It's lovely to meet you as well. You're really great with him. He's been so nervous to start a new school."

"I think he is going to fit in great here. I know a few other kids who are also big fans of our masked hero who would be glad to show him the ropes."

"Mrs. Davenport was hoping to take a look around the school today and hopefully start Greyson here on Monday."

Shawn stood with his hands clasped around the standard community packet they gave all new families.

"I think that sounds perfect. If you guys are still going to be around in a few hours and you have a few minutes after school, I'd love to sit down with you."

"That sounds wonderful. Thank you."

Ali was surprised to see Harper's eyes tear up, but neither of them acknowledged them.

"You know, they're still serving lunch down the hall if you guys wanted to stop in and grab something to eat. Today just happens to be breakfast for lunch day, too."

"Yeah, Mom! I'm hungry!" Greyson whirled on his mother.

"Okay, let's go eat. What do you say to Ms. Crawford?"

He turned his little body to her and looked her in the eyes. "Thank you."

"You are most welcome. I will see you in just a little bit."

"Here, I'll show you to the lunchroom." Shawn ushered them out of the room as they each gave her a smile over their shoulders.

Just as she sat back down to finish her yogurt, the whistle blew outside her window. With a speed that would horrify her mother, she shoveled the rest of her food in her mouth and tossed her trash into the bin on the way out the door to get her kids.

"You gave her a *key*?" Adam barked in his ear. "It's been, like, a month."

Kellen walked around the room, holding the phone to his ear with his shoulder, as he carried the dishes to the sink. "You say that like it's a bad thing."

"Oh, man. Addy always said that, when you went down, you'd go down hard. Sooo, when's the wedding?" Adam gasped. "Can I be a groomsman?"

Kellen just shook his head at his friend's theatrics and let him carry on, talking about ice sculptures and place settings, while he continued cleaning up his apartment. With only him here, it never got too dirty, but he accumulated clutter just like everyone else.

"But, in all seriousness, we like her. She seems solid and hot to boot." Kellen heard a smack on Adam's end of the call. "Hey! I'm allowed to say that because you said it first! You did, too. You literally just said that you knew Kellen would end up with someone just as hot as he was. And you don't see me gettin' all pissy about it." Adam quit bickering with Addison and got back on the line. "Anyway, my wife is way hotter, just for the record."

"Duly noted." Kellen grinned as he wiped down the kitchen counters.

Addy was beautiful, no doubt, but no one held a candle to his Ali.

"So, let me guess. You're bailing on poker night tomorrow."

That was why he'd called in the first place. He'd never bailed on poker night in the past, but he actually had tomorrow night off, and so did Ali. Those kinds of days had been hard to come by.

"Yeah, man, I am."

"And so it begins."

"Don't be like that."

"Nah, I'm just giving you a hard time. I remember how it goes. You guys do you, and we'll get you back in a month or two. Besides, you know Addy will eventually drag Ali into her girls' night. It's only a matter of time. Oh shit! I just thought of somethin'! Please, please, *please* tell me that Wade doesn't know any of this yet?"

"I don't see how he would."

But then again, Wade just seemed to know shit sometimes.

"Perfect! It's about time I get to one-up that asshole."

"Go nuts, man. Thomas isn't coming back, right?"

"Oh, hell no. I made Wade tell him that was a one-time thing."

"How'd he take it?"

"Fuck if I know, and I don't give a shit. All right, man. I've got to go. Give your girl a hug for us, and I'll catch you later."

"You got it. Same for Addy."

"Later, man."

"Later."

Kellen tossed his phone onto the wooden coffee table and straightened the pillows on the couch, remembering exactly how Ali had looked, draped across the back of it this morning. He'd never considered himself a lucky man before, but the way Ali looked at him made him feel like the luckiest goddamn person in the world.

He'd given her the key to his apartment on a whim, but he didn't regret it for a second. There had never been a girl he'd ever been close enough with to even consider sharing his space. It had always seemed too personal and too invasive. But not with Ali. He loved the idea of coming home to her after a shift, like he did this morning. She didn't belong out on the stairs. She belonged inside his apartment. In his space, in his bed. But the decision would be up to her now. She had the key, and he just had to hope she'd use it.

He was going to choose to err on the side of optimism. And, since he was the ass who'd fucked her on the back of the couch instead of feeding her breakfast, he was going to make sure he had everything he needed to make her dinner tonight if she decided to stop by after work. They should have a few hours together before he needed to head out.

Checking the time, he quickly made his bed and scrubbed the small bathroom. He figured, if he hopped in the shower now, he'd have just enough time to run to the store before she got off work.

Ali sat down at one of the little chairs with Harper in the seat next to her as they watched Greyson play with the blocks on the other side of the room. He was building a rather impressive fort for the Spider-Man action figure he'd brought with him.

She had been happy to see the pair waiting inside her room when she came back inside from sending the kids off to their parents and their busses.

"So, can I ask why you're switching schools this late in the year?" Ali had been wondering about that all day since they only had about six weeks left before summer break.

Harper turned her eyes on Ali, and she couldn't help but see the underlying sadness in them.

"It's a really long story." And not a happy one apparently. "But the short version is, my husband died about a year ago. That's an even longer story. We used to live in California, but we ended up losing our house a few weeks ago, so I figured it was a good time for a change."

"I am so sorry." Ali's heart ached for them.

Harper didn't look that much older than she did. Ali couldn't even imagine what they'd been through.

"Thank you. But we're just trying to get our lives back."

"What made you decide to move here of all places?"

"I'm from here actually. My family moved to California when I was still in high school, but I never wanted to leave. And, after living in the city for so long, I couldn't breathe there anymore. But I mostly did it for Greyson. We just needed a fresh start."

That was interesting. She'd have to ask her brothers if they remembered her.

"Well, if there is anything I can do to help make this transition easier for you or Greyson, I'm happy to help."

"Thank you for that. I appreciate it."

For the next half an hour, they sat and talked about Greyson and how best to help him make the transition. For such a little guy, he'd had a lot of change already.

After they left, Ali hurried to finish her stuff, so she could get home. She was itching to put that new key on her key ring to good use.

When Kellen pulled up to the curb, he looked up and saw his living room lights on, illuminating the window that faced the street. His heart started racing as the warm feelings in his chest grew tenfold.

She actually did it.

He hopped out of the truck, grabbed the two large grocery bags out of the backseat, and beeped the locks on his truck. Sprinting up the stairs, he took them two at a time. The front door was unlocked when he twisted the handle. As much as he loved the fact that she'd used the key, he wished she'd keep the door locked when she was here alone. They might live in a small town, but that didn't mean people should just leave their doors unsecured.

Kellen opened the door and looked around but didn't see her anywhere, so he called out, "Hey, Kitten, I'm home. Where you at?"

But there was no answer.

He reached out with his foot and kicked the door shut behind him, unease twisting up his stomach. He took one step toward the kitchen when pain exploded on the back of his head. He pitched forward, dropping the bags. The tomatoes rolling across the floor was the last thing he saw before everything went dark.

18

The first thing Kellen registered when he came to was a blinding throb. His head felt like it had been split open and then stomped on. He opened his eyes just a slit but didn't raise his head. He was sitting on one of his kitchen chairs in his bedroom. He subtly tried to move his arms, but they were bound behind his back with what he assumed was duct tape, given it was tied around his chest, too. Next, he tried his legs but found that they were secured tightly to the chair.

Shit.

This was bad.

There was no sense in trying to be stealthy about this anymore. Opening his eyes all the way, he raised his head, but it wasn't without effort. The shooting pain that shot down his spine made black spots dance in front of his eyes, but he pushed through it. He didn't have time for that shit again. Warm wetness dripped down the side of his face and off his jaw. He could see the blood trail down the front of his gray shirt. He must have hit his head on the kitchen floor when he went down, too.

Fucking perfect.

On the bright side, he could still feel his Glock digging into his ribs under the flannel shirt he wore over it. When he was off-duty, he rarely went anywhere without it strapped into his shoulder holster. He just didn't have any way to get to the gun, and his service pistol was locked in the safe behind him in his nightstand drawer. Either way, he had to get out of this tape first.

Kellen heard someone coming and wasn't surprised at all when Connor walked into the room. He should have been expecting something like this but not this soon. His brother had only been out of jail for about thirty-six hours. Regardless, it was stupid to have let his guard down.

"Good morning, sunshine." Greasy black hair hung in clumps over his forehead, and his dirty clothes were wrinkled and ripped.

Kellen had seen homeless men in better shape than the guy standing in his doorway.

"Hey, Connor. What's new?" Kellen glared up at his big brother.

Despite the cool temperature of the room, Connor was sweating through his shirt, and the skin clinging to the bones on his face was about three shades too white.

"Withdrawals suck, am I right?"

"Fuck you, Kellen." He wrapped an arm around his waist in pain.

"Yeah, those stomach cramps can be a bitch. When was the last time you used?"

He knew damn well that it had to have been since he got out, or he wouldn't still be this messed up.

"I don't know what the fuck you're talkin' about."

If he'd dragged his sorry ass all the way up here, that could only mean one thing.

"Let me guess. Somewhere in that fucked up head of yours, you still think we owe you money."

"You bet your ass you do! That money should have gone to me!" Connor screamed in his face, spit spraying from his mouth and landing on Kellen's face.

Kellen jerked his head forward and felt the crunch as Connor's nose broke under the force, making him stumble backward.

"I don't owe you jack shit." Kellen seethed as blood poured out from around the hand that Connor had cupped over his nose.

The pure hatred in Connor's eyes wasn't anything new as he glared down on him. Kellen saw the backhand coming, but there wasn't a damn thing he could do about it. The metallic taste of blood filled his mouth as his teeth sliced open the inside of his cheek.

"Tell me where Mom's money is!"

Turning his head to the side, he spit out a mouthful of blood onto the carpet. "I need you to clear your head and listen carefully, Connor. There. Is. No. Money."

"Stop saying that! I know she had life insurance!"

"That was almost ten fucking years ago! Of course there was a life insurance policy. How do you think we paid for Mom's medical bills? Their funerals? We didn't see a dime of that money."

"You're lyin'."

"Jesus Christ." Kellen hung his head. He had no idea how to get through to his brother.

Years ago, their mother's insurance agent had told them that there was a two-hundred-fifty-thousand-dollar life insurance policy and that only he and Finn were listed as the beneficiaries. Not once did that money ever see the light of day. They didn't have health insurance, and the hospital bills were every bit of that amount before it was over. And the funerals for both their parents, minimal as they were, had still cost them money they didn't have.

"I know Finn's going to that fancy school."

"You don't know anything about Finn." Kellen tensed at the mention of their brother.

Finn had worked his ass off to go to college. He'd gotten the grades that got him a full academic ride, but Connor would never understand that.

"I know that shit ain't free. Neither is this apartment or that fancy truck you pulled up in." Connor threw his hands out toward the window.

"It's called a job, you dipshit. But you wouldn't know anything about that either."

Connor sneered at him again. Looking around the room, he picked up a bronze sculpture of a grizzly bear from his dresser. The bear was standing on its hind legs and snarling. Finn had made it in high school and given it to him for Christmas a few years ago. It was one of his favorites. It was also about the size of a twenty-ounce soda and weighed a fucking ton.

"You do remember what I do for a living, don't you, Connor?"

"How could I forget?" He tested the weight of the sculpture. "You're a fuckin' cop. You've put me behind bars twice!"

Brandishing the sculpture like a bat, Connor swung forward and cracked it across his ribs. Kellen felt something break as the wind was knocked out of him.

That was when Kellen heard the front door open, and his heart stopped.

Ah, Kitten, no.

Blind panic seized him. He couldn't let her come in here.

He opened his mouth to holler at her to get out, but he couldn't get his lungs to work.

Ali stuck her key in Kellen's lock, only to find it already open. She was a little disappointed she hadn't been able to actually use it this time. It seemed rather unceremonious to just walk in, but he wouldn't have given her a key if he wanted her to knock first. She knew he was home because his truck was parked along the curb.

Pushing the door open, she paused with one foot over the threshold. His house was completely ransacked. The cushions on the couch were ripped open, and the drawers in the kitchen were all open and disheveled. Worry gripped her as she walked farther in, letting the door shut behind her.

On edge, she startled when the toe of her tan ankle boot kicked a can of tomato sauce. Looking down, she watched it spin across the kitchen floor. That was when she noticed the blood smeared along the tiles among the groceries that were flung everywhere, and her knees went weak.

Her heart in her throat, she called out, "Kellen?"

A faint grunt came from the bedroom down the hall.

She knew it was stupid, but she slowly made her way across the living room. Every horror movie *ever* told her that she needed to turn around and run out that front door, but she couldn't stop her feet from moving in the opposite direction.

You are a total dumbass.

She couldn't agree with herself more, but still, her feet kept moving.

If Kellen was hurt, she wasn't just going to leave him here. But she wasn't a total nutjob. With shaking hands, she reached in her sweater pocket and pulled out her phone. Looking down, she dialed 911. As soon as she dialed the last number, she heard the grunt again. Only, this time, it sounded a whole lot like her name and was most definitely Kellen, although he didn't sound okay. Not even a little bit. Her feet raced the rest of the way down the hall and into the bedroom.

Rounding the corner, she was stopped short when two arms wrapped around her from behind, trapping her arms at her sides, startling a squeal from her. The man was strong, squeezing her so tight that she thought she'd pop. Panicking, she lashed out, her phone flying out of her hand as she twisted, trying to break his hold.

"Let. Her. Go." The rasped words were breathless and broken and most definitely pissed off.

Ali stopped fighting and looked to her left, her heart stopping in her chest.

Kellen sat, taped to a chair, both his chest and legs tightly secured. Blood caked the side of his face and ran down the front of his shirt.

AMANDA KELLEY

Those beautiful eyes of his were absolutely murderous as he glared at the man behind her.

"Connor…let her go. This has nothing…to do with her."

Ali was worried about Kellen's broken speech. It sounded like he couldn't breathe.

"Shut up and let me think!"

Ali was jerked to the side and lost her footing. Connor almost went down with her but yanked her back to her feet before she could hit the ground. She was going to get whiplash before he was finished.

Looking to the mirror above the dresser, she caught a glimpse of the man behind her.

So, this is the brother.

At first glance, she could see the resemblance Kellen had mentioned. They were the same height and build and even shared the same coloring, but that was all. There was no kindness in his eyes or confidence in his stance. Connor was frail-looking, and his eyes were mean and cold. She was happy to see he hadn't gone unscathed. His nose was obviously broken, as blood dripped off his chin. She tried not to think about it getting in her hair because there were definitely bigger things to worry about, but she couldn't help it.

Apparently, her showing up had thrown a wrench into his plans because, from the looks of it, he was freaking the fuck out.

Welcome to the club, asshole.

Her heart was pounding so hard; she was a little worried about it legitimately bursting.

"Ali…look at me."

Her eyes swung from the mirror down to Kellen. Her vision went blurry as she looked at his bloody face, but she blinked the tears away. She could lose it later.

If there is a later.

That thought was unacceptable. There would be a later, damn it.

"Breathe, baby." Kellen's whisper was calm, helping her focus. When she locked on to his eyes, he nodded at her. "You've got this."

When his words broke through her panic, she realized he was right. She could get away from Connor.

Ali took a deep breath and reached up, hooking her fingers around the clammy arms banding around her chest. In one quick move, she dropped her weight, jerking him off-balance, and loosened his hold. She didn't waste any time, bringing the two-inch heel of her cute boot down onto the top of his foot and slamming her head back into his face, no doubt getting blood all over herself. Connor let out an inhuman roar as pain exploded across the back of her head.

Son of a bitch, that hurt!

She didn't remember her teacher telling her that head-butting someone would hurt her, too. But it did the trick, and he all but threw her forward as he let go to grab his face.

"You stupid, bitch!"

Ali landed hard on her knees at Kellen's feet.

"Run." Kellen's eyes pleaded with her.

Yeah, that is so not happening.

She scrambled over to him and tore at the tape around his chest. She almost had it when her hair was yanked back, flipping her over.

"Don't you *fucking* touch her!" Kellen was twisting in his chair, trying to break the last bit of tape.

Connor bent over, reaching for her hair again, but he didn't get that far. She planted her foot in his groin with every ounce of power she had, doubling him over. She kicked again, catching him in the side of the head, and knocked him down to the floor where he sprawled on his side, out cold.

"Ali, get...my gun. Under my left arm."

Getting to her feet, she tore away the last bit of tape and found his gun in his shoulder holster. With shaking hands, she aimed it at a still-incapacitated Connor on the floor while she knelt behind Kellen and used her keys to get through the tape around his wrists. As soon as Kellen's arms were free, he took the gun from her, and she gladly let it go. The only thing she'd ever shot at was a target. No matter how much he deserved it, she didn't want to actually have to shoot her boyfriend's brother.

She breathed a sigh of relief when she heard sirens in the distance, getting closer.

Kneeling down again, she freed Kellen's legs from the chair as well. As soon as he was loose, he stood up, but when he stumbled, she wrapped her arm around his waist, making him wince when her hand landed on his ribs for support.

"What's wrong? Are they broken?"

Turning into her, he laid the hand that wasn't holding the gun on her cheek. "Are you okay?"

"I'm fine, but, Kellen, you're scaring me. What's wrong?"

"Don't worry…about…about me." He paused, trying to take a deep breath but only got a little puff of air.

Something was definitely not okay. She jumped when she heard the front door bang open against the wall.

"WGPD! O'Connell, you here?"

"Back here!" Ali hollered in response. When Kellen smiled down at her, she shrugged. "What? I'm not completely senseless. I called them after I saw the blood in the kitchen."

"That's my girl."

Only he could make her heart soar with half his face covered in blood. Just then, two uniformed officers came around the corner with their guns drawn but stopped short when they saw them.

One she recognized as the cop who'd pulled her over last week, named Jones, and the other had *Holdren* sewn into his vest.

"What the fuck?" Holdren lowered his weapon and looked them over with a concerned eye. "Are you guys okay?"

Jones bent down and checked Connor for a pulse, apparently finding one because he called for an ambulance.

"Fine," Kellen rasped.

"You are not fine." She glared up at him before turning to the other cop. "He can't breathe. I don't know what's wrong."

She heard Jones call for another ambulance when Holdren walked over to them and lifted Kellen's shirt.

She gasped when she saw the discoloration on his ribs closest to her. They were already a horrifying array of cranberry red and black. Holdren gently pushed on them, making Kellen cough.

"They're definitely broken, and they probably punctured your lung. We need to get you to the hospital. What the fuck did he hit you with?"

Kellen nodded to the discarded bear statue on the floor.

"Jesus," Holdren muttered, looking at the heavy object.

Now, Ali kind of wished she had shot him.

"At least you took him down harder."

"Wasn't me." Another short breath. "All her." Kellen grinned down at her, full of pride.

Surprise flickered across the other man's face when he looked at her. "Badass, girl."

When the paramedics arrived, one of whom was her uncle Ben, everything moved quickly. She and Kellen were separated when he told her uncle that her head needed to be checked. *She* wasn't the one bleeding, but he stayed and checked her over anyway while the other took Kellen downstairs to the waiting ambulance.

"Uncle Ben, I'm fine. It's nothing some ibuprofen can't handle." She brushed his hand away and tried to move around him to follow Kellen.

"Damn it, girl, will you just hold still and let me look?" He gave her the parent look. The one that made any misbehaving kid sit up straight.

"Fine but hurry."

He poked and prodded and shone a tiny light in her eyes before giving her the all-clear.

"You're going to be just fine. But I expect you to tell your parents what happened here before they hear it from someone else. You got that?"

"Yes, sir." She hugged him. "Love you, Uncle Ben."

He returned the hug, a little flustered. "You, too, girl. Now, let's go catch up with that boy of yours. You can ride to the hospital with him."

There were two more EMTs checking over Connor, who had regained consciousness. He wasn't making it easy on them as he cussed up a storm while Jones and Holdren stood careful watch over him.

She had so many questions, but she'd have to wait like everyone else to get some answers. Right now, she just wanted to make sure Kellen was all right.

19

Kellen woke up groggy. The incessant beeping coming from the monitors next to the bed was enough to make him walk out of here regardless of doctor's orders. They'd insisted on keeping him for a couple of days to make sure there weren't any complications.

The broken ribs had caused what they called a pneumothorax, but it hadn't required surgery. They gave him a local anesthetic and shoved a tube in his chest. The relief was instant, but apparently, they needed to leave it there to give his lung a chance to inflate all the way. Then, the doctor taped up his ribs and checked his head. He'd ended up with thirteen stitches total. Some in the cut on his forehead and the rest on the back of his head where Connor had knocked him out, using a cast iron pan that Jones had found among the mess inside the door.

Kellen had given his statement to Sergeant Hoffman, who met him over at the hospital in Wellington.

Ali refused to leave his side, holding his hand the whole time. It had killed him, not being able to help her with Connor, but she hadn't needed him. She was amazing.

And he didn't care what kind of lawyer Connor got. There was no way out of this one. The doctors released Connor into police custody after only a few hours. He had a broken nose and a mild concussion, but he was going to live to spend the rest of his natural life behind bars.

Over the last few days, Kellen had had a revolving door of guests. Addison and Adam were the first ones here and waited with Ali while the doctors straightened him out. Everyone from the station had been in and out constantly for days now, too.

Finn had also driven up even though Kellen had tried to get him to stay at school. Adam and Addy had taken him home with them, and he'd been staying with them ever since.

To his surprise, Ali's entire clan had shown up at one point or another. Including her parents, Lee and Maggie. While he would have loved to meet them when he was more vertical, they were sweet people. Maggie had fussed over him and Ali until Lee had to drag her out at Ali's insistence.

He'd learned yesterday, only after she brought his key back, that Maggie had taken it upon herself to steal Ali's key and gone over to his place, cleaning it from top to bottom. Putting everything back together and throwing out what couldn't be saved. She'd done it like it was no big deal. But it was a huge fucking deal to him. He tried to thank her, but the words got stuck in his throat, and his eyes burned. Ali was sitting by his bed and reached out, squeezing his hand. He held on to that hand for dear life, trying not to lose it like a four-year-old.

Maggie seemed to understand because her eyes got a little glossy, too. Leaning down, she'd hugged him and whispered in his ear, "Welcome to the family."

He'd hugged her back as tightly as he dared. If this was the kind of love that Ali had grown up with, it was no wonder she'd become such an incredible person.

Kellen looked over at the girl curled up in the reclining chair next to his bed. It was the middle of the night, and she'd been sleeping in that damn chair for three nights now. That first night, a nurse had suggested Ali head home once visiting hours were over and was met with a death glare as Ali sat right back down and told her she wasn't leaving. Twenty minutes later, the nurse brought her an extra pillow and a blanket, and it was never mentioned again. Shelby had also brought Ali a bag of clothes, and no one had tried to kick his girl out since then.

Even in sleep, she had one arm stretched out, touching the edge of his bed. Kellen reached over and laid his hand over hers, causing her eyes to shoot open.

"Shh, it's just me. I didn't mean to wake you."

"Is everything okay?" She sleepily blinked her eyes.

"Everything's fine, Kitten. Go back to sleep."

Doing the exact opposite, she sat up in the chair, rubbing her eyes. She was wearing a pair of sweats with her hair piled on top of her head like a big ball of yarn, and she didn't have a stitch of makeup on. She was still the most beautiful girl he'd ever laid eyes on.

"Come here."

Ali smiled at him like he was joking, but he lifted the covers and held out his arm to her.

"You're serious?"

He'd tried to get her to lie with him every night, but she'd insisted on the chair. He was over it. It'd been days since he held her in his arms for more than just a minute.

"Get your cute little ass up here."

With a grin, she caved and crawled into the narrow bed with him. They'd taken the tube out of his side a few hours ago and stitched him up, but she was still careful as she wrapped her arm across his stomach.

"Is this okay?"

He lowered his arm around her and pulled her in closer. "It's perfect."

"How are you feeling?"

"More than ready to be out of this hellhole. Doc said he'd release me in the morning."

"When did he say that?" she asked, confused.

"About an hour ago."

"Why didn't you wake me up?"

"It's bad enough they wake me up every hour. At least one of us should get to sleep." He kissed the top of her head.

"When we get out of here, I want you to come back to my place with me."

"Okay."

"To stay. I want you to move in with me."

"Okay."

He laughed quietly, thinking that was way easier than it should have been. "You're awfully agreeable tonight. What's goin' on?" He squeezed her a little tighter and felt her shaky inhale. "Hey, what is it?"

"It's nothing."

He didn't believe that for a second.

"Come on. Talk to me."

"I just don't want to be apart from you anymore. I'm sick of only seeing you once or twice a week."

"Yeah, about that—"

"No, it's fine. I get our schedules will never quite be in sync, but if we're living together, we'll at least get to see each other every day. Even if it's only for a few hours."

"But it's not enough." Kellen squeezed her tighter. "Not for me. I want to be able to fall asleep with you every night and wake up with you every morning. That's why I asked my sergeant yesterday if I could switch to the day shift."

She abruptly sat up, jostling them both. "Wait, what? Really?"

"Turns out, Jones wants to switch over to the night shift anyway. I think it's so he can be closer to Amelia, but whatever the reason, Sarge said it's fine with him. When I go back to work in a few weeks, it will be on strictly day shifts."

"I never would have asked you to do that."

"I know." He cupped her cheek and ran his thumb under her eye. "But I need this. It'll be good for me. For us." She leaned into his hand, covering it with her own. "Besides, maybe then Addy will stop calling me Batman."

Ali turned a full smile on him then, and he swore, his heart skipped a beat. He was pretty sure he'd even heard the monitors lose their rhythm for a second.

"Do you have any idea how much I love you?"

She nodded as her eyes glossed over. "I think I've got a pretty good idea. Because I love you just as much. So much that I don't think I can stand it sometimes."

Pulling her down, he kissed her long and hard. Slipping his tongue past the seam of her lips, he deepened the kiss with a groan. He'd never get enough of the taste of her. He'd barely gotten more than a quick kiss out of her between the constant parade of nurses and doctors and family.

When the damn heart monitor started beeping rapidly, she pulled away, laughing, and he dropped his head back on the pillow. He couldn't wait to get out of this place.

"I want to ask you something, but it's totally fine if you want to say no." She went from laughing to somber pretty damn fast.

"What's goin' on?"

"Do you think that maybe we could look for a different apartment? I know that's your and Finn's place, and I don't want to overstep. It's just…"

"It's just that you don't want to see Connor every time you walk in there."

"No, it's not Connor." She dropped her eyes as she fingered the edge of the sheet. "It's you. Kellen…there was so much blood."

"Hey. Look at me." He waited for her eyes to lift to his again. "It's just an apartment. We can start looking tomorrow. Until then, how 'bout I come stay with you? As long as you think Shelby will be okay with it."

"What about Finn?"

He laughed, causing his ribs to ache. "Finn hates that apartment. The walls are too thin, and the neighbors are too loud. It's a terrible apartment, Ali Cat. He'll pack his stuff faster than either of us."

"Are you sure?"

"Positive. I don't care where we live. This is home." He placed his hand over her heart. "Nothin' else matters."

She nodded and launched herself at him, sealing her mouth to his. But, before she could pull away, he fisted her hair and held her exactly where she was, turning her quick kiss into something far more salacious. When the monitors started rapidly beeping again, one of his regular nurses came in, walking brusquely until she saw them. Kellen loosened his hold on Ali's hair but didn't let her go as he dropped his head back again.

"Goddamn it." He rolled his head to the side, looking at the nurse. "Can't you just unhook me or something?"

Ali buried her head in his chest as her body shook with laughter. The nurse gave him a cheeky grin as she rolled her eyes and left the room.

Guess that's a no.

Tomorrow couldn't come soon enough.

EPILOGUE

The incessant chirping of a bird woke Ali, and she grumbled. Kellen liked to sleep with the window open, and as spring fully settled in on their little mountain town, the birds had come out in full force.

Kellen radiated warmth as she snuggled against his chest, his arms tightly holding her. She wasn't ready to wake up yet.

Ali reached above their heads for a pillow to put over her ear, but her hand brushed up against cold metal instead. Confused, she opened her eyes and took a look around.

Last night, she and Kellen had taken the truck back up to the field outside of town. Their field. And, just like the first time, Kellen had turned the bed of his truck into...well, a bed. An incredibly comfortable bed because, apparently, they never made it home.

The air was cool, and their blankets were covered with a light layer of dew, making them feel wet to the touch. It was still mostly dark out, but the sky was beginning to turn a brilliant orange as the sun started to rise over the mountains.

"Hey." Ali rubbed her hand over Kellen's stomach. "Wake up."

His arms tightened around her as his whole body stretched before he kissed the top of her head. "Hey."

"We fell asleep."

"I know." Kellen's voice was still sleepy. "You started snoring, and I didn't have the heart to wake you."

"I do not snore." She playfully poked him in the ribs, making him twitch. Okay…so maybe she did but *only* when she was sick.

"Whatever you say, Ali Cat."

The way he used that asinine nickname made her heart soar like the lovesick fool that she was. She didn't think that there'd ever come a day when she tired of hearing it. She snuggled closer against him, and they watched the sky slowly brighten as an orange glow spread across the expanse of the field. Even the small white daisies that now flowed over the ground looked yellow under the glow.

Turning her head, she placed a kiss over his heart. "Sorry I fell asleep on you last night." She hadn't meant to, but the quiet sound of the crickets mixed with the way he ran his fingers through her hair had lulled her under before she could stop it.

"You've never got to be sorry for that."

His left hand was trailing lazy strokes up and down her back while his other hand lifted her left one from his stomach. They both watched as the early morning light glinted off of the pear-shaped diamond sitting on her ring finger.

He'd put it there last night while the stars danced above them, and she never planned on taking it off.

Since the day she'd seen him across the gym, they'd been headed right here. And right here was the only place Ali wanted to be.

IF YOU OR SOMEONE YOU KNOW IS STRUGGLING,
THERE ARE RECOURSES TO HELP.

US Helplines

Substance Abuse and Mental Health Services Administration
(SAMHSA) National Helpline

1-800-662-4357

National Domestic Violence Hotline

1-800-799-7233

National Sexual Assault Hotline

1-800-656-4673

National Suicide Prevention Lifeline

1-800-273-8255

ACKNOWLEDGMENTS

I want to thank my husband, Scott. Without his love and support, I wouldn't be able to do any of this. And thank God he loves to cook, or we'd all starve.

Thank you to my two amazing boys, who constantly cheer me on and help me celebrate every little success. Being your mom will always be my greatest accomplishment.

Also, I would lose my mind without my amazing friends and family, who listen to my ramblings and answer off-the-wall questions without batting an eye. I would go insane without you. I will never be able to thank you all enough.

This book wouldn't be complete without thanking everyone who had a hand in the final product. From my editor and formatter, Jovana, to my cover designer, Barb, and my team of beta readers, Kassie, Lori and Ricki—You have all been amazing.

Lastly, I'd like to thank everyone who gives my writing a chance. Your support and praise have been overwhelming! I know there are millions of books out there, so the fact that you choose to read mine is astounding. Thank you!

ABOUT THE AUTHOR

Amanda Kelley was raised in a small town in Wyoming where she met and married her high school sweetheart. Today, they live in Northern Colorado where she is lucky enough to be a stay-at-home mom to two incredible sons. When she's not attempting to write awesome love stories, she spends her days as an alarm clock, chauffeur, maid, nurse, chef, counselor, cheerleader, referee, finder of shoes and homework, giver of hugs, and pet whisperer. And she wouldn't have it any other way.